What the critics are saying...

80

5 Angels! "Eve Jameson creates a suspenseful story that leaves readers clinging to their seats with each turn of the page. The characters in *Bethany's Rite* are both imaginative and unbelievably realistic at the same time. The author has done an incredible job on balancing love, lust, passion, and fear into an intelligent plot. *Bethany's Rite* is a book that needs to be read by anyone looking for a flaming hot romance with a side of suspense." ~ *Fallen Angel Reviews*

5 Hearts "This is the first book in the *Ilyrian Destiny* series and starts the series off with a bang. This book combines action and adventure along with passion and intrigue to make one marvellous story. The relationship between Wyc and Bethany is intense and erotic is not the word for this couple. Eve Jameson is an author to watch and I can't wait to read the other sisters' stories in the Ilyrian Destiny series." ~ *The Romance Studio*

"Good golly miss molly, can *Jameson* write a sex scene. :) Get out a pen and start taking notes." ~ *Sequential Tart*

5 Hearts "...The premise is beautifully and masterfully created to rouse all of our sensual senses. All the dialogues and sequences blend in paired harmony to master the mind and enthrall the soul. This is a scorcher of a story that will take control and not let go until the very end!" ~ *Love Romances*

Gold Star Award "*Ilyrian Destiny: Bethany's Rite* is an amazing debut book. What an entertaining mix of suspense and sensuality! Ms. Jameson merges the best of classic paranormal/shape-shifter genre with a tight up-to-date style! This book is exceptional and definitely one I highly recommend." ~ *Just Erotic Romance Reviews*

Available in ebook: Brooke's Sanctuary

"This is the second book in the *Ilyrian Destiny* series and is just as incredible as the first one, *Bethany's Rite*. Eve Jamison shows remarkable skill for writing hot, seductive love scenes as well as creating characters that are both humorous and endearing to the reader. Rordyc is the ultimate Alpha male and Brooke is fun and sassy. I look forward to reading more of Ms. Jameson's work– she is definitely an author to keep an eye on!"~ *Euro-Reviews*

"BROOKE'S SANCTUARY is a fantasy tale that will enthrall the senses and boggle the mind. Rordyc is strong, sexy and his sheer determination to get his woman will have your heart jumping in your chest. Eve Jameson is doing an incredible job with the ILYRIAN DESTINY series and I can't wait to see what the next book will bring." ~ *Romance Junkies*

"Ms. Jameson has written a fantastic second book in the Ilyrian Destiny series. Brooke and Rordyc are a hot, erotic combination. I loved the way they interacted with each other. The volatile emotions and physical desires they release in each other are intense and highly arousing to read. I am anxiously awaiting the next installment to this series. ~ *Coffee Time Romance*

Eve Jameson

Bethany's Rite ILYRIAN DESTINY

ELLORA'S CAVE
ROMANTICA PUBLISHING

An Ellora's Cave Romantica Publication

www.ellorascave.com

Bethany's Rite

ISBN # 1419953451
ALL RIGHTS RESERVED.
Bethany's Rite Copyright© 2005 Eve Jameson
Edited by Briana St. James
Cover art by Syneca

Electronic book Publication July 2005
Trade paperback Publication July 2006

Warning:

Also by Eve Jameson

ᕫᴑ

Brooke's Sanctuary

About the Author

ᕫᴑ

I can't recall a time when I wasn't making up stories. As long I remember, they've played like movies in my mind and I love seeing what will happen next.

Why did I decide to become an erotic romance writer? Easy. I didn't.

One day I was minding my own business, writing a nice sweet story, and suddenly this incredibly sexy, all-things-fantasies-are-made-of man just jumped out of my pen. He smiled at me, winked and told me to follow him. What could I do? My feet were moving before my brain had a chance to lodge any reasonable objections. Thank goodness!

I've been on this journey with my muse ever since. And I gotta tell you, I'm loving it! He's introduced me to some gorgeous, alpha heroes and take-no-crap, sassy heroines and the adventure has just begun. I can't wait to introduce you to them and hope you'll have as much fun reading their stories as I have writing them.

Besides being whisked away by my muse, traveling, hiking and reading are in my top ten favorite things to do with a day, along with eating Mexican food and the most decadent chocolate dessert I can find. Drop me a line, I'd love to hear from you.

Eve welcomes comments from readers. You can find her website and email address on her author bio page at www.ellorascave.com.

Bethany's Rite
Ilyrian Destiny

ઠબ

Dedication

ஐ

My family, who have kept me in touch with heaven while I've walked through a personal hell. Always supportive, always loving, always there.

Bree, for whom I couldn't begin to list the number of things to say thank you without surpassing the length of this book. I'm grateful and blessed to be able to work with you.

RWS, who has forever made me a fan of CSI: NY.

Words can't begin to explain how you've encouraged and inspired me.

Trademarks Acknowledgement

The author acknowledges the trademarked status and trademark owners of the following wordmarks mentioned in this work of fiction:

Coke: The Coca-Cola Company

Harley: H-D Michigan, Inc.

Honda: Honda Motor Co., Ltd.

The X-Files: Twentieth Century Fox Film Corporation

West Coast Chopper: James, Jesse

Chapter One

෨

There were days when fulfilling your destiny could be a real bitch. Wyc Kilth held the beer bottle loosely between his thumb and forefinger, rolling the bottom edge in a small, slow circle on the cocktail napkin as he considered the number of such days—hell, *years*—he could mark off in his life. He lifted the beer to his mouth, lips pulled in a grim smile.

And then there were days like today.

Finishing off the bottle, he laid it on its side and sent it spinning with a distracted flick of his wrist. Keeping his long legs bent under the table, he rested his elbows on the scarred, thickly lacquered tabletop and let the shadows crisscrossing the back of the bar do their best to camouflage his broad shoulders. He ignored the women openly throwing him *come-fuck-me-now* stares and concentrated on his intended target through the dim lighting. Like the predatory animal that lived within him, he tracked every move Bethany Mitchell made.

Across the room, a customer shot up from his chair and backed into Bethany and the full tray of drinks she was carrying. In one fluid movement, she sidestepped and turned, lifting the tray over her head and out of danger. The action pulled her short black skirt higher up her thighs, the clingy material forming to every luscious curve of an ass he wanted desperately to get his hands on.

His gaze traveled down the back of her bare legs, her smooth skin pale as cream. He couldn't wait to fit her well-shaped calves into his palms, push her legs up high and wide and bury his face in her pussy until she writhed in ecstasy against his mouth.

He adjusted his position to give his swelling cock more room in his jeans and settled his shoulders back against his corner seat. On the opposite side of the bar, Bethany placed two drinks in front of a couple who needed to forget about another round and get a room. The woman pouted and reached for one of the glasses when the man pulled his hand out from under the table to reach inside his jacket for his wallet.

Bethany took the money and, unlike Wyc, ignored the man leering at her breasts. She might be used to men ogling her in her little skirt and tight T-shirt with the bar's logo printed in bright red letters across her chest, but he sure as hell wasn't. Too bad it was imperative for him to keep a low profile, otherwise he'd bash the guy's face in just for fun before teaching him a serious lesson about what could and could not be looked at.

Turning his attention back to Bethany, he watched her flip her long ponytail over her shoulder and return to the main bar for change. Until tonight, he hadn't seen her since their Matching Ritual that had taken place on her first birthday. Even as a baby, she'd had the same dark auburn curls and eyes the color of sunlit emeralds as her royal ancestors. Not to mention a scream that could curdle milk.

Though only nine at the time, he could recall every minute of the ceremony. The rebel insurgence had intensified in the previous weeks, and the Matching Ritual was completed in secret rather than in the normal, public forum. As a young boy, he had been more interested in the guards' weapons than the squalling baby that everyone else was clucking over.

Bethany smiled at something another waitress said as she passed, and Wyc's entire body tightened in response. He expected her to be beautiful as her mother and grandmother had been. But he hadn't expected the sight of her as a grown woman to seize the breath in his lungs.

Once again he cursed the attack that had panicked Bethany's mother, Magdalyne, into fleeing Ilyria with her children through an unmanned portal. Right into the middle of a damn society that would lock him up if he did what was his right—toss Bethany over his shoulder, carry her to a place where he could tear her clothes off and complete the final step in their ritual.

He should have taken her as soon as she stepped out of her car this evening, but he had wanted a chance to observe her unnoticed. To see for himself if there was any truth to the myths surrounding the traditional ceremony that bound an Ilyrian male to his life-mate. Since he was a child too small to stand against a stiff wind, he and his four cousins had the importance of joining Mystic bloodlines and royal ancestry pounded into their brains. Centuries ago, the ritual took place after a couple met and fell in love. But as the time for the prophecy's fulfillment drew near, that quaint custom had been discarded in favor of more practical methods.

Magdalyne had known the royal family would send a retrieval team into this world after them. She and her children were the strongest known line of Ilyrian Mystics. All her daughters, except the youngest, were already matched to royal heirs. Put in place for the prophecy's completion. What Magdalyne didn't foresee was that she'd not live to return to her homeworld, and her children would be separated and lost within the labyrinthine maze of this country's foster care system.

He and his cousins, along with a good number of royal warriors, had spent years tracking Bethany and her sisters. Twelve years ago this world, this country, had finally been pinpointed. Most worlds they'd searched, you went in, asked a question and got an answer—even if you had to take off a few heads to do it. But he had never seen the kind of screwed-up mess like this government's bureaucratic red tape. And with trails long cold, elusive evidence, false leads and sometimes only hearsay to go on, it had been like trying to capture a wisp of smoke by grabbing it with your hands.

Nothing could go wrong at this late date. The Guardian protecting his heart had already begun to fade. If he didn't complete the final rite soon, Bethany would be released not only from her obligations to her people and her birth, but also from his protection. She would be released from him.

A primitive rush of possessiveness surged through his veins. He would never allow another to claim her. She had been promised to him and she belonged to him. Her soul, her heart, her body. Bethany Mitchell was his.

He watched the man return to finger-fucking his date as soon as Bethany dropped off his change and headed toward another customer. She didn't know it yet, but this was her last night working in this dump. Fending off gropes, parrying unimaginative come-ons while trying to keep the customer happy enough to leave a tip. Her damn uniform barely kept her ass covered.

It was time, past time, for her to know her past and accept her future.

* * * * *

"There's a guy in my section who's been tracking you for the past three hours."

Bethany started to turn around, and Donna hissed at her. "Don't look. He'll know we're talking about him."

Letting out an exasperated breath at her friend's drama, Bethany brushed her bangs out of her eyes. Although tonight's crowd was no busier than normal, she was still tired from being called in on her day off yesterday. Last night was the first home game for the local college in this small Midwestern town, and the bar had been a zoo, complete with gorillas and jackasses.

"We are talking about him. If I have a stalker, I'd like to know what he looks like."

Donna snorted. "I wouldn't mind being stalked by him."

"Now I'm really going to look. Which table?" Bethany started to turn again, but Donna grabbed her arm.

"My corner table. Here, I'll let you deliver his drink." Donna plopped a beer onto Bethany's tray next to the other four drinks already there. Bethany immediately placed it back on her friend's tray.

"I have enough work to do. If he's so hot, you go for him."

Tucking a blonde strand of hair behind her ear, Donna let out a long-suffering sigh. "Believe me, I tried. But he barely peels his eyes off you long enough to order a beer. Probably hasn't even noticed that I'm cuter and have bigger boobs." She winked good-naturedly at Bethany and leaned in close. "Why don't you wander back there and let him down easy so I can soothe his broken heart after shift?"

"No thanks." Bethany hoisted her tray up off the bar. She turned, one hand balancing her tray and the other tugging down the ridiculously short black skirt that Barry insisted all his waitresses wear. Said the sexy outfit was good for business. In truth, it didn't hurt her tips any.

"Tell him he's wasting his time if he's waiting on me. I'm not interested."

Without intending to, she found herself scanning the back of the bar as she headed toward her tables. Her movements were jerked to a stop by the dark gaze fastened on her.

Are you sure?

The words—no, not words exactly, more of a distinct impression—floated through her mind. The difference between someone telling her the blanket was soft and touching the cashmere herself. And her mind had just been wrapped in one hell of a blanket. A sensual caress that had her body immediately reacting. Against her will, her nipples tightened and a burning awareness swirled low in her abdomen. Even from across the bar, she could feel heat arcing between them.

In the weak lighting, the man looked huge, dangerous. His body dwarfed the two-person booth he had chosen for his stakeout. Black hair brushed past his shoulders and his mouth alone supplied ample ammunition for countless lust-filled fantasies. The lines of his face were harsh, set off by a heavy five o'clock shadow.

Gorgeous was too nice a word for him, though she couldn't think of another that fit better. Drop-dead, damn sexy maybe. But she wasn't going to go there. Not with that voice, or whatever it was, messing with her head.

She frowned. What was up with that? The long shift was getting to her, letting her imagination run wild. One corner of his mouth tilted up, and she realized she had been staring at him while her thoughts wandered.

He wasn't the average college frat boy who frequented Straight Up. She wasn't interested in them. She wasn't interested in him.

With a toss of her head, she forced her attention back where it belonged. Table seventeen and its four customers waiting for their two beers, a vodka sour and a Coke.

* * * * *

Wyc smiled in pure male appreciation as Bethany turned and wove her way between tables and drunken coeds. Her heart-shaped ass swayed seductively with each step, and he couldn't wait to have it naked and bent over in front of him. He wanted to reach out and touch her with his mind again. Stroke her fantasies. Hell, from just one simple mental caress, her body had responded as if his hands had already been on her.

Seeing her nipples poke at the front of her tight T-shirt made his hands itch to be filled with her sweet flesh. He'd work those nipples into hard, puckered peaks that begged to be taken into his mouth. Would she like gentle flicks with his tongue or sharp nips with his teeth better? He was impatient to hear the sounds she would make when he put his mouth to work on her. Wanted to feel her passion ignite under his guidance.

With a grimace, he shifted in his seat again. Damn, this had been the longest night of his life. As much as he wanted to clear out the bar, spread and take her on a table, he'd wait. Compared to the years he'd already waited, a few more hours until closing time was nothing.

His line of sight was suddenly interrupted by tits the size of watermelons. The busty brunette leaned close and pressed a cocktail napkin into his hands. Her IQ was likely lower than her bra size, but by the way she licked her silicone-enhanced lips and presented her cleavage when she told him that her cell phone number — good day and night — was on the paper, he doubted she figured intelligence was a determining factor in her appeal. He nodded distractedly and shoved it into his pocket with the other six numbers he'd been given.

She turned to leave, and Wyc ignored the practiced pout from the Midwest's answer to the Rocky Mountains. He scanned the crowd. Bethany's auburn ponytail bobbed between two college boys. Her laughter carried across the crowded room as she expertly avoided their pathetic advances.

Good girl, Bethany. A proprietary satisfaction filled him at her ability to deal with their amateurish come-ons. If she'd been less able to handle them, he would have had to plow into the whole freakin' frat pack, and remaining inconspicuous would be a joke. Hard to stay unnoticed when you redecorate a public bar with broken furniture and bleeding boys.

A half hour before closing, he paid for his final drink and left the bar. He waited, hidden in the shadows next to Bethany's car. She had pointedly ignored him after their brief interaction. He smiled to himself. The woman had a stubborn streak, determination. He liked that. But he'd be damned if he'd let her ignore him again.

Forty-five minutes later, she exited the rear of the building with one of the bouncers. He smothered the growl that gathered in the back of his throat when the man said something that made her smile, spring up to her toes and give him a quick peck on his cheek. Unreasonable or not, he didn't care. Now that he had found her, he didn't want her mouth on any other man. Ever.

The back door opened again, one of the other waitresses yelling for the bouncer. The man gave a parting, two-finger salute and headed back inside.

Bethany walked to her car, digging through her purse for her keys. The woman needed some basic lessons on safety. Walking through a dark parking lot at the back of a bar with her head down and attention on anything other than the surrounding area was stupid. Especially for a woman. His woman. She'd learn to be more careful with herself. He'd make sure of it.

Wyc moved to stand beside her as she stopped beside the driver's side door. "Bethany." He purposely kept his voice low and unthreatening.

She dropped her keys, spun around and let out a startled shriek. Immediately, he moved to reassure her, but she plastered herself against the door of her car and opened her mouth to scream again.

He took half a step back and held up his hands. "I'm not going to hurt you. I just want to talk to you. I've been looking for you for a long time." The fear on her face was slowly replaced by curiosity. He smiled.

He swept assurance across her mind, letting her know she had nothing to fear from him.

Her eyes widened, incredible green eyes that flashed in sudden irritation.

"Is that you? Doing that freaky telepathic thing?"

He raised his eyebrows and let her feel his answer rather than hear it.

"Stop it. However you're doing it, stop it. I refuse to hold a conversation with someone who isn't talking. And if you do that whisper in my head thing again, I'm out of here."

"Okay. But I'd rather not stand in the parking lot to talk. We can take my—"

"Oh no. I don't know you from Adam, and I am not going anywhere with you."

She stooped down to pick up her keys and Wyc watched the skirt mold as tight as a second skin around her ass and slide up to within an inch of her pussy. He was becoming very fond of that little black skirt.

"Then I'll meet you at your apartment."

She turned to unlock her door and shook her head. "You are insane. And I'm leaving."

He smiled at her naiveté. She could run, but he'd catch her. She could hide, but he'd find her. The better part of his life had been spent searching for her, and now that he'd found her, there was no way in hell he'd let her just walk away. It wasn't only his future at stake here, but the future of his entire race. And suddenly even more important to him—her future, and possibly even her life, hung in the balance as well.

* * * * *

Bethany grabbed the handle to open the door, but stopped when the man's hand curled around her own. His touch shot electricity through her, focusing her senses on the stranger behind her. Despite the only physical contact between them being the light touch of his hand on hers, his presence surrounded her. Held her.

The heat radiating off his body warmed her back in the cool night air, and his breath brushed against her cheek as he said, "I will not hurt you, but I will not let this night pass without talking to you."

His voice, low and a little rough, coursed through her like the extremely expensive bourbon Barry kept hidden in his office. This man could probably talk a woman to climax. Every time he started to speak, her stomach fluttered like a butterfly on speed, and it had nothing to do with how he appeared out of the dark and scared the hell out of her.

Turning to face him, she swallowed a gasp at the determination in his eyes. She had a feeling that once he set his mind on something, he wasn't easily dissuaded.

He wanted to talk to her? Fine. She'd let him talk. Following her thoughts, her gaze dropped to his mouth. A sudden rush of need poured through her. The man might be irritating and overbearing, but he had the sexiest mouth and voice she had ever encountered. Firm lips, the bottom one a shade fuller than the top with a paper-thin, half-inch scar right underneath.

A slight breeze brought his scent to her. One of leather and exotic cologne that made her body hum in response. Pulled toward him, she instinctively lifted her face, aligning her lips with that fantasy-inducing mouth of his.

His hand lifted, and he traced her bottom lip with his fingertips. Then he closed his eyes and let out a long breath. "Bethany, sweet babydoll, you tempt me too much."

He could probably crack her spine in two without blinking, but the heat building in his eyes made it more than evident that other than being jumped, her bones weren't in much danger. There was no threat of harm either in his expression or in his hold on her. If anything, he looked like he was trying his hardest *not* to scare her with the fierce attraction whipping between them. His effort calmed her fears and stroked her confidence. With a kittenish smile of feminine gratification, she watched the very powerful man in front of her fight the need she stirred in him. "Who's running scared now, Mr. Macho?"

His hand slipped behind her neck, and he pulled her against him. "That mouth of yours needs some discipline," he breathed against her lips.

She tried to drag air into her lungs, but the feel of his chest against her breasts made it stutter out again on a low moan. His embrace tightened. His eyes narrowed, and she swore he was trying to inhale her perfume, only she wasn't wearing any.

Hot and hard, the furiousness of his kiss caught Bethany by surprise. What had spurred her into taunting him, she might never know. Fractured thoughts skittered like shattering glass through her mind. This was not a normal kiss, and it was quickly heading into dangerous territory. Their explosive chemistry had her arching into him and opening her mouth at the insistence of his tongue.

He swept in with a shocking possessiveness. Turning slightly, he pressed her against the car. His hands skimmed over the curve of her waist, down her hips and back up. When the heels of his hands pressed against the sides of her breasts, a soft moan of pleasure sighed out of her mouth. Needing more of his taste, she clutched at his shoulders, closed her lips around his tongue and sucked.

* * * * *

She had teased him, and he had countered her attack, not intending to take more than a quick taste. Just hard and deep enough to force her to recognize the bond she had to him.

He had controlled himself after drawing in her scent. A scent that he would recognize among a million others, one that was uniquely hers and belonged to him. Controlled himself after that first taste and the press of her soft body against his. Even when that goddamn fuck-me-now moan of hers slipped into his mouth.

Then her arms moved up around his neck and her body undulated in a slow wave against his. And when she closed those pink lips around his tongue and sucked, he was lost.

To hell with good intentions.

A violent shudder shook him, and his hands shot down and around to cup her bottom, lifting her until his throbbing erection pressed against her mound. He thrust hard against her, but she kept her thighs closely locked together. With a low growl of irritation, he lifted his head. Before he could tell her to open for him, she brought his face back down to hers and plunged into his mouth, her tongue on a fierce mission of seduction.

Her boldness surprised him. Pleased him. He rocked against her, once, twice, as he continued to plunder the sweet recesses of her mouth.

He wanted her. Here. Now. The need was brutal and ripped his common sense to shreds. The long years of searching were finally ended, and she was in his arms, where she belonged. Even if it took her mind time to catch up, her body and heart accepted him. Wanted him. Reached for him. Knew she was his.

The hardened peaks of her nipples pressed into his chest, and his senses expanded to completely capture her reaction. A risky move. He might not be able to rein back his own response once he set himself free to explore his mate's on every level.

He had been denied her for so long. Too long. He wanted to taste that passion already pulsing with indomitable force between them. Wanted to taste her. All of her.

He heard the pulse of her blood as it raced through her veins and the catch in her breath as her excitement grew. Heard the desperate desire in her thoughts as they swirled in confusion. Triumph roared through him as a yearning heat rose under her skin and her breasts plumped at the brush of his hand. The scent of her arousal speared straight to the center of his being. Knowing she was wet for him tempted him beyond endurance.

With a rough sound low in his chest, he shifted her, pulling her thighs open and wrapping her legs around his waist. She cried out, tightened her hold, and for a brief moment ground against him like a wild woman. Even through their clothes, the heat and soft give of her pussy against his cock fueled the need to have all that heat wrapped around him, milking him deep inside her sweet body.

With a rough movement, he slid his hands back up her thighs. His fingers had just dived under the hem of her skirt when she twisted her face away from his.

"No. Please."

Her ragged plea sliced into his desire. He forced himself to still as she planted her hands against his chest and tried to arch away from him.

She shook her head. "No more."

Lust still flamed in her eyes, but now it was mixed with panic. He took a deep breath and looked down at her hands curling into fists against his shirt. Not pushing him away exactly, but keeping a distance between them while she caught her breath. Her head fell backwards onto the roof of the car as she breathed in long and deep.

He watched her breasts rise and fall and wondered where the hell he went from here. Nothing like skipping from step one to step twenty-three in a well-laid plan. Involuntarily, he groaned at his own thoughts. Right now, the only thing he cared about being well-laid was the woman he held in his hands.

"Whew." Bethany patted his chest. "Time to put me down, big guy, and tell me your name."

He didn't want to let her go. The primal hunger for her body raging within him demanded he overwhelm her with kisses and caresses until she forgot about resisting him. Forgot about everything but opening herself completely to him.

Suppressing a violent curse of denial, he loosened his grip and allowed her to slowly ease down his body until her feet returned to earth.

His gaze drifted from her swollen lips, the surrounding skin red from whisker burn, to the pulse beating erratically at the base of her throat. He placed his hands on the car and reluctantly pushed himself away. Though no longer touching her, he couldn't bring himself to drop his arms, keeping her caught between him and the car.

"Wyc Kilth."

* * * * *

Nervously, Bethany licked her lips and looked up at the man who had just incinerated the memories of every other kiss she had ever received. Burned them to less than ash.

"I'm not sure what just happened here, but it makes me think I shouldn't be anywhere with you that isn't a public place." Her hands were still pressed against him and she tapped his chest, gauging the space between them. "A very public place."

"What are you scared of, Bethany? Me?" His voice rumbled low, the struggle he waged for control still evident.

She looked away from his gaze. "I don't think so. Though you haven't really given me a reason not to be. Any woman in her right mind would be at least a little suspicious of a stranger who sat and watched her for hours, then backed her up against a car and kissed her into oblivion."

The fierce lines of lust on Wyc's face softened to something less desperate, but just as dangerous. The change in his expression eased her wariness.

Wary? She was wary? She shouldn't be wary. She should be frightened as hell. But there was an aching familiarity about him that she couldn't explain. Like he lived in an elusive memory drifting on the outside edge of her consciousness. By the same token, she was certain Wyc Kilth was not a man any woman could forget.

If she believed in reincarnation, she'd think they had been lovers in some past life. But belief in anything along that route was parked strictly in the science fiction category. Emphasis on *fiction*.

He lifted her chin with the tip of his finger so she was once more staring into his unfathomable gaze. "What's the frown for?"

She still couldn't tell the exact color of his eyes. "How did you do that earlier? Talk inside my head? Was it some kind of subliminal suggestion?"

"No." He took a deep breath and, with the tips of his fingers, brushed her brow and over her cheek in a gentle touch. "Where do you want to go to talk? I promise. No kissing unless you ask."

"Don't hold your breath."

A dark flame leaped in his eyes. He leaned in close and whispered in that smoky voice, "There'll come a time, Bethany, when you won't only ask me to kiss you, you'll beg me to fuck you." The absolute certainty with which he spoke made her skin tingle with unwanted anticipation.

But from experience, she knew that anticipation would be all she got. Being cursed was the only explanation she could come up with. She'd never had a man go down on her or even give her a simple freaking finger-fuck.

A year ago she had tried nearly every night for a month to get laid. Different men, different bars, even different cities. Every single time, something happened to the guy she picked up, cutting the evening short well before she attained any hint of satisfaction. Whenever a man got close enough to do some good, he would get suddenly and violently ill, start cramping up, turn ghostly pale and thrash around in pain. One even passed out cold and scared the crap out of her.

Once, out of desperation, she had stripped and straddled a guy as soon as they got to his place. In a heartbeat, he had gone from grinning like a lottery-winning loon to screeching. A horrible, high-pitched shriek that sounded like a small, cornered animal and made her want to check to see if her ears were bleeding. He pushed her off and swore she had stabbed his dick, though when he checked, he was completely whole—and completely deflated.

No matter how turned on a man was with her, he never got close to finishing what he started. Much to her endless frustration. And men thought a woman with PMS was a bitch to be around. They had no idea.

Surprisingly, Wyc hadn't fallen prey to the curse. Maybe it was because she was still dressed when she started climbing up his body. She wondered if she could rub herself to climax against his erection through their clothes. If they had kept going, she might have found out.

She gave herself a mental eye roll. Right. Given a couple more minutes of close contact, he would probably have collapsed in agony on the asphalt beside her car. Still, his pain, her gain.

Blinking away images of Wyc bringing her to the point of begging, she drew herself up straight. "If you're trying to convince me to go with you, you're headed in the wrong direction."

"Perhaps this will aid my argument." He pulled a delicate gold necklace out of the front pocket of his jeans. At the end dangled a ring of intricately woven silver and gold.

"That's my ring." Her voice was a whisper of disbelief as she reached for it. "How did you get it? It was lost when I was a child." Even in the muted glow of the streetlight, the ring shone bright as if reflecting an inner fire that needed no external light to set off the complicated design.

"Are you sure it's yours?"

She turned it over in her hand, looking at it carefully. The elaborate scrolls ran around the entire ring and interlaced the two metals in a complex pattern she had never seen the equal to. She tilted it to the side and held it out to where he could see what she saw.

"Here. If you look closely, you can see the name Ilyria. That was my mother's name. At least that's what I think."

Wyc rolled the chain around his palm, bringing the ring back to his hand. Silencing a cry, Bethany watched the ring disappear back into his pocket. It had been the only link she had to her mother. When she was twelve, it had disappeared in the same fire that had killed her third set of foster parents. That ring was hers and she wanted it back.

He had moved while they talked, and the sudden light thrown from the back door of the bar when it opened illuminated his features. The eyes she had thought were dark brown were actually a deep blue. A mesmerizing, midnight blue. His thick black hair had a slight wave to it she hadn't noticed before. High cheekbones and a square chin framed that hard mouth she desperately wanted on hers again, damn it. This man made her lose all sense of modesty, and it pissed her off.

Jim, one of the older bartenders, exited the building. He headed across the lot, but stopped when he saw them standing there.

"Everything all right, Bethany?"

She waved at him and smiled. "Just fine, thanks. Have a good night."

After a moment of hesitation, he nodded and climbed into his truck. Neither she nor Wyc spoke until Jim had pulled out of the parking lot.

"Does this mean you're coming with me?"

Bethany returned her attention to Wyc and frowned up at him. "Hardly. It means I'm willing to listen to what you have to say. But not right now. It's late, I'm tired and I need to think. Something I can't do at the moment."

The muscles around his jaw tensed for a moment. "Tomorrow it is."

She shook her head. "No. I have a date."

"Break it."

"Excuse me?" Her voice sharpened in reaction to his command.

He seemed to take no notice as he captured her between his body and the car again, resting his hands against its roof, one on either side of her.

"I said, break it."

She crossed her arms over her chest and lifted her chin. "I don't think so."

His leaned in until his eyes were even with hers. "Bethany —" his voice rumbled in a low growl.

"No. I am not going to break my date for you. He's a really nice guy, and I'm not going to stand him up. But I may change my mind about talking to you."

Wyc lifted his head and stared out into the night. Angry tension vibrated from him, and she resisted the urge to fidget. For a long minute, he didn't move. Then taking a deep breath, he unclenched his jaw, dropped his arms and straightened. "I'll meet you for breakfast then."

"I have plans."

"Damn it, woman. Are you always this difficult?"

She smiled. "Are you always this bossy?"

He glanced around the empty parking lot and muttered a curse.

"Why are you in such a hurry? I told you I'd talk to you. For being such a big scary guy, you should consider that progress."

"A big scary guy?"

"Long black hair, six-foot what? Four?"

"Five."

She tapped his shoulder. "Leather jacket, black work boots. You probably have a Harley parked around the corner. Not the kind of man my mother would approve of."

"Your mother's dead."

Her good humor abruptly fled. "How do you know that?"

"I told you. I've been looking for you a long time."

"Why?"

He shook his head and backed up a step. "Not here."

She ran her tongue over lips suddenly dry and closed her eyes. When she opened them, he was still there, still waiting. Filling the night, watching her with those dark eyes and sexy as hell.

God, she was attracted to him. She didn't want to be, but he was the type of man who shattered the civilized restraints on a woman's basic, primitive need to mate with the Alpha male. Her body hummed with the desire to capture him inside her, regardless of how medieval she knew the whole idea to be.

It was a good thing she was so tired, or she'd be sorely tempted to find out where that kiss could have taken her. Wyc Kilth was fantasy rolled up in pure lust. She needed the bright light of day to take the edge off his mystery. To put her reactions in perspective.

"Fine. Tomorrow then. I'll meet you at the diner across the street at noon for lunch."

He frowned, but nodded.

She reached out a hand to stop him as he turned to leave. "Just tell me one thing. How did you get the ring?"

Wyc looked down at where her hand clutched his arm, and then up at her face. "Tomorrow."

Chapter Two

ℭᴏ

Bethany stood across the street from the coffee shop and checked her watch again. 11:59. She should go in. She should go home. She let out a sigh. She should make up her mind.

Looking around the busy intersection, she was pleased with her meeting choice. She didn't think he'd try to get under her skirt again in such a public place. Just in case, she had worn jeans. She fell in with the tide of people rushing along the crosswalk, hoping that with lots of witnesses, she wouldn't be tempted to climb up his body again either.

Half believing the whole seduction by a bad boy in black leather had been the weird waking dream of an overactive imagination, Bethany opened the diner's glass door, a tinkling, tinny bell ringing over her head. The smell of burnt coffee and old grease rolled over her as she nodded to a couple of regulars seated at the counter to the right of the door. She ate lunch here several times a week—whenever she worked the early shift at the bar. With an entire page of meals for $3.99 or less, it was a perfect fit for her budget and gave her time to relax before facing the tried and tired flirting techniques of the latest fraternity crowd.

"Hey, sweetie," Sharon called out as she bussed by with a tray full of hamburgers and lunch specials. "Hot chocolate as usual?"

She nodded and Sharon gestured with her free hand. "Go ahead and grab a seat. I'll be right with you." Her friendly smile pulled one from Bethany in return. With a swish of ample hips and brown polyester, the waitress continued winding through tables to a family seated at a six-top by the front plate-glass window.

Bethany felt a hand on her shoulder and turned. There was no one behind her, no one touching her. But across the crowded space she spotted Wyc watching her from a table in the back. The intensity of his stare as much a physical force as his fingers on her skin last night.

Seated in a packed-out restaurant in the middle of the day, he looked as dangerous as he had in the dark, deserted parking lot. His black jacket had been exchanged for a navy T-shirt that stretched over wide shoulders. He shifted, and she watched the play of muscles across his chest and biceps, her fingers itching to more intimately explore them.

When she glanced back up at his face as she slid into the seat across from him, a hint of amusement lightened the dark blue of his eyes. Unbidden, her gaze fell to his lips. A sudden, fierce desire to taste that mouth again fired her with a passion she couldn't rationalize.

"Later."

It took a moment for the blatant promise permeating his tone to sink in. The dark, husky sound of his voice had her clenching her thighs together as lust washed through her. She couldn't help it. After last night, she was more than curious to see what else that talented mouth could do. If just thinking about it made her pussy cream, there was no telling what his mouth could accomplish if it moved out of her thoughts and onto her body.

She blinked and tore her eyes away from Wyc's mouth. The temperature was kept too warm in the restaurant, and she wished she'd worn a cotton blouse instead of a sweater. The heat was making it hard for her to breathe. This wasn't good.

Wyc reached across the table and covered her hand with his. Turning her hand over, he stroked the pulse point vibrating in her wrist like a trapped bumblebee.

"Don't worry. I won't push you. Though your responsiveness tempts me to drag you out of here and see just how fast I can make that heart of yours beat before you scream my name in ecstasy."

Bethany swallowed and pulled her hand out of his gentle grasp. Arrogant bastard. She looked up with relief when Sharon approached the table.

Plunking a cup of hot chocolate in front of her and refreshing Wyc's coffee, Sharon asked, "So you two made up your minds yet?"

Bethany glanced at Wyc, caught the flare of arousal heating his gaze as he said, "I know what I want."

Biting her bottom lip, she tamped down another hormonal surge. *So, so unfair that with a few words he can make me desperate to do him right on this table.* Crossing her arms over her chest, she glared at Wyc and ordered. "The lunch special's all I want."

Sharon turned toward Wyc with a knowing smile and cocked a hip. "Anything on the menu you want?"

A sexy grin stole over his face before he turned back to Sharon. "A number four. Rare. Extra fries."

"Gotcha." With a wink, Sharon turned on her heel and headed toward the kitchen, hips sashaying enough to sway the ends of her apron bow from side to side. Bethany watched until she disappeared through a swinging door, studiously avoiding the man sitting across the table from her.

She hadn't expected him to have the same effect on her in the middle of the day as he had in the dark when she was tired and alone. If anything, the magnetism of his attraction had increased. She didn't understand his pull on her. It made her want to strip him naked, take him in her hands, her mouth, her body. Made her wish she hadn't stopped him last night.

She shivered. He made her want to run like hell and never look back.

Wyc reached across the table and brushed her cheek with his fingertips. Her head jerked up to see concern crowd the desire in his expression. "This isn't going to be easy."

She shook her head. "I'm not sure what you're talking about. I just want to know how you got my ring."

He leaned back and leisurely placed one arm across the top of the empty chair beside him, as graceful as a panther at rest. His position was relaxed, yet the air around him seemed stretched taut by a barely leashed power.

"Okay. We'll start there. Your ring actually belongs to me." He fished in his pocket and brought out the intricately crafted gold band.

She took it out of his hand when he offered it to her. With a frown, she slid it over her thumb where it dangled loosely around her knuckle. "This isn't mine. It's too big."

"That's because it's mine." Wyc took it back and slid it over the middle finger of his left hand. "They were crafted at the same time, by the same artisan."

Bethany felt hope swell in her chest. "You know where they were made? Do you know who had them made? Anything about my family?" She gripped the table so hard the edge of it bit into her palms. She welcomed the sensation. It kept her grounded enough not to launch herself over their drinks and shake the information out of him.

Before she could rattle off the other dozen and more questions on the tip of her tongue, Wyc bolted from his chair, grabbed her hand and pulled her out of her seat.

"What are you doing?" She pulled against him, but he ignored her protests as easily as he ignored her struggles.

He didn't look back as he dragged her through the swinging door leading into the kitchen. They nearly ran Sharon over as she turned from the pass-though with a tray full of dishes.

"Hey," she shouted, grabbing a plate of fries and chicken strips before it could slide off her tray. "You can't come back here."

Wyc glanced around. "Which way to the back door?" The sharp bite to his question made Sharon take half a step back.

Wyc growled and glared at the older woman. His grip never lessened on Bethany's hand. "Which way?"

"There." Sharon pointed to the left and immediately Bethany was hauled in that direction. Past a surprised busboy who barely managed to escape being mown down by the six-and-a-half foot mass of fury and motion Wyc had turned into.

A cook was opening the large, walk-in refrigerator when Wyc shoved it shut to pass. The man spun around with a curse and Wyc shouldered him out of the way as easily as he would a skinny, eight-year-old girl. Bethany turned to apologize, but only got out a few stuttered syllables before Wyc yanked her through the heavy delivery door at the rear of the kitchen and slammed it shut behind them. Once in the back alley, Wyc thrust her between two large garbage dumpsters.

She jerked out of his grasp and spun to face him. "What the—"

"Stay put and be quiet."

For a moment, she was shocked enough to actually obey his command. But it was a brief moment. Then she grabbed enough of her wits to give him a piece of her mind, but he had already turned to face the alley, granting her his back. Furious, she launched herself at him, pushing against his shoulders with as much force as she could muster in the small space he had stuffed her in.

Her palms slapped against solid muscle. Warm muscle under soft cotton that didn't budge even when she braced a foot on the brick wall behind her for extra leverage. The only effect she seemed to produce was irritation as he shot her a quick glare over his shoulder.

Wyc's wide shoulders blocked her view into the alley, but his relaxed stance assured her that whatever reason he had for dragging her out of the restaurant couldn't be too serious.

"Thought that was you, Kilth. And just when this retrieval assignment was getting boring."

The words originated somewhere just in front of Wyc, and a chill passed over her skin. She sank against the diner's back wall. Though unable to see the man addressing Wyc, she recognized the ugly threat in his voice that went beyond menace. It rolled over her like oily sludge, and she fought down a shudder.

Wyc made a derisive noise and shook his head. "You're more delusional than normal, Enath, if you think there's anything here for you. And as much as I'd love to pound your ass into the ground, I'm running a little short on time today."

A low chuckle slid around Wyc to scrape along her scalp. "I know she's behind you. I can smell her. And she's ripe for harvesting. You can move, or you can die. Either way, I'm taking her with me."

"She's matched."

"There are ways around that. Not much fun for her, but a hell of a show."

Wyc's response was a low snarl, more animal than human. Definitely a scary sound.

No matter how she took it, this was not a normal exchange, even between two men fighting over a woman. The whole dash through the restaurant hadn't unnerved her nearly as much as this conversation.

He could smell her? Harvesting? And what the hell did Wyc mean when he said she was *matched*? She didn't like the sound of any of it, and wondered if both these guys weren't flying high on whatever was their chosen poison. She hadn't gotten that impression from Wyc when he was sitting across the table from her, but he could have been hiding it.

Maybe he was simply humoring the wackjob in front of him. Making things up to go along with the guy's insane comments to distract him. Whatever, she wasn't going to stick around to find out.

Pressing her shoulders back into the wall until she was certain that the bricks would leave permanent marks in her skin, she waited for the first opportunity to flee.

* * * * *

Wyc glanced down the alley. No one else was in sight, but that wasn't likely to be the case for long. Especially since the asshole in front of him probably hadn't been very polite as he followed them through the kitchen. It was a good bet the police had been called and were on their way.

He didn't have time for cops. If the Predator had tracked Bethany to this place, the Sleht's bred destroyers weren't far behind. If Enath's retrieval was unsuccessful, Slayers would be set loose on Bethany's scent. And their brutality and thoroughness made the Predators' threat look as dangerous as newborn puppies.

As the time drew near for the Ilyrian prophecy to be fulfilled, the Sleht were desperate to keep the promised sons from being born. For centuries, they had stalked Ilyrian women of Mystic descent through the different worlds and times where they were hidden.

In the past, Predators would take them back to the rebels and they would be used to breed bastards in an effort to mix Sleht blood with the powers passed down through the women. Once found, if a woman couldn't be retrieved or was already fully matched, she had not been left alive to continue the Ilyrian lineage. If they were now taking matched women, then the rumors were true. The images that filled his mind at the thought made his stomach turn in revulsion.

Enath took a step forward. "So what's it gonna be? Are you going to step aside, or are we going to play? I just hope you're a better fighter than your brothers. At least I'd get to enjoy grinding you to dust before I take your woman."

Primitive, brutal fury tore through Wyc's veins. The commitment and need to avenge his younger brothers' deaths nearly blinding in its intensity. Wyc had known a Sleht Predator killed his brothers. Even knew it was one of three.

Until this moment, he had never known which of the three was ultimately responsible. Not that he wouldn't have taken out each one. Simply existing as a Predator was reason enough to die. But he wanted to know who had murdered his twin brothers. Wanted to have that knowledge when, by his hands, the one who took his brothers' lives was forced to surrender his own. The time had come. At long last.

He stepped forward and took a deep breath. Bethany's scent filled his nostrils. With a hard jolt, her presence brought him back to reason. She was in mortal danger. His woman. His future and the future of his people. His first priority was to protect her. Even at the cost of delaying personal vengeance.

He watched the scum before him shift his feet further apart in anticipation of attack. Mottled skin pulled too tightly over eyes and nose stretched even more grotesquely in an expression Wyc supposed was meant to be a smile. With such an ugly face, who could tell? He had the Sleht beat in height by several inches, but Enath was built like a solid block of cement. If he ever had a neck, it had been swallowed by his shoulders ages ago.

There was only one thing Wyc wanted more than to see Enath's lifeblood pouring out into this garbage-filled alley, and that was to get Bethany to safety. He felt her rising panic and didn't want her to do something stupid that could cause her harm.

The back door to the café opened a crack. The cook stuck his prominent nose out and shouted that the police were on their way, adding invectives after nearly every syllable.

Enath's head swung toward the sudden noise. Wyc didn't wait for another chance. With a lightning-fast spin, he executed a perfect roundhouse kick and planted the heel of his boot in the Sleht's face, sending him crashing into a pile of empty boxes. The café's door snapped shut, and Wyc stepped forward to slam Enath's face into the asphalt. He wanted to finish the son of a bitch off, but if he killed him, the Predator would return to his natural form and tonight's local news would look like an episode from the *X-Files*.

"Today's your lucky day, you bastard," he whispered as he straightened over Enath's unconscious form.

Time to get Bethany the hell out of here. He turned around just in time to catch sight of her tight little ass disappearing around the corner.

Damn it, why couldn't the woman stay put like she was told? Didn't she know she could get herself killed by not doing what he told her? He wouldn't let that happen. Not to her. Not again.

* * * * *

Bethany's hands shook as she dug her apartment keys from the pocket of her jeans. She couldn't believe that Wyc had kicked that guy in the face. He had been rude, threatening and possibly insane, but that was no reason to beat someone to a bloody pulp. She shivered, remembering the animal ferocity of Wyc's attack. Enath hadn't stood a chance.

The key scraped along the outside of the lock several times before she managed to ram it home. The lock clicked open and she breathed a sigh of relief.

A solid heat pressed against her back as a large hand appeared in front of her face, pushing the door open. She drew a deep breath to scream, but an arm of iron snaked around her waist, and the hand that had been on the door clamped around her mouth. She twisted and fought, her heels finding their targets in shins and insteps.

"Jesus, Bethany," Wyc hissed in her ear, "would you get out of the hall?" He pushed her into her apartment and slammed the door shut behind them. For a long moment, Wyc said nothing, simply raked a harsh glare over her from the top of her head to her feet.

Against her will, she felt her body responding to his openly sexual scrutiny once he passed her chin. With her heart still racing from the encounter in the alley, his thorough perusal only increased her irritation. She had never noticed before how irritation caused her nipples to harden and her pussy to cream. She clenched her sex, repressed a shudder of pleasure and then fisted her hands in anger. Why the hell couldn't she control her reaction to this man?

When his gaze returned to settle on her face, his dark eyes burned into her as he shoved his fingers roughly through his hair. "I told you to stay put."

"What?"

"You ran off. You could have been hurt. Killed. You have no idea what you're up against."

"You're insane. Get out of my apartment." She started to step around him and reach for the door, but he grabbed her shoulders and backed her against it instead.

"How the hell am I supposed to keep you safe when I can't trust you to obey me?"

"Keep me safe? I was perfectly fine until you showed up. Now I'm getting dragged through restaurants and threatened with harvesting. What the hell does that mean? I'm not a crop in a field."

Her voice had risen steadily with each statement. Taking a deep breath, she forced herself to calm down. When he opened his mouth to respond, she shook her head sharply, cutting him off. "No. Don't explain. I don't want to know. I don't care. I only want you out of my house. Out of my life."

The harsh flash of anger in his eyes faded slightly. He moved nearer. "This isn't the way I wanted to explain things to you—"

"No. Stop talking. I don't want to hear what you have to say. I just want you to go away." Her words ended on a desperate, whispered plea as she flattened her palms on his chest and pushed.

He didn't back up. Instead, he moved in until her hands were caught, pressed between his chest and her breasts. She looked up into his face, terrifyingly close to her own. The hard, steady rhythm of his heart pounded under her palm. Seemed to pulse through her hand until it fueled the hammering of her own heart.

"I can't do that, Bethany."

The finality of his tone staggered her. He was not going to let go. She hated being afraid, yet Wyc frightened her beyond anything she had ever known. And the most horrifying part was that in spite of her fear, she was struggling with a frantic desire to throw herself as deep as she could into this man.

She felt, rather than heard, the rumble deep in his chest against her palms as his face sharpened with desire. He leaned down, his hands on the door on either side of her face. His thighs pressed against her, and his hips pinned her body in place, the softness of her belly giving way to the solid length of his hardened cock.

She took a quick, deep breath and inhaled the same exotic scent she had thought was cologne last night. It wasn't. The strange mixture of spice, musk and man that sent her senses reeling for want of his touch wasn't aftershave or soap. It was him. And once again, she found herself being inexplicably drawn to him. Felt something hidden so deep within her that she hadn't even known of its existence rise up, shake to awareness and reach for him.

It terrified her.

"What do you want from me? I don't even know you." Her voice was less than a whisper, her words a prayer for release. Not from him, but release from the escalating need within her for him to fuck her deep and hard. She didn't understand this need he created in her, but no matter how much she fought it or tried to ignore it, it wasn't going away. Every minute in his presence intensified her body's demand until she burned for his touch. Wild and fierce, he surrounded her with a presence that exceeded his obvious physical dominance. As if he were literally sinking into her skin, burrowing past her defenses into places that had, until now, been hers alone. Asserting ownership over her very heart and soul.

He lowered his face toward hers, intent clear in his eyes. He wanted her — all of her. And he was going to take her. Mark her as his. As his mouth closed over hers, she felt the branding begin.

Chapter Three

ಐ

I don't even know you.

Bethany's words echoed in Wyc's head. He cursed the twisted, malicious hand of fate that had kept him from her for so long. She should have borne him at least one child by now. Instead, she was telling him to get out of her life. Wanting to escape from him.

Except she wasn't going to escape him. Not now. Not ever. The sooner she realized that, the easier this would be on both of them. He'd planned on explaining her heritage and family to her before fucking her. Explain how he was her future, how she was his.

But now her hands pressed against his chest, her breath was coming in short, quick pants, and her eyes darkened with increasing arousal. Her scent rose to taunt him. She wanted him. Reaching past her fear to touch him.

And she was going to stand there and tell him to go away? Like hell she was.

Already tense muscles tightened further. When she refused to go with him last night, he had wanted to push the issue. More than just push. He had wanted to throw her over his shoulder and haul her back to his home. Back to where she'd be safe. Where she belonged. Where he could lay her out and feast until he was sated.

That's exactly what he would have done if her mother hadn't panicked and jumped through the first portal she came to with Bethany and her sisters. He wasn't the only one who cursed the fact that they hadn't entered a different place and time. A more reasonable world where it was acceptable to ride in and simply take what was yours.

Anger stirred his lust, and he took her mouth with the ferocity of a warrior bent on absolute conquest. Conquest without negotiation. Without compromise.

She let out a startled gasp, but he didn't pause or gentle his attack. Instead, he took advantage of her opened mouth and plunged his tongue inside, insistent, dominating. Letting her know in no uncertain terms how he was going to take her body. Just the thought of finally being inside her tight, hot little cunt had his cock throbbing painfully for release.

He swept his tongue over her teeth before returning to fill her mouth with fast, pulsing strokes. Her tongue swirled tentatively over his and his desire spiked in a violent rush. He growled and shoved his fingers into her hair, angling her head and holding her in place to give him greater access to the sweet honeyed taste of her mouth.

With a soft whimper, Bethany fisted her hands in his shirt and arched into him. He dragged his teeth over her bottom lip and then bit it lightly. Pulling back, he looked down into her face. Her lips were swollen from his kisses, her cheeks high in color. Her wide eyes, dilated with her own desire so that only the thinnest rim of green circled her pupils.

She was stunning. So incredibly sexy she stopped his breath.

He would be her first lover. That safeguard had been taken care of at her first birthday. He closed his eyes and tried to think past the sharp slap of need pounding through his blood. He had to slow down. Had to take his time, make sure he was in enough control not to hurt her more than necessary.

She flexed her fingers, scraping his chest through his T-shirt with her short nails. He ground his teeth together as his restraint wavered at her touch. When she flexed her fingers against him again, this time slower and pressing harder, his lust clawed to be free of its leash.

"Bethany." He didn't attempt to smooth the ragged need in his voice.

She licked her lips, pushed up on her toes and placed an openedmouthed kiss on his neck. She sucked his skin between her teeth and bit down hard enough to leave a mark.

He wrapped her tightly in his arms as she licked the spot she had bitten. "Do you have any idea what you're doing to me?" His blood rammed through veins on fire, and every thought in his head involved her naked and open.

She nipped at his neck again, and then stretched against him like a cat rousing from a long nap. He released her long enough to pull her sweater over her head and drop it. A second later, her plain white bra was on the floor next to it. His eyes narrowed as he took her breasts in his hands and molded them to his palms.

Mine. The word tore through him with a surge of possessiveness that bordered the line of insanity. He didn't understand it, but he didn't question it. At least one Matching myth—fierce possessiveness—was true after all.

He circled his thumbs around her nipples and watched them pucker into coral-colored peaks. Bethany dropped her head back and let out a low moan that went straight to his cock. He lowered his mouth to her breast and ran his tongue around the tip. Pulling the hardened bud into his mouth, he drew on it forcefully until she was twisting her fingers through his hair and writhing against the door.

He kept her other breast cupped in his hand, feathering his fingers over and around the nipple. When it couldn't get any tighter, he pinched and tugged it in rhythm to his sucking of its twin.

She jolted, and her fingers dug into his head. "Oh my God, Wyc. Stop. Please. I can't breathe."

He chuckled and slid his free hand over her belly and unsnapped her jeans. She tried to push him away, but he ignored her, lowered her zipper and slid his hand inside her panties. He released a harsh groan when he found her hot and slick.

"You're wet." He pressed his fingers between the lips of her sex and started to spread her dampness around and over her clit. "So wet and ready."

She rocked against his hand again and again, her body tensing, reaching for release. Her juices coated his fingers as he increased the pressure on her clit. He pressed her swollen nub between his index and middle finger. With a moan, she bore down hard.

"You like that, don't you, babydoll." He moved his fingers faster, harder against her clit.

"Oh God. Oh Wyc. Oh God." She panted out each phrase over and over and her palms flattened on the door behind her. He squeezed her breast and pushed a finger up inside her pussy.

Suddenly, her body shuddered and her cunt spasmed around his finger. Her eyes went wide with surprise, her ivory skin flushed with the heat of her climax. Her thighs clamped around his hand and she let out a low keening sound. Panic flashed through her eyes, and she shook her head hard enough to send her hair flying around her face.

"Let it go, Bethany. Now." He flexed the finger within her pulsing cunt, skillfully forcing her orgasm to continue long past when it would have faded on its own. When the tremors slowed, her body slumped against the door, her hands on his arms for balance. He withdrew his finger and she sucked in a fast breath. His hand lingered on her mound, teasing her with gentle swirls of his fingers in her soaked curls. Another violent shudder racked her body.

"See what I can do to you? And I'm going to do it again and again. Starting now."

* * * * *

Bethany bit her bottom lip until the pain helped clear the euphoric fog from her brain. She forced herself back to reality when all she really wanted to do was melt to the floor in a puddle of sated desire. What the hell had happened between her telling Wyc to leave and those mewling sounds that had just come out of her?

Wyc yanked her jeans and underwear down her legs. "Lift your foot," he said. She did.

He tugged off her shoe and sock at the same time he removed one leg of her jeans. Repeating the process, he finished stripping her and straightened. In one fluid movement, he dragged his own shirt up and off.

The sight of his bare chest made it difficult to think. He had a faint tattoo of a dragon on his left pec. Very sexy. Too sexy. She took a deep breath and focused. On the ceiling.

"Wyc, wait."

"I'm past waiting, Bethany. And so are you." He shoved his hand between her thighs, pressing his fingers into her damp heat. Her head snapped back down. His unrelenting gaze burned against her bare skin like a furnace blast. As if to prove his point, he thrust a long finger up inside her, making her gasp.

"But I can't—" She cut her own words off with a moan when he started tracing small circles on the inner wall of her vagina with his finger.

"You already did."

She tried to catch her breath, catch the reason he wouldn't be able to go through with this. A small voice at the back of her brain begged to keep her concern to herself. The louder voice of her conscience won out.

"I mean, you can't."

He pulled his hand away from her and began undoing the button fly of his jeans. "The hell I can't, babydoll."

She swallowed, trying to focus on what she wanted to say and not on what he was doing.

"You don't understand. No one has ever been able to fuck me."

That stopped his movements cold. His eyes held an arctic gleam that shot a shaft of alarm through her.

"And how many men have tried to fuck you, Bethany?" The ice in his tone could have frozen a sunbeam.

"Enough. And they all wound up sick or hurt. I'm trying to tell you that I'm cursed—"

He pushed his jeans down over his hips. "Not cursed. Protected. Kept for me."

There was something fundamentally wrong with his statement, but all coherent thought streamed out of her brain at the sight of his erection so suddenly and fully revealed. He was huge. Thick. Long. The head of his cock dark red, almost purple in color. Dark veins ran down the length, standing out in stark relief. His balls were already drawn up tightly under his shaft.

He was planning to put that inside her. Doubt and disbelief rolled through her. Fear started to win the battle against lust, but before she could move, he gripped her thighs and lifted her off the floor. Her back pressed against the door, and her hands flew up to grasp his shoulders. Spreading her legs, he opened her body. He looked at her exposed cunt, and the planes of his face sharpened with a mixed expression of possessiveness and want.

He lifted her higher and stepped into her, pressing her wet pussy flush to his stomach.

"Wrap your legs around my waist. Now," he growled when she hesitated. His cock prodded her bottom and she squirmed, trying to move higher and locking her ankles together behind his back.

He shifted her, his fingers biting into the cheeks of her ass, until her sex slid along his shaft. She looked down. He wasn't entering her, just moving her slowly up and down. His cock started to shine as her juices spilled out and over him, more each time he pushed her up and then allowed her to slide back down his length.

"That's right, baby. Watch." The sexy timbre of Wyc's voice drove her lust up another level. "Look at how wet you're getting me. I can feel your heat, smell your need. The way you're creaming all over my cock is driving me crazy."

She couldn't tear her eyes away from the straining head of his penis trapped between their bodies. The heat of his cock scorched her pussy and made her whimper in need. Pre-cum beaded out from the slit at the top, glistening and pearly white.

Giving in to the urge to taste it, she reached down, wiped it off with the tip of her finger. As she brought it up to her mouth, the heavy musk smell of his sex invaded her nostrils, and she realized that he had stopped sliding her over his cock.

His chest didn't move with a breath, his eyes didn't blink, his hands didn't shift from their almost painful grasp where he held her in place. The only thing that kept him from looking completely frozen in time as his eyes focused on what she was doing was the ticcing muscle at the side of his jaw.

Her mouth curved into a slight smile right before she parted her lips, slipped her finger inside and sucked. Slowly, she pulled her finger free.

"Mmmm," she hummed, pressing her lips together. Bethany watched in amazement and alarm as dark lust—wild, fierce and primal—flamed in Wyc's eyes.

His body jerked, bucked once against her and a strangled noise forced its way free of his throat. His mouth branded hers with a kiss so violent and base in its taking, she was lost. Completely engulfed by him.

She felt a release in her soul, heard him murmur against her lips before crushing them under his again. He positioned one forearm underneath her butt, rocked his body seductively against hers until her cunt was clenching with a need to be filled.

He continued the rocking motion and slid first one, then two fingers up inside her. Pushing them up until her virgin barrier stopped them. He pressed against it, and she stiffened from the brief stab of pain. He pulled his fingers back and began stretching her opening until three fingers were able to slide inside her.

It was uncomfortable, but not unbearable. The rocking motion of his cock against her clit overrode the slow burn of muscles being stretched, and his consuming kisses kept seizing her attention. She twisted her hips, seeking the release he was building her to. He changed position slightly. A wave of apprehension rolled over her as she realized he had replaced his fingers with the hot, smooth head of his cock. Its steady ingress unyielding and insistent.

He worked just the head in as he maintained the rocking motion of their bodies. The fit was tight, and she squeezed him hard, afraid to move either up or down. She shook with the effort to remain still. The need to have him fully implanted within her struggled against the overwhelming surge of emotion and pain at having him invade her body.

He withdrew slightly and then pushed in again, deeper. She sucked in a breath and dug her nails into his shoulders. Once again, he pressed against the barrier, only this time, the pain was sharper. She shook her head and closed her eyes, trying to push up off him.

He didn't release her. Instead, he lifted her up a couple of inches. The relief was immediate. She let out a deep breath and opened her eyes to tell him to put her down.

Vivid resolve gleamed in his eyes and harsh lines of intent carved his face. She realized what he was going to do too late to stop it. Before she could take in another breath, he pulled her back down. His hips shot up hard and quick and he embedded himself completely inside her.

She was shocked by the sudden, searing pain and her fingernails bit into his skin until they drew blood. After a few frozen seconds, she consciously sucked in a shallow, testing breath, and tried to get her lungs to work. The first, piercing sting began to fade seconds after he pushed fully in, but her muscles continued to throb in resistance to his invasion. Her entire body felt battered and tense, her mind confused and her emotions frighteningly off-center.

Wyc wrapped his arms around her, managing to hold her firmly in place and at the same time cradle her body gently against his own. Though he nuzzled the curve of her neck with surprising tenderness and scattered soft kisses over her cheek and temple, his voice was gruff when he spoke.

"It's done, babydoll. You're mine. Try to relax your muscles and let your body adjust to having me inside of you. It'll be better in a minute."

She nodded and noticed that even that slight movement eased the ache within toward pleasure. She tightened her thighs and pressed her pelvis forward. Warmth circled her lower body, the throbbing turning hurt into need.

Her nipples became almost too sensitive to bear as she moved against his chest. She tried clenching her sex and gasped at the intimate feeling of holding Wyc so solid and deep inside her. Sensation spun out from her cunt to spike in her clit and echo clear through to her toes. She moaned and clamped her thighs more forcefully about his hips.

Wyc groaned and moved his hands to cup her bottom. "Damn, woman. You're making it impossible for me to wait."

She tightened her muscles around his cock again. "Don't wait," she whispered as she shivered from another pleasure spike. She wiggled her butt and tried to get him in deeper. "Not another second."

With a sharp intake of breath, he pulled out of her and then slowly pushed back inside. Bethany let out a hiss of ecstasy as he repeated the process.

The third time, she rocked hard against him, impatient with the deliberate pace he was keeping. When he didn't increase the tempo of his thrusts, she pinched his shoulder.

"Damn it, Wyc. Fuck me harder," she rasped. "Faster."

The change in him was immediate. The last vestige of control disappeared and his fingers dented her flesh with a biting grip on her legs. His upper body leaned heavily into hers, crushing her to the door.

Her hands slipped off his sweat-slicked skin. As she struggled to hang on, he began hammering into her. Slamming their bodies together. The only sounds were the stark slap of flesh against flesh, ragged breaths forced into lungs on fire and her own desperate cries each time his cock struck the opening of her womb.

She licked her lips and groaned at the salty tang from his skin still lingering there. Her entire existence distilled into this one volatile act of joining until the brightness of it blazed through her blood like a flame searing across a trail of gasoline.

And suddenly she felt Wyc. Not just his body filling and pounding into hers, but in her heart, wrapped around her thoughts and touching her emotions. The intensity of having him so undeniably claiming her on so many levels started a quake from the center of her being, sending tremors of growing magnitude pulsing over every nerve ending until she was screaming his name. Lost in a place beyond reality, existing only as an explosion of pure sensation, rocketing past colors, smells and sounds. Where the only truth was Wyc turning her inside out with the universe.

Chapter Four

ഇ

Wyc slammed furiously into Bethany as she screamed his name. She bucked and writhed against him. Her thighs squeezed his hips and her fingers dug into his arms. He was helpless to stop the low, feral sound that burst from him as her cunt gripped his cock in greedy, clutching spasms.

With another hard thrust, he felt himself breaking over her emotions like a relentless, inexorable flood. He surged through her. Filled every corner of her mind and heart. Claimed them. Marked them as surely as he was about to mark her body by filling her with his seed.

Her soul seized his, inundating him in the sensations of her climax as the storm of release swept through her.

Wyc's world burst into flames. Never before had a woman been able to weaken the hold he kept on his control. Made him slip in his ability to impose his will over his actions and responses. But Bethany didn't just loosen his grip on his legendary self-control, she ripped it clean away as if it had never been.

Suddenly it didn't matter that this was her first time, that she was so incredibly tight and would be sore as hell by the time they finished. That all this was new to her. That she knew nothing of matching rituals, soul bonding or the claiming rites of Ilyrian males to their mates. None of it mattered. The only thing that mattered was pounding into Bethany's hot, wet cunt until he exploded into paradise with her.

With her body quaking around his in orgasm, Wyc felt the hard pull at the base of his cock, the final swift rush toward ecstasy. He drew back just enough to see Bethany's pussy stretched taut around him. To see his cock ram inside his mate one last time before succumbing to a pleasure so fierce and blinding, so intense and demanding, he could do nothing but grind into her cunt, throw his head back and roar.

* * * * *

Wyc had no idea how long he held her — arms locked under her butt, forehead pressed against her front door — trying to stop sucking in great gulps of air. Hoping like hell his body, unlike his soul, wasn't trembling around her, shaking like he was standing in the middle of a damn earthquake.

Bethany's arms and legs fell limply from around him and her head lolled against his shoulder. The way she was laying against him, she would drop to the floor like a bag of wet sand if he let go of her. With a groan, he leaned back, shifted one arm around her for better support and forced his legs to move.

A glance around the small apartment revealed a tiny blue-and white-tiled kitchen off to the right and a cramped living area to the left with a yellow flowered loveseat as its only seating. A sixteen-inch TV on a plastic stand was pushed to the far wall. Evidently, she didn't spend much time watching it since stacks of paperback books leaned against its sides, front and so high on its top they looked ready to topple any moment.

Straight ahead, on the back wall between the kitchen and living room, he found what he was looking for. A door stood halfway open, and just beyond it, an unmade bed with at least half a dozen pillows tossed across it. Big, fluffy pillows that would prop Bethany up at just the right angle when he flipped her onto her stomach to take her hard and fast from behind.

Still nestled inside her slick warmth, he began to harden again. The thought of having her sweet ass bent over in front of him gave him all the motivation he needed to get them both to the bed.

Bethany slipped from his grasp as he lowered her to the bed. Her legs and arms flopped over pillows like a rag doll's might. With her eyes closed and her deep steady breaths, she looked unconscious. The only thing that gave away her true state was the slight, satisfied smile that graced her lips.

Intending to turn her facedown as he pulled away, he ran his hands down her body. Over the sides of her breasts, pressing the heels of his hands into those full curves. He took full enjoyment from the way they plumped together and created a tempting valley for his cock to slide into. God! There were so many things he wanted to do with and to Bethany's luscious body.

Slowly, he let his hands drift down to her waist and admired the soft paleness of her skin. The color of rich cream. Soon, he vowed, he would lap it up like a voracious, insatiable cat, not sparing a single inch.

He cupped his palms around her hips to flip her over, marveling at how perfectly her silky flesh molded to his hands. Then he saw the blood. Her inner thighs were smeared with it.

Christ. How could he have forgotten? He glanced down. The evidence of her recently taken virginity was on his swollen cock as well.

What the hell was he thinking, planning to take her again so soon? The woman really had gone to his head. And she must have pushed out all his common sense on her way in. No way would she be ready for him again so soon. Especially in the hard and rough manner his body clamored for.

Damn it. The desire to slam into her tight cunt from behind was so intense that he began to shake with the wanting of it. In his mind, he could already see the rounded cheeks of her ass positioned high, her back arched to expose her glistening, swollen pussy. Could hear her whimper as he rammed home. The wet, sucking sounds of her sex pulling on him as he drew back to repeat the motion again and again. Her screams as she came. Her nails clawing at the sheets—

"Wyc?"

His eyes flew open at her worried whisper. Her green eyes no longer glowed in passion as she frowned up at him. He realized his fingers were digging into her hips, and he immediately let go of her, leaving behind bright red marks on her skin.

"Relax," he said, his voice strained and harsh. "I'm going to get something to clean you up with."

She murmured something indiscernible and let her eyes fall closed. Wyc wiped himself down in the bathroom before running a washcloth under warm water and bringing it back to the bedroom. Bethany hadn't moved.

He sat on the bed beside her and pushed her legs wider apart. Her only response was a grunt of irritation at having been disturbed, which quickly turned into a soft sigh as he placed the warm cloth between her thighs. With gentle swipes, he meticulously cleaned her, taking the opportunity for a close study of her intimate flesh that brought him so much pleasure. With every stroke he memorized her response—her little hums, slight flinches, flexing hands and tensing muscles—discovering where, even here, she was the most sensitive.

Her quiet laugh brought his head up to meet her gaze.

"I think I'm clean," she said.

He sat up and gave her a knowing smile. "I always like to do a thorough job with anything I start."

"So I've learned," she said with a languid stretch that pointed her toes, arched her back and pushed her hands into the pillows above her head. When she was done, much too soon in his opinion, she rolled to her side and rested her head on her arm and curled her legs up to her stomach.

"God, I can't believe the curse is finally broken. Sex is amazing. All these years and this is what I've been missing." She gave him a wide smile. "I have a lot of time to make up for."

His eyes narrowed as anger washed through him. "You'll make it up with me, Bethany. Only me. Do you understand? Besides, the Guardian is still in place. I'm still the only man who can fuck you."

She frowned. Leaned up on one elbow. "You mentioned that guardian thing before. What are you talking about?"

He pushed her left leg back and circled the mark high on the inside of her right thigh. She looked down. As he ran his fingers over it, the light birthmark stain darkened and a perfect picture of a dragon appeared. Fierce and terrible looking, it came complete with claws, scales and a wicked snarl wrapped around dagger-sharp teeth.

"Oh my God. How did you do that? Is this another one of your tricks?"

She rubbed at it until her skin was bright pink. Wyc lifted her hand and threaded his fingers between hers.

"There's a lot we need to discuss." He nodded to the mark on her thigh. "That's a good as place as any. I put it there on your first birthday."

"What? What kind of a psycho—"

He squeezed her fingers. "We're never going to get through this if you interrupt me." He loosened her fingers and brought them to his lips to brush a kiss across their tips when he saw fear settle on her face.

"I have not, nor will I ever, hurt you. And everything that's been done was with the purpose of keeping you safe. Trust me on this. Besides, if I had meant to hurt you, it would have happened long before now."

"Gee whiz. I wonder why I don't find that exactly reassuring?"

He held back a grin. At least part of her fear was being replaced by peevish irritation.

"First, you were born in a place that matches females of certain ancestry with the males from another, specific ancestry at the female's first birthday. You were matched with me."

"But I'm not there—"

"Do you ever want to get fucked again?" he asked with some rising irritation of his own.

"What? Of course I do. Hell yes."

"Then it matters. Now be quiet and let me explain."

Bethany narrowed her eyes at him and tried to tug her hand free, but he held tight.

"We were matched in a ritual held on your first birthday. Bound together in front of our families, the prophets and the acting sovereigns—"

"Acting sovereigns? What happened to the real ones?"

"The ones allowed to ascend to the thrones have yet to be born. Twelve centuries ago—"

Bethany shook her head. "How long? And unborn kings? You're not making sense."

"It will make sense. Eventually."

"Okay. Back to the guardian thing and sex."

He smiled. "Priorities. Part of the Ilyrian—"

"Ilyrian?"

"Jesus, woman. Would you let me finish a sentence?"

"Are you always this grumpy after sex?"

Wyc let out a breath that came out as a low growl. Why was he even trying? "Maybe I should give you something to put in your mouth to keep you quiet." He brought her hand to his erection and wrapped her fingers around it. Holding her hand firmly in place as he guided it in stroking him from base to tip, he said, "I'd love to see that smart mouth stretched around my cock. See how much of me you can take."

Her eyes widened and she yanked her hand away. Pushing herself up to a sitting position, she scooted backwards toward the headboard but didn't get very far before the piles of pillows stopped her progress. When she started to pull her legs up close to her body, he wrapped his hand around her right ankle and gave it a warning squeeze.

"I'm listening. No more interruptions. I promise."

He didn't believe her. But at least he had her attention. For the moment. He loosened his grip and traced small circles just above her ankle with his thumb.

"Part of the Ilyrian Matching Ritual is the Guardian placement upon the female's inner thigh and the male's chest. Its purpose, if the two are separated, is to guard the man's heart for the woman and the woman's virtue for the man."

Bethany made a very unladylike snort. "Oh, please. What group of Neanderthals got together and came up with that rule? So this Guardian is some kind of curse that keeps any man, except the one she's matched with, from entering the woman's forbidden territory?"

"That's a crude definition, but basically true."

Suddenly, she sat up ramrod straight. "Wait a minute. What about *your* virtue?"

Wyc shrugged. "A man's virtue is not considered something to be protected among our people."

"So while I've been living with forced chastity all these years, you've been boinking any and every woman you get the urge to?"

"Bethany —"

She jerked her leg out of his grasp and rose up to her knees. "Don't 'Bethany' me." She pointed to her thigh. "Take it off. Now. Right now."

"I can't. It was put in place with an enchantment spell during the ritual. Even if I could, I wouldn't."

With a scream of frustration, she shot off the bed and ran through the door. "If all the men in this Ilyria place are as big of assholes as you, it's no wonder you have to curse your women to keep them," she yelled.

Wyc followed hard on her heels as she raced into the kitchen. She grabbed a large carving knife out of a drawer.

"What the hell are you doing?" he yelled. With an abrupt motion, he captured her wrist and trapped it against the counter.

"I'm cutting the damn thing out, and you're getting out of my apartment." For someone wielding a large kitchen knife, her statement sounded remarkably matter-of-fact. As if slicing into a tattoo were the most sensible thing to do, and as if he would just turn around and walk out her door because she said to.

He pried the knife from her hand and dropped it in the sink. "I don't think so."

She kicked out at him and he backed her against the refrigerator, effortlessly holding his body flush to hers regardless of the struggle she put up to push him away.

"I know you're upset about this—"

"Ya think?" She bent forward and bit him on the shoulder.

"Shit!" He jerked back, and she used the extra space to take a swing at him. Her fist connected with the side of his head and for a second, there were two Bethanies in front of him hissing and scratching like cornered bobcats.

"That's it." Not bothering to restrain a snarl of aggravation, he bent down and threw her over his shoulder. He ignored her outraged protest and her nails raking over his butt and back, and hauled her back to the bedroom to dump her unceremoniously on her ass into the pillows. She bounced once, arms and legs flailing, before he pinned her to the bed. Taking her arms by the wrists, he stretched them above her head and held them pressed to the mattress.

She twisted and shoved herself against him. He let his weight settle more firmly over her body.

"You can keep bucking underneath me like that if you want, but I don't think it's having the desired effect." He rocked his erection into her belly. "But it is having an effect."

Instantly, she went still and sank into the mattress. "Bastard."

He laughed and lowered his head to nip at the top of her left breast. "Actually, I'm a direct heir of the royal Ilyrian line."

"Great. That's just fucking great. Congratulations. Now get off me."

He shifted, pushing apart her thighs with his knee. "We're not done talking. You keep interrupting." He kissed the pulse throbbing at the base of her neck.

"We can talk in the living room. I promise not to say a word until you're completely through."

He kissed his way up to her ear and tugged on her lobe with his teeth. "I've heard that before. I don't believe you." A shudder ran through her body when he traced the shell of her ear with the tip of his tongue. Pressing his thigh into the juncture of her legs, he felt the warm cream of her arousal and a sharp flare of lust shot through him.

A long conversation would soon not be an option. He was already having difficulty concentrating on anything but devouring her delicious body a thousand different ways. He was going to have to make this quick. Details could wait.

He lifted his head so he could watch her face as he explained just who and what she was and why she was forever his.

* * * * *

Bethany wanted to scream. She had just experienced the most bone-melting sex of her life, albeit the *only* sex of her life not involving batteries—but she was pretty sure that by any standards, it would have rated as bone-melting. Maybe beyond bone-melting, though she wasn't sure what came after that. And then he had to go and ruin it by being some crazed psycho with a penchant for cursing virgins. Life sucked and the situation demanded a good, loud scream.

She looked straight into his eyes, took a deep breath, opened her mouth—and found it filled with his tongue. His mouth covered hers, adamantly demanding her response as the kiss continued, hard and hot. The deep thrusting of his tongue brought back his other, most recent thrusting moves with a liquefying rush. The fire began just under her skin again as his body moved on top of hers in perfect rhythm to his kiss. If his purpose had been to kiss every thought out of her head, he was accomplishing it in spades. He rocked his thigh insistently against her pussy and she moaned.

He stilled, pulled back and glared at her.

"What?" she asked, arching up to maintain the heated, glorious contact of skin on skin.

"I'm never going to get through an entire explanation."

"Totally your fault. I didn't say a word."

"You didn't have to. That was a 'fuck-me-now' moan if I've ever heard one."

"Again. Totally your fault." Damn the man. Didn't he know she hadn't had sex in at least twenty minutes? And had remained a very frustrated, unwilling virgin for the twenty-five years before that? At the moment, she didn't want explanations. She wanted sex.

He didn't move, just looked down into her eyes like he was trying to decide something. Her body was burning, and he was laying there like there might be something else he should do besides fuck her blind. She squirmed underneath him, desire held in frustrating limbo. A low growl escaped her throat, and she considered biting him again.

With a smile, he transferred both her wrists to one hand. Then he slid the open palm of his free hand down the length of her inner arm to her breast where he traced around her areola in ever-shrinking circles as her nipple puckered tightly.

Bethany closed her eyes and let out another fuck-me-now moan. Maybe he would get the hint.

His hand settled possessively on her breast. He let out a breath that sounded frustrated and resigned. She opened her eyes to find his face set in harsh lines of determination. His midnight-blue eyes locked onto hers.

"Short version. Years ago the ruling houses of Ilyria decided that instead of ruling their kingdoms, it would be better to go to war with each other. They nearly destroyed everything before the gods intervened and cursed them, fracturing and locking their powers inside a line of Mystics. The curse can only be broken if, at the seventeenth generation, the eldest living heir from each of the five houses binds himself to the other four in a vow never to bring war between their houses again.

"Before you and your sisters, your mother was the only survivor of one of the last undiluted Mystic lines."

Questions whirled around her mind. Too many to pick a single one out of the morass to ask. Though she was far from believing any of it, she couldn't doubt the sincerity of his belief in what he was saying.

But swimming in the middle of a sexual haze was not the best time to try and figure out why he had decided to explain his presence with such an outlandish story. Maybe the guy was into metaphors. Perhaps he was a philosophy major and saw life as one big fable of cosmic proportions. Maybe he had played those imaginary world-building games just a little too often as a kid.

He squeezed her breast and suddenly she didn't care.

Wyc's gaze dropped to her mouth. He closed his eyes and drew in a long breath before continuing at a clipped rate.

"When the Mystics began dying out, a law was passed that a female child of that line be matched on her first birthday to ensure she would not become mated to someone outside one of the royal families."

"What's wrong with marrying outside a royal family?"

He opened his eyes and stroked her breast. Plumping it up, he bit gently at its nipple. "Nothing. But the powers locked inside the Mystics are only manifested in their male children when the father is a royal."

"And what happens to a royal when the mother isn't a Mystic?"

"Depends on the purity and percentage of Mystic blood passed down from his fraternal grandmother. Either way, the powers, which were already splintered, are greatly diminished even more."

"Was your mother a Mystic?"

"Half."

"Oh my God. We're related?"

"No. My mother was from a different line than yours. That's taken into consideration, among other things, by the Prophets when they choose a match. In Ilyria, when a man and a woman complete The Matching Ritual, they are bound together for life."

He paused to kiss around the side of her breast to the underside.

"So it's only to release these powers that we were matched?"

"There are other reasons." He rolled her nipple between his fingers and she let out a small mewl of pleasure. "But right now, what you need to understand is you were, and are, matched to me."

The last of his words broke through the blood-pounding need he had created by teasing her breast. They resonated through her with what felt terrifyingly close to truth.

Something deep in her subconscious stirred, making her want to believe him, but there were too many impossibilities, unanswered questions. His story didn't fit her conception of reality. A reality that involved working at the local bar and saving money for another semester at college where her advisor, after taking one look at her transcripts, had told her to get off the smorgasbord plan and pick a major. In fact, she had taken off this semester to decide exactly what she wanted to do with her life. Running away with a delusional foreigner who beat up strange-looking men in alleys was not at the top of her list.

"I don't believe you."

He dropped a kiss on her chin. "You will."

"You say that like you're sticking around. What if I don't give you that option?"

His eyes hardened, and behind them, she saw a very scary look of resolve settle into place. She had seen that look before. Right before he fucked her against her front door.

"Your life is in danger. If I hadn't been with you at the café, Enath would have had you halfway back to Ilyria by now."

"First, I always thought Ilyria was my mother's name, not a place—which by the way, I've never heard of. And second, the difference between going with you versus going with Enath would be what?"

"My purpose is to protect you. Enath's primary purpose is to force you back any way possible, and keep you hostage for breeding. It's a very painful process for the woman when forced to conceive by someone other than her matched mate. If he can't get you back to Ilyria, he will try to kill you."

"Kill me?" The words squeaked past the obstruction fear had lodged in her throat. She took a deep breath, reminded herself that this man, as sincere as he appeared, was quite possibly crazy, and forced herself to speak in a more normal voice. Hard to do with a gorgeous, naked man on top of you talking about breeding, pain and killing. "Why would he want to kill me?"

"The Sleht are our ancient enemies. A cruel, brutal and base race that will stop at nothing to gain control of our land. Their evil was controlled when we held our full power. But as the Ilyrian strength declined, the Sleht's increased. Enath is one of their soldiers bred for Mystic retrieval."

"Bred?"

"Yes. Specifically to track and abduct Ilyrian females who carry the Mystic bloodline. The Sleht don't want the prophecy to come to pass because when it does, they'll be crushed like vermin. But the prophecy can't be fulfilled if there are no Mystics left to marry into the royal line."

She blinked hard. And again. And struggled to swallow. She tried not to believe him. Really, really tried. It wasn't working. Not with the memory of the horror-movie mutant attack in the alley. And as much as she hated to admit it, Enath had frightened her to the core, and Wyc had made her feel safe.

Well, as safe as one can feel wedged between garbage and surrounded by testosterone-enhanced insanity.

"So how did you find me? How did he find me? And what the hell am I doing in the middle of Iowa if I have psychotic killers after me, and why hasn't anyone bothered to let me know this before now?" She was shrieking by the time she stopped to take a breath.

Wyc cupped the side of her face with his hand, stroking her cheek with his thumb. "There was an attack and your mother panicked. She took you and your sisters and ran. Before we could find her, she died and her daughters disappeared into the foster care program. We've been searching for you for years."

"Sisters?"

"Three of them. You're the second youngest. Your mother disappeared three weeks after your first birthday. That's why you don't remember."

Shadows of memories that had roamed free through her dreams and haunted her days shifted and slithered in the back of her mind, glimpses of faces and voices. Elusive and alluring, but not solid enough to ground his explanation in a certainty she was willing to accept without further proof.

Still, she had always wanted to be a part of a real family. Not just a temporary add-on. It was a normal desire, and if he had been looking for her, he probably knew she had been bounced around and could be using that to draw her into his deception. Refusing to take the tenderness and concern she saw in his expression at face value, she narrowed her eyes.

"How do I know you're not the bad guy in this whole crazy story you're trying to sell me?"

He let out a loud, gusted breath that blew her bangs off her forehead. "You are the most stubborn woman I've ever met. Mystics are supposed to be known for their excellent intuition."

"Well, pardon me. But I just found out I'm a sex-cursed Mystic, have sisters I've never heard about, and have maniacs out to breed or kill me. If my intuition seems a little slow on the uptake, that's too damn bad. Personally, I'm feeling the need to start this day over and forget everything that's happened."

His smile, slow and sexy, combined with the gleam in his eyes, made her stomach dip in a flying-over-the-edge-of-a-cliff way.

"Everything?" he asked, rocking suggestively against her.

She tried to ignore the amazing way his body felt rubbing over hers and her own body's rioting response. "If I'm in so much danger here, why aren't we running like hell instead of lying here naked?"

"We will be leaving. Soon. And don't worry, Enath will be out of commission for at least twenty-four hours. Predators are a very competitive sect and always work alone. They refuse to share information among their ranks, afraid that someone else will beat them out of a retrieval."

"Why?"

"The only thing that gives a Predator value in the eyes of their people is the ability to retrieve Mystics. Without that, they're worth less than spit.

"You're being hunted, Bethany." He paused and combed his fingers through her hair. An oddly comforting action incompatible with his words.

"Now that you've been discovered alive, Enath won't stop until he's found you, or he's dead. And when he's dead, there are others like him who will come for you. That's why we're not staying here. I'm taking you back to my home where you'll be safe."

Ilyrians, Sleht, Predators, Mystics. The terms and pieces of the story swarmed through her head until it all buzzed together and made her dizzy.

"Is there any possibility you've got the wrong person?"

"No."

Bethany scrunched her eyes shut and pressed her head back into the mattress. Her life had never been much to speak of in the first place. There were more ragged edges and frayed strings to it than on her favorite pair of faded old blue jeans.

Once she turned eighteen and gained her freedom from foster care, she had started moving around a lot. Tried to find a place to belong, to get her life straightened out and headed in a specific direction. Any direction, as long as it kept her from feeling like life was constantly coming unraveled.

Whether or not Wyc was telling the truth—bizarre as it sounded—didn't matter. He was not leaving her life any time soon by his own admission, and if he was right, there were a whole lot of nasties on her trail as well. Shit. So much for her biggest worry being whether to choose nursing, counseling or business for a major.

If a prince had to appear in her life, why couldn't he have been a normal prince, one with four white horses, a crown and a castle full of money?

* * * * *

Wyc watched her sink away from him. Her eyes filled with acceptance and then defeat. And then they closed.

His heart twisted. He wished he could make this easier on her. Was surprised at the intensity of that emotion. He'd do anything to change the situation and make her happy. Well, not anything. He wasn't about to release her as his mate.

When he and his cousins set out to reclaim the women, he had gone into the pursuit with the single-minded determination of bringing his mate back any way he had to. Her emotions were never considered. He only needed her to accept her position as his mate, and she could do that regardless of how she personally felt about him.

He had even entertained thoughts of wishing a simple abduction was a possibility. Taking her from this world to lock her in his own until she had given him several sons, and then releasing her. Clean and quick, with no emotional entanglements. He had learned his lesson about the treachery of emotions years ago and his brothers had paid the price for that mistake. He had no intention of clouding his judgment with sentiment ever again.

And he had succeeded. Until he held Bethany against her door this afternoon and she looked up at him with those clear green eyes and told him to go away. Suddenly, every carefully chained-down emotion had roared to the surface. Anger. Lust. Protectiveness. Possessiveness. All those and many more.

A complex layering of emotions that he couldn't identify, never mind explain. Yet each feeling and instinct, primitive and raw, pitched through him like an ocean wave slamming against cliffs edging a stormy sea. He needed to wrap her in himself until she and everyone else acknowledged that she belonged to him.

As much as he wanted it to only be about keeping her safe and gaining heirs, it wasn't. She was a part of him now and he'd give his own life up before releasing her. At the thought, the primal desire to claim raised its head, pushing him to be inside her body again.

"You're going to be all right, Bethany. I won't let anything happen to you." He brushed his lips over hers. "Trust me." He kissed her again, not quite so gently. Her eyes opened, wary and unsure.

"But you have to do what I tell you," he said, unaware of how much he needed to hear her assent to his words until she frowned up at him. He moved his hand to hold her jaw still when she started to shake her head. He kissed her hard, smashing her lips against her teeth.

When he lifted his head several seconds later, he didn't release her face. He forced her to meet his gaze. "Understand?"

He watched as indecision, confusion and anger played tug-of-war for dominance on her expressive face. He expected the confusion. Could deal with the anger. But indecision was not an option. He had to know she would obey him when he told her to do something. Her life depended on it.

When she still didn't respond, he gave her head a little shake. "Understand?"

Her expression cleared to one of undiluted anger.

"Yes," she snapped.

"Good." His hold softened, and she immediately tugged on her arms. He realized he still had them pinned above her head.

She glared at him and pulled on her arms again, her tongue darting out to lick her lips in agitation. "Well, now that we have that settled, get the hell off of me."

He slid his hand around to cup the back of her neck. "No."

Chapter Five

ഔ

"No?" Bethany couldn't believe, after all he had told her and expected her to accept, that now he was adding insult to injury by pissing her off and then refusing to get off her. Next time she got her hands on a knife, it wouldn't be her thigh she'd aim for. "What do you mean, no?"

Automatically, she tried to dislodge him by pushing against his bulk. Her effort only managed to remove all space between their naked bodies and force his erection harder into her belly. His eyes darkened and she immediately dropped away from him.

"I mean," he said, dragging a finger across her bottom lip, "no. Earlier you were upset about missing out on certain experiences." His hand trailed down her neck and over her breast. "We're going to start rectifying that."

He pinched her nipple. She sucked in a breath at the bolt of sensation that arced from her breast straight to her cunt.

"Oh God." Damn. She really wanted to stay angry with him. Hard to do when, with a touch, he made her soak through her panties. Or would, if she were wearing any.

To hell with it all anyway. She'd be pissed later. After the day she'd had and the curse she'd been under, she deserved another round of volcanic sex. Wyc tugged on her nipple, lifting her breast just enough to nip at its tender underside with his teeth. Oh yeah. Being pissed later was a great plan.

He slid his hand down the center of her body to cup her mound. She bit her bottom lip to keep from screaming *yes*, but couldn't completely repress her entire reaction.

"Ah, there's what I was waiting for," he said with a smug smile.

"What's that?" she asked, trying to keep from sounding too breathless.

"Your fuck-me-now moan. It's a sound I'll never get tired of hearing."

He began stroking her clit, and she started to pant. His eyes roamed down from her parted lips to where her breasts were rising and falling in quick bursts.

She felt wanton and exotic. Stretched out beneath him, completely at his mercy. Trapped by the weight of his body and the pinning of her arms by a man so savagely masculine, she would ache for years simply from the thought of him. His long black hair falling about his shoulders in enticing waves. Midnight eyes that scoured her body as if there wasn't time to ever see enough of her. The hardened muscles that wrapped every bone beneath golden skin, and the pulsing proof jabbing her thigh that his desire for her was very real, very immediate.

He slid two fingers deep inside her, and despite the tremendous pleasure he was bringing her, she winced.

Wyc stilled his movements. "You're sore."

She nodded. "A little. But I'll be fine."

He shook his head and withdrew his fingers. "I'm not going to hurt you, Bethany, no matter how much I want to be inside that incredibly tight cunt of yours."

When she started to protest, he kissed her soundly. "Don't worry, I'm going to take you every way a man can take his mate. Eventually."

"Goddamn it, it is so unfair," she bit out. "I've been able to do nothing but fantasize until today, and now that I've got a man able to fuck me, he won't."

Wyc's face lit up with a sexy, arrogant grin. "You've been fantasizing about me, huh?"

"Sex. I've fantasized about sex."

"Tell me," he said, teasing her breasts. Cream from her pussy still clung to his fingers and spread over her nipples as he played, wetting them and making them pucker up tighter. She shook her head. He cupped her breast, pushing the nipple up for his mouth.

"Tell me," he insisted, lowering his head to lick her nipple. He closed his eyes on a groan, and his hand squeezed her breast in a reflexive action. "You taste so damn good." He finished licking her cream off her nipple and then switched to her other breast.

Bethany held her breath, waiting for his mouth to cover her other breast. He stopped a mere fraction of an inch from her straining nipple.

"I want you to tell me your fantasy." He bit the very tip of her nipple hard enough to make her jerk in surprise. "Now."

"Which one?"

"Your latest one." He flicked her breast with his tongue and she gasped. As he began to run his fingers up and down her abdomen, closer and closer to her mound, she closed her eyes and tried to focus enough to articulate what she had only dreamed.

"Umm...I'm at work, after hours. The bar is mostly dark. I'm cleaning the table by that big mirror near the back. I lean over it to wipe if off and I see a man behind—"

"Me."

Bethany opened her eyes. "What?"

"Me. You see me come up behind you."

She was about to protest, but Wyc pulled her nipple deep inside his mouth, doing something wonderfully wicked with his tongue. God, at this rate, he could star in any fantasy of hers he wanted.

* * * * *

"Yes. God. Fine. You come up behind me."

Wyc smiled as Bethany's words stumbled over erratic breaths. He released her wrists and cupped her breasts, pushing them together. Relishing the perfect combination of soft and firm, he dragged his teeth over one nipple and then the other. He lifted his head, raised his eyebrows.

"You were saying?" he asked.

"I can't do this if you keep doing that."

"Hmm. Then we have a problem, because I'm not going to do this—" he drew on one breast long and hard until she fisted her hands in the sheets and arched up off the bed. He released her suddenly, "—if you stop doing that."

"You are so evil." She took a deep breath and started talking fast. "You're behind me. But all I can see is your shadow in the mirror. And your eyes. They're glowing with lust. For me."

"Mmm-hmm." Wyc kissed the valley between her breasts and then dragged his tongue down the center of her torso until he reached her navel. "And?" he asked when she paused.

"And then you slip your hands under my shirt…lift it over my head."

He brushed the underside of her breasts with a feathering touch as his mouth moved across her belly. "Describe your bra."

"Black. Lace. You reach around. Pull it down to play with my nipples."

He rolled onto his side. "Put your feet flat on the bed and pull your knees up," he instructed.

A nervous expression clouded her eyes. "I'm not really—"

He pushed her legs apart and repeated the command. "I want to see you as you tell me your fantasy. I want to watch you get turned on as you talk about it."

Slowly she pulled her legs up. He moved to lie between them, placing his hands high on her inner thighs and pressing them even further apart.

If there was anything more amazing than a woman's pussy, he didn't know what it was. So pink and soft. He wanted to run his tongue down and around the silky folds and suck her clit until she screamed herself hoarse. But he didn't want her climaxing yet. He wanted to draw this out for her.

He rubbed his thumbs over the tender flesh of her inner thighs and gave her a little nipping kiss.

Wyc glanced up at her. "Show me."

"I'm already showing you everything I've got."

"Your nipples. Show me how I play with them in your fantasy." She blushed, and he wrung out her courage by running his tongue down the crease at the top of one thigh and then up the other.

She swallowed. Cupped her breasts. Gave them a tentative squeeze. Then circled the areolas with the tips of her index fingers until the nipples tightened. She glanced up at him and he gave her a curt nod to continue. Her eyes closed and she began to lightly pinch and tug on the peaks.

Wyc's eyes began to sting from needing to blink. No way in hell was he missing one moment of Bethany giving herself pleasure. He continued to massage her inner thighs with his hands and occasionally laid down an openmouthed kiss above her mound as he watched.

"Then what happens?" he asked, surprised by the roughness of his voice.

Bethany kept her eyes closed as she began to speak, her fingers tugging harder on her breasts.

"You kiss my neck. Below my ear. I push against you. Wanting, *needing*, to feel your heat. Your cock is hard. Pressed against my ass." She let out a little moan and twisted her nipples. "I want it inside me."

Wyc's cock pulsed with the demand to accommodate her. Right now. Right fucking now.

He shoved the thought away and shifted until his mouth was directly over her pussy.

She lifted her hips, but he pressed her back down into the mattress, holding her in place. He slid his thumbs down to her entrance, wet them with her juices and slid them back up and over the lips of her sex.

"Wyc," she whispered. "Please. Touch me."

Her nub had swollen so sweetly and was just begging for attention. He ignored it and repeated the spreading action with his thumbs over and over, until she was completely slick with her own cream. Every part but her clit.

"Keep going," he said and teased the top of her cleft with the very tip of his tongue.

"You bend me forward. Over the table. Push my skirt up to my waist. Rip off my panties."

Wyc cursed. Damn. He was going to come just listening to her.

He clung to his control and used his tongue to lick the cream off her pussy even as he continued to spread it up and around with his thumbs. Bethany twisted under his hands, but he refused to let her lift herself against him. Her breaths echoed harshly around her words and she reached down to bury her fingers in his hair.

She was so turned on her skin was hot to the touch. Her bottom lip was swollen from where she had bitten down on it when he started using his tongue on her sex. Her cream was flowing in a steady stream and dampening the sheet beneath her ass. He had never seen a woman so responsive before. He shifted to alleviate some of the pain in his groin, and the friction of the bed against his cock nearly made him explode.

"You unzip your jeans," Bethany panted out. "I want to slide to the floor, but you hold me against the table. Tell me to spread my legs. Push your hand between them. See if I'm wet enough."

Wyc scraped his teeth across her inner thigh, letting the whisker stubble on his cheek graze her clit. Bethany jumped.

"And are you wet enough for me to take you?"

"Oh yes. God, yes," she breathed out. Bethany opened her eyes and speared Wyc with a look sharp with passion. "Wet and ready."

He circled her clit with his tongue and she pushed up on her elbows. Damp tendrils of curls framed her face. Her eyes glowed like green fire and her cheeks were flushed a bright red.

"Finish it," he demanded.

"You watch my breasts in the mirror. Put your cock to my cunt. I try to move back...take you in. You won't let me. You hold me in place with one hand. Reach around to touch my clit with the other."

Wyc followed her words by laving her clit with his tongue. Her head fell back and she moaned. He circled her clit and licked again. And again. Faster.

"You stroke it. I beg you to fuck me. Suddenly you drive your cock in hard and fast—"

Wyc burrowed his face against her and stabbed his tongue deep inside her cunt. Bethany screamed. Struggled. Bowed up and fell back. Pulled and pushed at him. Begged him to stop.

Wyc took her to the peak and demanded more. And more. Until her screams faded to whimpers and his own release spilled onto the sheets. Until neither one could imagine a world without the other in it.

* * * * *

Resting his head against her leg, Wyc closed his eyes and inhaled the satisfying scent of his woman's release. If he had a choice, he would stay right here and love Bethany until they didn't have enough strength to roll over, never mind pack a suitcase and hit the highway.

But there wasn't time. He turned his head to place a kiss on her inner thigh, right above her Guardian, and couldn't resist sucking that tender flesh against his teeth and tasting it one more time.

Bethany whispered his name and feathered her fingers through his hair. The desire to take her in his arms, gather her close and hold her next to his body for the next century crashed over him. So intense, it was nearly impossible to remember that Bethany's life was in danger and he needed her in a place he could better protect her. And naked in her bed in an unsecured apartment was not the best option.

The anger at not being able to totally eliminate Enath rose again and focused him back on his mission. "Time to get dressed." He stood, took her by the hands and pulled her off the bed. He held her steady until her knees quit wobbling and he was sure she wasn't going to sink straight to the floor. That he had done that to her brought out an arrogant smile on his face.

"Not much for afterglow, are you?" she asked, stepping away from him.

"Not with a Predator on our trail."

"Then why—"

"Enath's injuries take at least twenty-four hours to heal. As long as you're with me, he won't risk coming after you until he's at full strength. But I'm not willing to push our window of opportunity too far.

"Now," he said, turning her toward the bathroom and swatting her on the butt, "get cleaned up so we can go."

Bethany stopped abruptly and spun back around. "Go? Go where?"

"Where I can keep you safe. If you want a shower, better get in there, because in twenty minutes, we're leaving."

"I'm not going anywhere."

"Clock's ticking, Bethany. I suggest you argue after your shower."

Wyc headed toward the living room to gather up their clothes while Bethany muttered unladylike curses and stomped into the bathroom. The shower had just started when he heard her shout.

"Oh my God! Oh. My. God!"

The door to the bathroom crashed into the wall with the force Wyc used to push it open. Bethany was standing outside the bathtub, screaming at the water.

"What? What's wrong?" He scanned the small room. More blue and white tile, but no threat that he could see. Unless there was a homicidal midget hiding under the sink. She turned a horrified gaze toward him. When he reached for her, she flinched away.

"You didn't use a condom. That's what!"

Tension rolled off his shoulders and he let out a loud breath. "Shit, woman. Next time you scream, it better damn well be because you're hurt or in trouble." He turned to leave.

"Don't you walk out on me. You could have gotten me pregnant. Oh my God. I could be pregnant right now!" Bethany was shrieking by the end of her rant.

That she found the possibility of carrying his child so appalling really ticked him off. Sure, it might be too soon to pick out names—he had planned on finishing the Matching Ritual and getting her back to Ilyria first—but never had a woman so blatantly despised the idea of having his baby. Hell, there were dozens of women who would stand in a freezing rain for a week to be given the chance.

Slowly, he backed her up against the tile wall. "If getting pregnant is such a concern of yours, why aren't you on birth control? And not once between your moans and your screams did you bother mentioning a condom. And believe me, I was listening very closely."

Bethany's cheeks flamed. She shifted her eyes from his and he watched anger, guilt and panic flood her expression. Damn it all to hell. He had a Predator on their trail, his entire team waiting for their arrival and had just fucked this woman to within an inch of her life. But instead of packing, leaving or fucking again, she was standing there looking like she wanted to cry, right after she found a sharp, serrated object to ram through his gut.

If this was what finding your mate did to a man, no wonder women said men were crazy. They made them that way.

He gritted his teeth and stifled the urge to growl. Instead, he took her face in his hands and held her still while he smacked a hard kiss on her lips. "You have nothing to worry about. An Ilyrian male can't impregnate a woman until she's taken him as her mate."

She looked at him, doubt clear in her eyes. "We didn't just mate in there?"

The growl he had been repressing escaped. "No. When an Ilyrian woman takes a mate, there's more to it than fucking."

"Are you sure?"

"Yes, babydoll. I'm sure. Now will you please get in that shower?" He leaned down and gave her another quick kiss. Wrapping his large hands around her waist, he lifted her over the edge of the tub and placed her in the middle of the pelting water. He immediately withdrew his hands before he followed through with the urge to slick them down her hips and join her in the shower. "Don't worry. We will get to the mating part. Soon. When you've settled down some." He whipped the shower curtain closed. "You're down to ten and a half minutes."

By the time she was done in the bathroom, he had found a duffel bag in the bottom of her closet and stuffed enough clothes in it to last her several days.

"What are you doing with my stuff?" she asked.

He zipped the bag closed. "I told you. We're leaving."

"And I told you, I'm not going anywhere." Her stubborn statement was reiterated in her posture—chin lifted, fists propped on her hips and feet braced apart. The corners of Wyc's mouth tugged upward. It was hard to look intimidating when one was only dressed in a skimpy little towel, but Bethany was giving it her best effort.

He advanced toward her until he was within an inch of touching her, forcing her head to tilt back to keep eye contact. He glanced down at the top of her towel. Her defiant posture had her breasts nearly popping out of their restraint. He hooked a finger in the terrycloth at her cleavage and tugged. The towel opened and slid down until it was stopped at her waist by the hands still on her hips.

"I suggest you put some clothes on, otherwise I'll be hauling your pretty ass buck naked to Colorado."

Her eyes narrowed, but she didn't move. "I won't be threatened into doing something."

"Would it make a difference if I said please?"

"No."

"I didn't think so." With his hands under her arms, he picked her up and moved her out of the way. Before he set her down, he kissed her left nipple. When she gasped and dropped the towel to take a swing at him, he let go of her and ducked into the bathroom, closing the door behind him.

He waited. Nothing but silence. He yanked the door open to find Bethany leaning over the unzipped bag, pulling clothes out. Many were already strewn around the room. Caught, she looked up at him, anger snapping out of her eyes.

"With or without clothes, I'm taking you with me when I leave here. If you want to meet my family in your birthday suit, you just keep unpacking that bag. I won't be packing it again."

He closed the door and started the shower. The rushing water did little to drown out her barrage of epithets that greatly maligned his character and birth. Her verbal assault was interrupted only by heavy thuds that sounded like she was pelting the bathroom door with her never-ending supply of paperback books.

He sighed and stepped into the shower. Was nothing going to be easy with this woman? Ten minutes later, he was finished and relieved that her temper tantrum had apparently ended.

Then she screamed. A high-pitched, fear-filled scream.

His heart clutched, and he followed her cry into the kitchen. Backed against the little, two-person dinette table, Bethany was twisting and scratching, trying to pull out of a Predator's grip. A broken vase and flowers lay scattered across the kitchen floor. As Wyc came through the door, the Predator plunged a tiny syringe into her arm.

Wyc roared and immediately called up the beast within. The room wavered before his eyes, like looking through rippling water. Animal senses sharpened as the *kyltar* took over his body, focused on the threat.

The Predator spun to face Wyc, and the tiny needle fell to the floor. Shock washed over Bethany's face as she turned from the Predator in time to see Wyc's transformation. She clutched her arm where she had been pricked and crushed herself against the table.

Shapeshifted into a large, panther-like cat, Wyc lunged and landed on top of the Predator. Bethany's eyes stretched impossibly wide before they fluttered closed. In the next instant, she sank beneath the table, unconscious.

For a Predator, this one was small and young. He tried to ward off the beast with flailing arms and legs. The battle was brief, but bloody. Fear was the last emotion that crossed his face before a final swipe of the *kyltar*'s claws shredded flesh and cartilage. The Predator fell to the floor in a heap. The *kyltar* shook once, sending a spray of blood from its pelt across the kitchen wall before withdrawing deep back inside Wyc.

The Predator was still as death, but Wyc wasn't fooled. He knew that if he left him as he was, he would soon recover from even his worst injuries. The Sleht had spent decades biogenetically engineering retrieval soldiers that regenerated nearly every body part quickly.

Now in human form again, Wyc waited for his heart to quit beating at nearly twice its normal rate before bending over the Predator, sinking his hand into its neck and closing off the air passage. Once the tube fused to itself, the Predator would be truly dead and no longer a threat to anyone.

Wyc pulled back one of the Sleht's eyelids, checking for the clear white eyeball signifying death. Once assured, he moved to see about Bethany.

He checked her pulse and pupils. Her pulse had slowed and her pupils were dilated. Shit. The bastard had injected her with their traveling serum. Just to make sure, he picked up the discarded syringe and brought it to his nose.

The distinctive odor of boiled cauliflower rose to meet him. The first of a two-part drug designed specifically for use on Ilyrian Mystic females of breeding age. It came from a plant that was thought to have been eradicated centuries ago. Wyc grimaced to himself. Sort of like the Sleht threat.

The name for the plant had been lost, and Wyc had never seen it in any other form than the liquid one found in the hands of a Predator. Among his soldiers, the drug was known as *Yes Master*. The first dosage rendered the victim unconscious for twenty-four hours and then groggy and lethargic for up to seventy-two hours after that. But its main purpose was to interact with the second injection.

The second dosage made the woman completely malleable to commands from the first voice she heard after being drugged. This effect lasted for as long as the initial drug was in her system, normally upwards of three weeks. A very important consideration for the Predators since they couldn't force anyone through a portal. In order to pass from this world to Ilyria, one had to be awake and willing.

Now that Bethany had been given the first injection, he had to make sure that no one had the chance to get close to her with the second. There was an antidote to the first, but none to the second.

He checked his watch. He couldn't administer the antidote until the first seventy-two hours had passed. And the antidote was in the safe house in Colorado, over a twelve-hour drive from this little Iowa town.

He picked Bethany up and carried her to the couch. He was furious that another Predator had tracked them down. Even more furious at himself for not having grabbed her and left the moment he knew who she was.

She would have screamed and fought. But she'd have been conscious to do it, goddamn it. Would have been fighting him and not another Predator.

He shook his head to clear it. He could curse himself to the moon and back later. Right now, he needed to get Bethany to safety. And he could use some help.

He wasn't excited about being alone and out in the open with her in this vulnerable state, but most of his team was spread out, tracking down leads on the other sisters. They weren't scheduled to meet up at the house for two days.

The fact that another Predator had shown up on Bethany's doorstep less than two hours after the first worried him. Never had Predators worked together. He glanced back at the dead Sleht. Then again, since when did they start sending green Predators into otherworld tracking situations? This was the youngest and most inexperienced retriever he had come across. Could be a rogue, but how the hell he found them so quickly made Wyc very nervous.

He went back into the bathroom and dug his cell phone out of the pocket of his jeans. Punching in Rordyc's number, he held it between his ear and shoulder as he pulled on his clothes. It was still ringing when he went in search of his shoes.

"Give me some good news, cuz." Rordyc's voice came across the line with unusual exasperation for a man so laid-back he normally made yoga instructors look tense.

"Tough day?" Wyc asked wryly.

"You have no idea."

Wyc smiled at the disgust in his cousin's voice and glanced at the bloody mess that was one side of the Predator's face. At least Bethany's kitchen floor was tile. Easy to clean.

"Have I ever told you how much I hate paperwork?" Rordyc asked. Wyc ignored the question.

"I was wondering if you were ever going to answer your phone."

Rordyc cursed. "I was in the records room of the downtown library when the damn thing went off. Had the librarian all over my ass because of the noise."

"First time I've ever heard you complain about having a woman all over any part of your anatomy."

"Not this one, dude. I'm pretty sure she was a man not too long ago. So what's up? And please tell me it doesn't involve musty files and scary librarians."

"We might have a problem."

Suddenly, all teasing in Rordyc's voice disappeared. "Is Bethany all right?"

After Wyc had spoken to Bethany last night in the bar's parking lot, he had followed her home to make sure she arrived safely and then called his team. He let them know the first sister had been found and that she was his mate, as expected from the paperwork they had on her. He hadn't even needed the confirmation of her matching Guardian tattoo. As soon as he had seen her, he had known.

"She'll be fine. We've had two Predator attacks and—"

"Two? Shit! What'd you do? Advertise in the local paper?"

"The attacks were less than two hours apart and Bethany got a first dose of *Yes Master*. She's out cold. I need to get her to Colorado. Think you could take a couple days off from your librarian to ride shotgun?"

After laughing at Rordyc's response concerning what Wyc could do with the librarian, he rattled off Bethany's address. Less than forty-five minutes later, Rordyc was banging on the door.

"Damn," Wyc said as he pulled the door open, "break any speed limits?"

"Only the posted ones." Rordyc stepped into the apartment and Wyc closed the door behind him.

For as long as he could remember, he and his cousin had been mistaken for brothers. At night, when you couldn't tell that Rordyc's eyes were dark brown and his were dark blue, they easily passed for each other—until Rordyc opened his mouth. Inevitably, his cousin managed to come up with the one smartass remark to land him neck-high in trouble with whomever he was speaking to.

"Are you on your bike?" Wyc asked.

"Is there any other way to travel?"

Wyc shook his head. The only thing Rordyc liked better about this world than Ilyria were the motorcycles. He rode them fast and reckless and went through several in a year. Presently, he was on a Harley kick, and last Wyc heard, he was still riding a custom West Coast Chopper.

"Guess we'll be taking Bethany's car. Kinda hard to transport an unconscious woman on the back of a bike," Rordyc said.

He walked over to the couch and squatted down beside Bethany, giving her a good once-over. An expression crossed his face that Wyc couldn't place. It was gone in an instant, replaced with a wicked grin. "But I'm sure I could manage to hold onto her if I got just the right grip."

Wyc jerked the younger man up by the front collar of his motorcycle jacket and, pushing him against the wall, got right in his face.

"That's my mate, you son of a bitch. If you so much as lay a finger on her, they won't even be able to feed you through a straw and the question of you having children will be a moot point. Got it?"

Lifting his hands in a gesture of surrender, Rordyc shook his head. "Jesus, man, you know I'd never touch her. I was kidding."

"I'm not."

"No shit," Rordyc muttered when Wyc let go of him and stepped away.

Wyc was an inch and a half taller than Rordyc, but it if came to a fight, it would be close. No one could fight dirty like his cousin. Still, he knew that his best friend would have been dogmeat if he had touched Bethany. Hell. The damn woman was driving him crazy even when she was unconscious.

"So, where's the Predator?" Rordyc asked, his easygoing tone returned, though he shot Wyc a look that made it clear he was worried about his sanity.

"Dissolving in the tub." He tossed the duffel at Rordyc and then the keys to Bethany's car.

Catching them one-handed, Rordyc flipped them over. "A Honda? Tell me it's at least an S2000."

"Sorry, *dude.*" Wyc grinned. "Late-model Civic. Gray. No upgrades."

Rordyc grimaced. "I think I'm starting to miss the records room. I need to call someone to pick up my bike."

"From the car. I don't know where the Sleht are getting their information, but I'm not waiting around here to find out."

Wyc bent down and slid his arms under Bethany. He settled her against his chest. And groaned. The simple weight of her body on his was enough to make him want her. He took a deep breath, inhaling her scent.

He straightened and nodded to Rordyc to lead the way. He hoped no one was in the hall. It'd be hard to explain why two six-foot plus men were carrying an unconscious woman out of her apartment and driving away in her car.

* * * * *

Bethany opened her eyes. Blackness. Then images. The flower deliveryman handing her a vase full of daisies and carnations. Looking into his eyes. Enath's eyes. But not.

Watching a needle sink into her arm. Wyc coming out of the bedroom. *Wyc.*

She tried to scream. Nothing but a crackling croak emerged from her throat. She tried to kick with her legs. Lash out with her arms. Nothing moved. She tossed her head from side to side, fear mounting into full-blown panic.

"Hush, Bethany. You're all right." Wyc's arms were around her. Cradling her against him.

"Y-y-you're not a m-m-man." She licked her chapped lips and tried to angle away from him. "I saw you. Y-you changed."

"Shhh." He kept rocking her. "I am a man. An Ilyrian man. As human as you are."

"I don't turn into a-a-an a-animal." She tried pulling away from him again. Nothing. "And why the fuck won't my arms and legs move?" Frustration and fear had tears spilling down her cheeks.

Wyc gathered her firmly against his body and nestled her head under his chin. He brushed the tears from her face, murmuring comforting words that made little sense but calmed her nonetheless. He stroked her hair so tenderly, it broke her heart. How could she want to be held so much by a man who turned into an animal?

"What you saw, babydoll, was the power the gods gave me through my mother's bloodline. Using it to protect my mate. It's the ability to change into the *kyltar.* An ancient beast that used to roam free in our homeland. The closest thing you'd be able to compare it to is a large panther, but with a spiked tail."

He continued to run his fingers through the length of her hair, letting it fall in wispy strands against her shoulders and back.

"Your arms and legs will be fine. That Predator injected you with a drug that will eventually wear off. But for the next couple of days, you'll be groggy and lethargic. You'll sleep a lot. But that's normal. And I'll be here." He tightened his hold on her briefly and kissed her hair.

Bethany tried to take what he had said and make sense out of it. She couldn't.

"Are you an alien?" She was nervous enough, asking the question. It didn't help anything when he burst out laughing.

"Oh babydoll, you constantly amaze me. In the strictest sense, yes, I suppose I am. But no more than you are. We are from the same home world, Ilyria. But it's not in outer space, it's in a different dimension, entered and exited by portals."

"Portals?"

"Doorways through dimensions."

"Of course."

Wyc chuckled, and the soft laughter echoed in his chest against her ear. "It's believed that the same race that settled Earth, settled Ilyria. Though there're no records that go that far back. But the Sleht are a different matter."

Bethany felt him stiffen at the mention of his enemy. She had so many questions she wanted to ask, but her eyelids kept insisting on closing. She was having a hard time following Wyc's words as he wove together stories of the world he claimed she came from. Finally, unable to fight the drowning sensation a moment longer, Bethany drifted into a deep sleep and allowed the comfort Wyc offered to seep into her heart and soothe her dreams.

* * * * *

Thump. Bethany frowned. Tried to open her eyes. Too much light. Too bright. Scrunched them shut again.

Thump. Her entire body jarred from the impact. What on earth? She tried the open eye thing again. One eye, narrow slit. There was a blonde Amazon leaning over her. *Thump.* Kicking her bed.

She blinked and tried to open both eyes. The Amazon frowned.

"Are you awake enough to eat?" The Amazon was not only built like a brick house, stunningly beautiful with blonde hair that fell in a long braid over her shoulder and light, clear blue eyes, she had a voice that sounded like she stole it from an angel.

"I think so," Bethany croaked. Sometimes life sucked. She pushed herself up to her elbows, thankful that her arms were working once again. She kicked her legs under the covers. Yay. They worked too.

She sat up, dragging herself up to rest against the headboard. She had been naked the last time she remembered waking up in Wyc's arms. Now, she was covered in an extra-large, black T-shirt. Wyc's, she supposed. It was odd to think of someone dressing and undressing her without her knowledge, even if she had screamed in that person's arms.

The Amazon lowered the tray she was carrying down onto the bed over Bethany's lap. And then stood back up and continued to stare at her. Bethany picked up the orange juice and took a large gulp. She hadn't realized how hungry she was until she took her first bite. Ravenous. She continued to stuff eggs into her mouth as the Amazon watched.

Bethany finally paused long enough to ask, "Are you the maid?"

Amazon's nostril's flared as she snapped her spine straight, her breasts jutting out enough to cast shade. "I'm the captain of Wyc's personal guard. Myrra Lansyr."

"Oh." Bethany stabbed a piece of ham. "Is he here?"

"No."

"No?" That bothered Bethany. A lot. He said he'd be here with her and the man had left. If she wasn't so hungry, she'd take a moment to snarl at the male gender in general. Instead, she finished off the ham.

"No. He left me in charge."

Not reassuring. "How long have I been here?"

"Almost two days."

Bethany chocked on a bite of biscuit. "Really?" Myrra's answer was to simply raise an eyebrow. Jeez. She'd had better conversations with a wall.

"Did Wyc say when he'd be back?"

"No."

Bethany polished off the final biscuit and looked under the napkin to see if there was a piece of toast hiding. No luck, so she settled for draining the last of the juice. A wave of fatigue hit her suddenly. She pushed away the tray and couldn't stop a huge yawn.

"So what's it like, captaining a personal guard?"

Myrra removed the tray. "I can't speak for others in similar positions, but personally, working under Wyc is an honor and a privilege."

As the frozen blonde goddess left the room, Bethany was pierced by a sharp shard of jealousy and wondered exactly what "working under Wyc" entailed. And if Myrra had "worked under" Wyc since they'd arrived.

Even if she had, it wasn't like it mattered. Not to her. Bethany sank down and punched her pillow. He could screw an entire pantheon of goddesses as far as she was concerned. She didn't care. Damn it.

Chapter Six

ହୠ

"Wyc?" Bethany rolled into a warm, hard body as the bed dipped. His arms came around her, and he pulled her next to him. Then with a grunt, he sat up and pulled the large T-shirt off her before drawing her to him once again.

"That's better," he said, weariness evident in his voice.

Bethany pressed her cheek to his shoulder. His damp skin smelled of soap and warm man. "What time is it?" she asked.

"Late." His answer was muffled against her hair.

She slid her hand over his chest and around to his back. He was so solid. The way the hard lines of his body countered her own curves amazed her. How long had it been since he had made love to her? Too long. Arching slightly so her breasts flattened against his chest, she let her hips cradle his hardening cock and kissed his shoulder.

He didn't respond. She licked the spot she had just kissed, rocked her hips into him once.

A rumble shuddered low in his chest, and his hand flexed on her back before moving down to cup her butt. "Go to sleep, Bethany."

She smiled against his shoulder and slid one leg up so her thigh rested high on his hip. When he still didn't take the hint, she slipped her hand between their bodies and wrapped it around the one part of him that was reacting. She finally got a response.

Wyc cursed, sat up again and flipped her around so that her back was to his front. He wrapped his arms around her, pinning her own arms in front of her, and tucked her into the curve of his body.

"Now go to sleep," he hissed.

She stared into the darkness and tried to make sense of Wyc's actions. Why the hell didn't he want her? Even with a hard-on the size of Mount Rushmore prodding her in the ass, he didn't want her.

Myrra. The name seared across her mind as she remembered the cool look of assessment that had been in the woman's eyes earlier. Not jealousy, just a cold curiosity. As if Myrra were sizing her up as the competition and finding her lacking. She had been unconscious for close to two days. He could have been sleeping with the other woman and she'd never know it. The only reason he was with her now had to be because they were matched, and he didn't want her screwing that up. Whatever the hell that meant.

The ache of acute loss wrapped around her heart, exhausting her clear to the marrow of her bones. She tried to shrink away from Wyc, but he held her too tightly. His skin burned against hers, mocking the desire it flamed to life in her body.

She refused to give in to tears. It wasn't the first time she had thought someone cared for her when, in reality, they were just using her to fulfill some personal agenda. She had learned that lesson a long time ago as a foster child the state paid people to take into their homes. Her "parents" hadn't cared about her so much as the money. As a child, she had yearned for a real home to belong in. One that she would be welcome in even if the money stopped coming.

A stupid dream. One she wouldn't make the mistake of dreaming again. This time she wasn't wanted for money, but for her bloodline. It might be a new reason, but the pain arrowed straight to the same wound. With everything that had happened in the last several days, this was the one threat experience had prepared her to handle.

Bethany closed her eyes and cocooned herself tightly under layers of self-preservation toughened through years of use. She didn't need to belong with Wyc or Ilyria. She belonged to herself. And that was enough. It had to be.

* * * * *

Wyc frowned as Bethany stiffened against him. Felt something shift between them. As if she had pulled away from him without moving. Sliding deep within herself.

He reached out with his mind and hit cold emptiness. His concern deepened, and he tried again. She was there, but hidden so deep he could only faintly sense her emotions. She was upset and feeling rejected. Damn.

He hadn't meant to hurt her. Had, in fact, been trying to protect her. As much as he wanted to bury himself deep and hard into Bethany, he wouldn't. He was barely holding on to the edge of his anger at the increasing threat to her life. If he took her body now, the moment her cunt wrapped around his cock all the emotion burning through him would roar in untempered lust. Violently. Desperately.

Hell, he had been too rough the first time because she had pushed him beyond his control. And if he fucked her tonight, the first time would seem sweet and easy by comparison.

It was pure torture simply holding her body against his without taking what she had offered. But it was a torture he was helpless to deny himself. When she had closed her hand around him, his need had momentarily blinded him, he wanted her so much. He used the last of his fading willpower to fight the desire to crush her beneath him and ram his cock into her hard and deep.

The final, straining thread that held him back was the memory of the shock on her face when she saw him transform into the *kyltar*. He didn't want her to go from seeing him as an animal to him fucking her like one.

His back teeth ground together. He had to quit thinking about fucking Bethany before he ignored wisdom and rolled over and into her anyway.

He tried to push assurance and comfort into her mind, but the extremity of her withdrawal managed to keep him blocked out. Without the connection of being completely mated, he was unable to break through the thick walls of her resistance. He stroked her stomach and rested his cheek on the top of her head. He'd smooth things over tomorrow, when he had a tighter rein on his lust.

His hand skimmed over her silky skin. The gentle swell of her belly reminded him of kissing her there before moving down between her legs. A rush of furious heat surged through his cock. He closed his eyes and silently cursed.

He forced his thoughts on the information Rordyc had brought back tonight and shared privately with him and Amdyn. After nearly forty-eight hours without sleep, he was too exhausted to fully wrap his mind around the possible implications it suggested. His cousin's report had arrived on the heels of two days spent tracking and closing down a Sleht portal.

Myrra had felt the gateway forming between worlds last week. As a Keeper, she was extra-sensitive, and he was damn glad. They had caught one Predator and a team of Slayers coming through as they were shutting it down.

They were finally closing in on Magdalyne's daughters after decades of searching, and the Sleht had somehow gotten wind of it. Information was being leaked. There had been too many coincidences for any other possibility.

Though the second oldest of his cousins, even he had been too young to take part when the search first started twenty-four years ago. It had taken twelve years to find which world Magdalyne had jumped into, and by that time, he and Amdyn were leading the hunt. They were working with a handpicked team here, but the military handled things in Ilyria. Top men in the Special Services, but there were many neither he nor Amdyn knew personally.

Bethany shifted in his arms, bringing his attention back to the one thing in his life that had finally worked out right. She sighed in her sleep and his heart twisted with emotion. To keep her safe, he'd interrogate every single soldier himself if he had to. He nuzzled the nape of her neck, breathing in the sweet scent of woman. His woman.

Tomorrow he and Rordyc would work on the new information, but for tonight, he was going to hold on to his reason for living.

* * * * *

When Bethany woke up, Wyc was gone. She ran a hand over his pillow. Cold. With a sigh, she flopped onto her back and stared at the ceiling. Nothing of interest there. She stretched and glanced around.

It was a beautiful room. Dark wood furniture, deep golden walls, white bedding on a huge four-poster bed and filmy, cream-colored curtains. So warm and romantic, it was depressing.

Even with all the insanity Wyc had brought into her life, she had started to fall for him. Hard. Those mesmerizing deep blue eyes had cast a spell on her that she had quit fighting somewhere along the line. Wanting to believe he was starting to care for her too, she had begun to open her heart to him. To hope again.

His rejection last night still stung. More than she wanted to admit. It had struck the center of her insecurity. Right now he needed her, wanted something from her. Once he got that, she'd be tossed aside. The story of her life — same book, next chapter.

Resentment swelled to douse her bout of melancholy defeatism. This time would be different. She refused to wait around until her usefulness had expired. She'd find out how to fight or hide from the Predators, and then she'd be gone. Wyc could find another Mystic to help fulfill his destiny and that of his people. She had sisters. He could damn well go get himself matched to one of them.

A physical pain shot through her at the thought, making her chest ache and her throat constrict. She cursed and threw the covers off. She couldn't think about him anymore or she might let emotion cloud her decisions. Forget it.

Forget him.

She pushed herself out of bed, glad to find more strength in her legs than the last time she had gotten up to pee. Padding into the bathroom, she ignored her reflection in the mirror, knowing she probably looked half dead. She didn't care anyway. Maybe "The Living Dead" look would encourage Wyc to keep his distance long enough to gather the information she needed and get the hell away from him.

The bathroom carried the romance theme of the bedroom to the next level. Complete with adjustable lighting, Italian marble and enough candles to set Rome on fire, it was a sensual enticement complete with a double whirlpool tub sunk into one corner. Designed for the decadent at heart and, obviously, for her personal agony. Oh well. If one had to suffer, might as well suffer in style.

She was rotating the taps on to full blast when she saw it. The bottle of jasmine and orchid bubble bath. Her favorite. Her bottle. The one she had peeled half the label off of during her last long soak after a hard night of waitressing. And Wyc had thought to bring it along. Damn him.

She dumped some of the bubble bath into the streaming water and refused to think about that. A show of thoughtfulness on his part was too dangerous to her recently acquired equilibrium. It was nothing more than coincidence. She wouldn't let it be anything more.

With a sigh, she slipped into the water and let the heat saturate her body. The bubbles rose around her, covering her in a mountain of soft scent. She waited until the water was lapping close to the edge of the tub before shutting it off. She adjusted the dials on the whirlpool to the lowest setting, let out a deep breath, and sank down until only her face was above the water and bubbles.

* * * * *

Frustrated, Wyc pushed his hair back from his face as he made his way up the front stairs of the large, two-story farmhouse nestled off a forgotten road high in the Colorado Rockies. He thought the meeting with his cousins would never end. But the fact that two Predators had attacked within a couple of hours of each other was a grave concern.

Predators never worked together. They were fierce, cunning and trained solely to track and retrieve Ilyrian Mystics, no matter the cost to them or their enemies. But they couldn't abide being with another of their kind. They prized their retrieval and/or kill ratio above all else and would sooner die than help another Predator track down a Mystic. Something the Sleht had not been able to breed out of their systems.

Born into one of the "specialized" branches of the Sleht, they had the ability to alter their appearance enough to fit in almost any world as long as the inhabitants were basically humanoid in form. The one that had drugged Bethany had the flat, black eyes of a Sleht youth, without the yellow flecking that came with age.

The neophyte mistakes of his attack led Wyc to believe that he hadn't been sent out through the usual channels in the Sleht hierarchy. Whatever the Predator trainers were, they weren't stupid, and they'd never send a beginner into an otherworld situation.

There was the added fact that though Predators were always a constant threat, there had been no indication that any had been on his or Bethany's trail for months. And then to have two attacks within the same day seemed more than just a little coincidental.

All were agreed that a traitor operating within their own lines ranked as a high possibility, but little more than hunches pointed toward any single person. As usual, Rordyc and Amdyn had fallen onto opposite sides of the discussion, their temperaments as dissimilar as their looks.

Rordyc, with his black hair and dark eyes, always wanting to jump straight in and deal with consequences as they came, push until someone pushed back. Amdyn, his white-blond hair and light blue eyes stark against his dark olive skin, would consider everything from a million different angles until all possibilities were exhausted. He refused to condemn anyone without solid proof. It didn't help the volatile situation around the table that Amdyn's younger brothers, Cirryc and Kayn, loved to add to the mix by egging the arguments on.

The entire time Wyc was trying to concentrate on the problem of security, he kept picturing Bethany as he left her that morning. In his bed, sweet, soft and warm with sleep. He had wanted to wake her with slow caresses and deep kisses. But she was still fighting the aftereffects of the drug and needed all the rest she could get.

And this afternoon, he'd be giving her the antidote. He grimaced. He'd never had to administer the antidote before, but had heard that some of the side effects, though short-lived, could be extreme. Fever, cold and the shakes reported most often. He hoped that due to her unmixed bloodline, she'd be spared the worst of it.

It ate at him like acid that she might have to endure any of it. He'd rather not give the antidote to her at all and let the drug work through her system naturally. But with Predators stalking her, he refused to leave any opportunity for Bethany to be given the second injection and be at their nonexistent mercy.

Sitting around the kitchen table with his cousins, his mind had flashed to the memory of Bethany's curves pressed against him in the night. His cock pressed into the cleft of her ass, the back of her thighs sliding along the front of his every time she moved in her sleep. The image immediately had his cock going from semi-aroused to painfully hard.

He had shifted in his chair and tried to adjust himself to a less agonizing position. When he caught Rordyc looking at him with taunting amusement, he had called an end to the meeting.

Quietly, he opened the bedroom door. If she were still sleeping, he didn't want to wake her. He frowned. The bed was empty. The room silent.

"Bethany?"

No answer.

A burst of panic flared through him when she didn't respond to a second, louder call. Taking a stranglehold on his emotions, he rushed into the bathroom. His heart dropped to his feet when he saw Bethany almost completely submerged in the tub, her pale face floating barely above the water.

The possibility that, fatigued from the drug, she had slipped or fallen asleep in the bathtub had him shouting her name again and thrusting his hands into the soapy water. He shouted a curse, grabbed her by the arms and lifted.

Bethany's eyes flew open and she screamed. Lashing out, she knocked his hands from her slippery skin. Free of his grip, she immediately fell backwards into the water and went completely under.

"Damn it," Wyc hissed as he shoved his hands under her arms and lifted her straight up. Bethany stood in the tub, sputtering, choking and slapping at his arms. He released her and abruptly pushed her hair out of her face, his scare making his movements rougher than he intended. "Are you all right?"

She pinned him with a glare. "I was fine until you tried to drown me."

"Drown you? I was—"

Wyc was cut off by Bethany's shriek as her gaze darted over his shoulder. She wrapped her arms over her breasts and dropped back into the water so fast, a wave of water sloshed over the side of the tub. He spun around to find Amdyn, Kayn, Cirryc and Rordyc barreling through the bathroom door.

Rordyc took one look at the situation, cocked an eyebrow at Wyc and left. The other three just stood there and stared. Amdyn at him, Kayn and Cirryc at Bethany. Wyc roared and stepped toward his younger cousins, blocking their view.

"What the hell are you looking at?" he bellowed.

Their gazes snapped to his.

"Get out!" Wyc yelled. "Now."

Kayn and Cirryc glanced at each other and backed out of the room.

Amdyn only widened his stance and propped his hands on his hips, his face set into sharp lines of anger. "You're the one shouting like the damn house is on fire, and you're angry because we came running to help?"

"I'm in a room with a naked woman in a bathtub. How much help do you think I need?"

"Beats the hell out of me. I'm not the one yelling."

"Both of you," Bethany demanded from the pile of bubbles she had gathered around her, "get out. Right now, get out!"

Wyc ignored her and continued to glare at Amdyn until, with a curse, his cousin stalked out of the room and slammed the door behind him. Wyc turned his attention back to Bethany and watched her eyes widen as he stripped.

"What do you think you're doing?" she asked. She lunged for the towel she had placed close to the tub, but Wyc reached it before she did. He tossed it across the room.

Bethany scooted to the far side of the tub as he stepped into the swirling water. When he sat down, she smacked the water and splashed him in the face. "I don't want you in here. Get out. Go back to Myrra."

He wiped bubbles from his eyes and grabbed her hand.

"Myrra? What are you talking about?"

For a moment, she froze. And then glared at him before sending another splash of water flying toward his face with her free hand.

With a quick tug, he pulled her to his chest. Shifting her to sit between his legs with her back to his chest, he stifled a groan as his cock pressed up against her butt. He held her tightly until she stopped struggling.

"Did Myrra say something to you?"

"It was more what she didn't say."

"Are you jealous?" His smile was stopped by a sharp elbow to his ribs.

"Of course not. I just don't appreciate you thinking you can screw her and then come get naked with me. It's not going to happen." She wiggled her ass deliberately. "No matter how high your…hopes are."

She reached for the sponge. "So you might as well get out now and stop wasting your time. And mine."

Bethany's voice had turned cool and detached. Since he had made it obvious he wasn't going to get out, she seemed determined to snub him. He wasn't about to let that happen.

Having been hard for her closing in on three days, he was past the point of patience. Since the drug had kept her mostly unconscious, he had had no way to slake his need without simply using her body while she slept. A thing he refused to do.

But now, his need for her raged hot, and he would have her.

He took the sponge out of her hand. "First, I never waste time," he said, picking up the bottle of bubble bath and squeezing some onto the sponge.

Slowly, he massaged the sponge in front of her until it was frothy with lather. "Second, no matter what Myrra did or didn't say, she's my captain, and I wouldn't sleep with her for that reason alone."

Wyc lifted her wet hair from her back, twisted it into a thick rope and draped it over her right shoulder and breast, letting his fingers graze her nipple as he released her hair. He kissed the left side of her neck before running the soapy sponge up her arm and across her shoulders.

"And third, you scared the shit out of me. What the hell were you doing, floating in the tub like that?" He was trying to be calm, but the picture of her pale face floating in the water was still too raw in his memory.

"I was trying to relax."

"Underwater?" Despite his efforts, his voice vibrated on a jagged growl.

She leaned forward to turn the water back on. He followed the curve of her spine down with the sponge until it disappeared under the bubbles. "The hum of the whirlpool made it easier to think."

Suddenly, the same emotional coldness he had experienced from her last night surged against him. She slid forward, breaking the contact of their bodies. Her shoulders stiffened, and he caught her hurt as it pitched through her mind. She was fighting her desire. Mentally and physically trying to distance herself from him. No way in hell. Not again.

Wyc caught her around the waist and brought her back to him. "I'm not finished."

She shook her head. Her body tensed, but she refused to answer him.

Wyc laid the sponge on the ledge. "Bethany, what's wrong?"

"You want the full list?" she asked, tossing him a sardonic look.

"I'm serious. What changed between last night and this morning?"

Bethany turned back around and hunched forward, crossing her arms over her chest. "Nothing."

He curved his shoulders around hers, wrapping his arms completely around her and snugging her into him. He rested his chin on her shoulder. "Tell me."

* * * * *

Bethany struggled to hold on to her resolve. He hadn't wanted her last night. Wouldn't want her again. Better to deal with the raw feelings of rejection now before he had a chance to insinuate himself into her heart any deeper.

Against her will, her breath stuttered out. He tightened his hold on her, and it felt so damn good. Too damn good. Like she was really protected and cherished. "You didn't want me."

His body went rigid around her. She stopped breathing, wishing she hadn't said a word. He kissed the curve where her neck met her shoulder.

"No, babydoll. I wanted you too much." He leaned back, taking her with him, until he was reclining against the tub with her resting on his chest. "I still do."

As if she couldn't tell from the uncomfortable rod prodding her lower back. But just having him want her body somehow wasn't enough.

She stretched and turned off the running taps with her foot. The movement pressed her butt into his groin, and she reveled in the low sound of need it produced from Wyc. "What makes you think I want you?" she asked.

"Give me a chance to convince you."

He nipped her earlobe, and that little action sent a jolt of lust spearing straight into her cunt. Bethany licked her lips. How, in a tub full of water, could her mouth be as dry as the Sahara?

Wyc kissed her shoulder, her neck, and then raked his teeth gently over her earlobe again. A husky sound of desire rumbled in his chest and vibrated through her body.

Her body began to riot under his attentions, and her determination to ignore his carnal allure weakened. She'd have to remember not to make any rash resolutions in the future when they were both naked. She didn't have the willpower to keep them in the face of such temptation.

"I've needed to touch you all day, Bethany." He splayed his hand over her ribs. The need in his voice magnified her own.

Maybe he didn't care for her like she had foolishly thought, but he wanted her, and she wanted him. If he could use her, then by God, she would use him right back. She would just have to keep sex and emotion separate. Free her body and guard her heart. She could it. She had to.

"Wrap your arms around my neck," he whispered, his lips brushing her ear.

Bethany did as he said, her back arching and her breasts lifting as she reached behind her. She was immediately rewarded with another dark growl of approval that set loose swirls of sensation low in her belly.

He slid his hands down her hips and over her thighs. Gripping her legs, he pulled them up and over his so she was totally open for him. He moved his legs further apart, until her calves pressed against the side of the tub and her sex was stretched wide.

The hum of the whirlpool jets lulled her as the water softly churned against her pussy. The humid air pressed down on her with the smells of wild, tropical flowers and wild, virile man.

Wyc's hands began making slow journeys up and down her body. Over her thighs and up her hips, his fingers barely brushing the edge of her curls as he passed her mound. Caressing her stomach, exploring her navel, teasing her breasts. Repeating the process down, and then up again. Down again.

He nudged her head to the side to give him full access to the side of her neck. With the tip of his tongue, he traced the edge and whorls of her ear, flicked at her earlobe, pulled it into his mouth and sucked. His hands continued to roam up and down.

Long minutes passed as he nuzzled and kissed her neck, paying particular attention to the spot he found just under her ear that made her moan when he kissed it and then laved it with his tongue. And still, his hands never ceased moving. Never straying from the path he had set, only varying the touches, pressure and pace.

Bethany wasn't sure how much of this slow torture she could stand. Every time his fingers rubbed over her inner thighs she desperately hoped he would stop and stroke her throbbing pussy before moving on. The eddying water against her clit was enough to heighten her arousal, but came nowhere near satisfying it.

She furrowed her fingers in his hair and twisted her hips in invitation. He brought his knees slightly higher, holding her still again.

He cupped her breasts and circled her erect nipples with his thumbs. "Do you have any idea how beautiful you are?" he asked.

The sexy husk of his voice melted any hiding reserve she had been harboring. He wanted her. Badly.

"All morning I had to sit around a table with my cousins, talking and planning, and all I could think about was being inside you again."

His hands skimmed down her body until they rested at the juncture of her inner thighs. With deliberate care, he began to massage closer and closer to her aching clit. And finally — God — *finally*, his fingers were brushing against its sides. She whimpered in relief.

He shifted sideways and reached behind him with one hand. She heard him turn the whirlpool dial as he positioned her in front of a jet. Before she could say anything, the gentle pulse of water changed into a powerful stream of force and heat. The pounding water slammed against her clit and deep up into her cunt.

The feeling was so intense after his extended loveplay, she cried out and curled forward. He brought her back flat against his chest with one arm wrapped around her chest while, with his other hand, he kept her labia pulled apart and her pussy vulnerable to the onslaught of the pounding water.

Her fingers scrabbled over the slick sides of the tub as she vied for purchase. Her body tried to bow and arch, but Wyc refused to let her escape. He pulled back the hood of her clit, exposing the almost painfully sensitive nub to the unrelenting pressure of the jet. Gently, he tapped it once, twice.

Bethany's entire body tightened and then convulsed with a climax so violent, it tore her heart from its moorings and she was set adrift, helpless. She closed her eyes and dug her nails into her palms, unable to fight the brutal pleasure conquering her.

Terrified at being so completely out of control, she reached for Wyc with her mind. Found him. As her body continued to quake under the power of her release, she buried herself into the feelings he surrounded her with. Warmth, assurance. In the safety of his embrace, she rode out her ecstasy.

When she opened her eyes, one of Wyc's hands was cupped over her pussy, the other was cradling her breast and his cheek rested next to hers. He was breathing hard and the strain of his muscles made his body feel as yielding as iron.

"Are you all right?" he whispered.

She smiled. "Mmm-hmm."

"Good." He grasped her hips and lifted. "Bend your knees."

Bethany grabbed the sides of the tub for balance. "What?" The euphoria of the orgasm was slow to clear and his instruction didn't make sense.

"I need to be inside of you." He raised her higher. "Bend your knees."

Her legs flopped a bit, but she managed to get them bent underneath her. When she was on her knees, Wyc reached between them to position his cock.

"Lower yourself down, babydoll. Take me into that honey slick cunt of yours."

Her pussy still sensitive, she dropped her head forward on a moan as his thick shaft nudged against her opening. She wiggled her hips and he began to slide in.

He groaned as the head of his cock slipped in completely. "Oh yeah. That's it."

The raw savagery of his voice brought the cooling embers of Bethany's desire back to flame. She lowered herself further, and Wyc groaned louder. She started to bounce in a slow, shallow rhythm. He ran his hands up and down her back as she moved.

"Put your hands on my knees. Arch your back for me."

When she complied, he hissed out a curse and ran his large, rough hands down to grip her ass. This angle pressed his cock into the front of her vagina and when she bounced again, it rubbed a spot that sent a small shockwave up her spine. Oh yes. God yes. She began to bounce harder and faster.

"Like that, babydoll. Just like that." His voice rumbled out low and ragged. He squeezed her butt. "You have a great ass. It looks amazing sliding up and down with my cock buried inside of you."

A moan of pleasure was the only response Bethany could make. Being able to control the depth and tempo of their lovemaking gave her an incredible sense of power. She rode the feeling like she rode him. Hard and furious, deep and fast.

Water sloshed over the edge of the tub by the bucketfuls. Every time she slammed herself down on him, the water slapped against her thighs and pussy. The contractions started low and slow. Unlike the previous climax that tore at her suddenly, this one rose steadily and flowed over her like melted wax. With a gasp, she let herself roll over into exquisite bliss.

A harsh growl erupted from behind her. Wyc grabbed her hips and held her still as he thrust up into her. As his release shot into her, she shuddered with the flood of heat that filled and burned her from the inside out. Her cunt spasmed around him.

His face pressed against her back. "What do you do to me?" he whispered into her skin. "What the hell do you do to me?"

Bethany slumped forward. Wyc's arms around her kept her from falling face-first into the water. She straightened her legs and collapsed backwards into his chest. Her breath gushed out on a well-satisfied sigh. Her body had turned to mush, every bone melted from extended exposure to mind-numbing orgasms.

Wyc kissed her shoulder. "Tired?"

"Yes—"

A harsh grinding sound came from the whirlpool jets. Wyc smacked the dial and turned them off. "You splashed all the water out."

Bethany glanced at all the water puddled on the floor and would have laughed if she had the energy. "I had help."

She shivered, and Wyc ran his hands down her arms.

"Let's get you out of here before you catch cold." He sat her up and stepped over the edge of the tub.

"You really need lessons on afterglow," she mumbled as he padded across the bathroom to grab the towel he'd flung away earlier.

"What?" he asked, bringing it back to her.

"Nothing," she said, and wrapped herself in the towel.

He scooped her up and carried her to the bed. Quickly, he toweled her off and pulled the comforter over her.

Her eyes were already closing as he tucked the blanket under her chin and around her body. She wanted to offer to clean the mess they had made in the bathroom. Wanted to scoot over and invite him under the covers, but her bones had yet to solidify.

"Rest. The drug's still working through your system. Once you feel up to it, I'll introduce you to everyone."

Her eyes fell shut and she heard him move away and rummage through a dresser drawer. She pried her eyes open for a second to look at one truly amazing body. Broad shoulders and biceps corded with muscle. A sculpted back tapering down into a narrow waist and straight into the most fantastic ass she'd ever seen. And those thighs. Even from across the room and looking at him sideways, they appeared strong, powerful.

She must have made some sort of noise, because Wyc snapped his head around and looked at her. The heat in his eyes told her she had been caught.

"Go to sleep, Bethany. Don't tempt me to wear you completely out."

Obediently, she closed her eyes. And smiled.

A couple more drawers scraped open and closed, followed by slopping sounds from the bathroom. Sleep was pulling her under for the last time when her right arm was lifted from beneath the covers and a ring slid onto her middle finger. Wyc kissed the middle of her palm, and although it might have only been a dream, she heard him whisper, "Mine."

Chapter Seven

ᔆᕞ

"I was coming to get you," Wyc said, and stopped two steps up the staircase as Bethany continued down it. Her long hair was caught up in a ponytail, and the dark green of her sweatshirt made her emerald eyes look impossibly deep. Though normally he preferred skirts on a woman, watching the sway of her hips as she descended in those snug jeans was going a long way to change his mind. She looked good enough peel out of those clothes and eat.

She stopped on the stair just above his, placing herself in a very accessible position.

"I'm starving," she said.

His gaze moved upwards, over her breasts, her neck, her mouth. By the time he reached her eyes, he was grinning and she was frowning.

"For food," she clarified.

"Damn." He leaned into her, wrapped his hands around her waist and kissed her. As soon as his lips touched hers, her mouth opened on a soft sigh, and he entered at the invitation. She smelled like flowers. Like the bubbles in the bath they had taken together earlier. The memory of her slick body riding his, the feel of her ass in his hands as she raised and lowered herself on him, abandoned to her pleasure, had him pressing against her and deepening the kiss.

She tilted her face away. "I really am hungry."

"So am I." With one hand, he cradled her head in place and then kissed her with intent. He slid his other hand under her shirt to cup her breast though her bra. When he teased her nipple to a sharp peak, she whimpered softly into his mouth and circled his neck with her arms.

"Not that I don't enjoy a good show," Rordyc drawled from behind him, "but you two are blocking the stairs."

Bethany pulled back from the kiss and turned a bright red, her eyes darting over his shoulder to find, he was sure, his cousin's amused smirk.

Wyc didn't turn around. Didn't take his eyes off Bethany's mouth or his hand off her breast. "So use the back stairs."

Bethany's tongue darted out to nervously lick her lips. Wyc's hunger flared at the sight. He squeezed her breast and leaned in to capture that pretty pink tongue. She hissed at him and tried to surreptitiously tug his hand out from under her shirt.

"Myrra's got the drug ready." Rordyc's tone was no longer teasing.

Wyc sighed and released Bethany. "We're on our way." He gave her another quick kiss and took her hand. Her face was lined with concern.

"A drug?" she asked as he led her down the stairs and toward the kitchen. "Is this one of those alien things where you guys have to take something in order to survive while you're here on Earth?"

Her question was directed at him, but said as they turned the corner, causing conversation to come to a sudden standstill in the spacious kitchen. Bethany froze beside him, her eyes going wide as she took in the group scattered around the kitchen. Wyc held back a grin. For once, he wasn't the only one Bethany managed to annoy with one of her exasperating comments.

* * * * *

Oh shit. Bethany looked around the warm kitchen done in shades of deep red and dark wood, but all she could focus on were the scrutinizing stares of the men and women before her. Close in height and breadth to Wyc, the men all exuded a palpable strength and a darkly sexual intensity that could melt the panties off a woman at a hundred feet. The women were stunning in their own right, and wore authority as other women might wear perfume. And she had just called them all aliens. Oh *shit*.

She took a step backwards and bumped into Wyc. Damn. When had the man moved behind her? He settled his hands firmly on her shoulders. Not reassuring so much as restraining. He was starting to read her too well.

"Bethany," Wyc's voice rumbled past her ear, "I'd like you to meet my cousins and part of the team that's been searching for you.

"You've met Myrra—" the woman gave a curt nod of acknowledgment that managed to show deference to Wyc and disapproval toward her at the same time, "—and Rordyc."

The dark-haired man had one hip cocked against a counter and his arms crossed over his chest. At Wyc's introduction, he gave her a quick once-over, winked and said, "Bubbles are a better look on you." The growl of warning that rumbled out of Wyc's chest only widened Rordyc's grin.

"The man next to him is Jordyn." Intense was the only word Bethany could put to the hard, sinewy man standing next to Rordyc. From under dark, thick eyelashes halfway lowered, his silver-grey eyes took her in with cool assessment, and the only movement he made at their introduction was to blink.

Wyc used his hands on her shoulders to turn her toward the center of the kitchen. Two Nordic gods and a fairy princess-looking woman bearing a startling resemblance to Wyc were seated around the table.

"Amdyn—" the largest Nordic god with the somber expression and sky-blue eyes tilted his head, "—and his brother Cirryc." The younger Nordic god nodded and a section of long, ridiculously golden blond hair fell forward over his shoulder. Any one of these men could be the poster boy for a woman's most wanted fantasy. She glanced around the kitchen again. Make that poster *man*.

"Beside him," Wyc continued, "is Shyrana, my baby sister."

Shyrana briefly narrowed her eyes at Wyc when he emphasized the word "baby", and then graced Bethany with a smile that undoubtedly got her anything she asked for from every male she encountered. With the possible exception being her brother.

"Welcome," Shyrana said.

Bethany managed to keep her mouth from falling open, though it wasn't easy. Wyc's sister had a voice that sounded like flowers opening to a beautiful spring day. It purred over her skin like a promise and made her shiver.

Wyc bent down so his lips were next to her ear. "You'll get used to her voice." His whisper caused Bethany to shiver again.

He straightened and nudged Bethany forward. "You'll meet the rest later."

"There are more?" she squeaked.

"A few." He gestured to a chair. "Have a seat."

The only open chair was between the Nordic gods. "No thanks."

Myrra moved forward and laid an open box on the table. Inside lay a small, five-pronged syringe. "It's ready," she said.

He gave Bethany another nudge toward the table. Harder. "You'll want to be sitting when you receive the antidote to the drug you were injected with."

Bethany snapped her head around and twisted out of his grasp. "What? What antidote." She shook her head and took a step back. "No thank you. I feel fine."

"Bethany —"

"No! No way in hell." She spun around to run and slammed into Amdyn's chest. One quick look confirmed that everyone but Shyrana had moved to block every possible flight path. She fought down the panic that had bile rising in her throat. "Oh my God. This is an alien abduction, isn't it?"

Rordyc tipped his head back and laughed out loud. Everyone else glared at Wyc.

"You haven't told her?" Shyrana's question was laced with astonishment. "You expected her to just sit quietly while you stuck her with a needle?"

"She knows she can trust me," Wyc said.

Shyrana raised her eyebrows and pointedly looked from the warriors crowding Bethany to the syringe. "Uh-huh. Nothing to make a woman nervous here."

Bethany began to shake. She was hungry, tired and had a roomful of beefcake aliens intent on drugging her. As calmly as she could, she turned and faced Wyc. "I'd like to go home now," she said.

* * * * *

Wyc cursed under his breath and reached out to pull Bethany to him. She didn't resist, but stayed stiff in his arms. Shyrana's censure was justified. He had gone upstairs with the intention of telling her about the drug and its antidote, but she had distracted him with her kiss.

This was the third time he had meant to explain something to her, only to be set off-track by his desire for her. He would set a damn record if he didn't regain some of his control where she was concerned. His arms tightened about her when her body quaked slightly against his own.

"Everyone out," he commanded. His sister started to rise. "Except you, Shyrana. You stay."

Though Myrra gave him a look of surprise, she turned and left with the others without a word. Normally, she would be the one to administer the drug, but Bethany still appeared uneasy around her. Captain Lansyr unnerved seasoned warriors with a look, but was one of his most dedicated soldiers, and as unfaltering in her pursuit of Magdalyne's lost daughters as his cousins who had been matched to them. Though he'd already explained her jealousy as groundless and she had no other reason to fear his captain, he'd grant Bethany some time to adjust.

He waited until the others had cleared the room before settling Bethany at the table beside his sister. He had asked those not on patrol to gather so Bethany could meet them. The introduction of the antidote was a simple matter of bad timing on Myrra's part.

The show of force from his cousins at Bethany's refusal had been unintentional. In their eyes, taking the antidote was a given for Bethany's own safety. Their actions were an automatic gut response out of concern for her as his mate and as one of their own. They'd seen what a Predator did to a Mystic under the influence of *Yes Master*. Every last member on his team would put themselves in harm's way before allowing Bethany to be hurt, even at the hands of her own stubbornness.

He pulled a chair around to sit catty-corner to her and lightly brushed her cheek with his fingertips. Her chin was stuck at a willful angle, but her face was pale and her full lips were pressed together until they were no more than twin slashes of thin pink lines.

With a nod toward the syringe, he said, "That's the antidote to the drug you were given by the Predator at your apartment."

Bethany's eyes darted to the needle and then away. Briefly, he explained the purpose and effect of the drug the Predator had used on her, and what would happen if she got the second dose. Not once while he spoke did she look at him. She kept her eyes fixed on a spot on the table. When he was finished, she sat silent and unmoving for a long moment.

"So other than knock me out," she finally said, rubbing at the place on her arm where she had been stuck, "the first injection doesn't do anything else until I get the second shot?"

"As far as we know," Shyrana's velvet voice cut in. "But we've had very little to work with. What we are sure of is that this particular combination of drugs only affects females of the Mystic bloodline."

She gestured to the needle still nestled in the box. "We were able to create an antidote that counteracts the interactive properties of the first dose so that even if you did get the second shot, it wouldn't affect you. But as of now, there is no antidote once both drugs are in your system."

Bethany picked up the syringe and slowly tilted it first one way and then the other. The thick, tarry substance oozed from one end of the glass vial to the other.

"But couldn't I just wait it out? Eventually, it will have to work through my system. All drugs do, right? And what are the chances of running into another Predator who just happens to have the second dose of a rare drug on him?"

"Less than slim to none," Wyc said, "and over my dead body." He wrapped his hand around hers that held the needle. "But even those are odds too great for me to risk with your safety at stake."

When she turned her eyes to him, the tortured look in them made him want to howl in protest and beat the crap out of someone.

"Do I have a choice?"

He let out a deep sigh. "No."

She released the needle into his palm. He handed it to Shyrana and then pushed up one of Bethany's sleeves. Shyrana tore open an antiseptic pad and cleaned a spot on the inside of Bethany's elbow.

"Shyrana's given the antidote before." He took her hand again, squeezed it in reassurance. "She knows what she's doing."

"I'm going to inject it right into the bloodstream, Bethany. It'll work faster, and if there are any side effects, they'll be over quicker this way too."

"Side effects?" Bethany tried to jerk out of his grasp, but he held her in place. "What side effects?"

Shyrana paused and looked at him. "You might want to let her lie down on the couch."

Her body went rigid and her fingernails dug into the fleshy part of his hand. Though her voice was demanding and even, panic flared in her eyes.

"Tell me about the side effects," she insisted.

Shyrana turned her deep blue eyes to her and the unique melody of her voice sent some measure of comfort through Bethany. "Sometimes a fever accompanies the healing process. The degree of discomfort varies. Would you be more at ease if we did this upstairs in your room?"

"I'd be more comfortable if we didn't do this at all."

Wyc slid one hand up to cup her elbow and the other circled her wrist to hold her arm steady. Shyrana held the syringe over Bethany's arm and looked at him, waiting.

Bethany let out a small sound of frustration. "Just do it and get it over with. The sooner it's done, the sooner I'm going home."

His fingers hardened around her arm, but he didn't respond to her comment other than to nod his head at Shyrana to continue. Bethany was home. With him. Her constant refusal to accept that fact was really going to piss him off one of these days.

There was a lot for her to get used to. A lot to accept. But the sooner she started, the easier it would be. Because she wasn't going to leave him. He wouldn't allow it.

Bethany winced as the five tiny prongs were inserted into her flesh. As Shyrana depressed the plunger and the inky substance disappeared under her skin, she let out a slow hiss.

Quickly, Shyrana removed the needle and placed a bandage over the prick marks. When Bethany pulled her arm away this time, he let her. She held her arm to her stomach and covered the bandage with her other hand, pressing against it. The little color remaining in her face quickly drained away.

Her reaction worried Wyc. He looked at Shyrana for an explanation. It didn't make him feel any better to see concern deeply etched on his sister's beautiful face.

"What's wrong?" he asked.

"Nothing's wrong. It's just a side effect. It stings some when injected."

* * * * *

Bethany pressed against the point where the needle had gone in. Sting some, her ass. It was burning like liquid fire being poured through her veins. She could track the progress of the medicine as the inferno spread from her arm to her shoulder.

Damn. She couldn't just sit here and think about it. She had to get her mind off what was happening, or she was going to faint from the pain blasting a path under her skin.

"Does everyone in your family turn into cats when they get mad?" she asked between clenched teeth.

"What?"

Wyc looked at her like she had just blurted gibberish. She didn't care. Hoped he got angry. She was in the mood to fight, thanks to the solar flare that just erupted in her chest.

"Cats. Do they all turn into those big, black, damn cats like you do?"

Wyc shook his head distractedly and reached for her hand. She thought he was going to hold her hand as an offer of comfort. Instead, he checked her pulse.

"No," he said, "Our powers were fractured by the curse, leaving us all with different abilities."

"Like what?" She pulled her hand back and wrapped her arms around her stomach, doing her best not to double over and roll out of the chair and onto the floor.

"You'll have to ask them."

When she glared at him, he shrugged.

"It's not my place to reveal their secrets, just as I wouldn't reveal yours to them."

She blinked and tried to clear the tiny black spots that were starting to dance in front of her eyes. "I don't have any secrets."

Wyc's grin was tense. "Sure you do. And each time I take you to bed, I discover more."

Damn man. How could he think of sex at a time like this? He better have a good memory, because after this little stunt, he'd be building snowmen in hell before *discovering* more of her secrets.

Another wave of fire shot through her body, this time reaching to her toes. She hissed and hunched her shoulders. "What happened to the Predator that gave me the drug? Did you kill him?"

"Yes." His answer was curt, harsh. She looked up to see brutal rage wash over his features.

"Did you bring him with us? I'd like a chance to take an ice pick to his body."

"No, I left him in your bathtub."

Despite the pain, Bethany shot straight up out of the chair. "You did what? Damn it! What if my landlord checks on my apartment while I'm gone? He'll find a dead alien in my bathroom and I'll never be able to get my apartment back, not to mention my deposit. You owe me two hundred bucks."

Wyc leaned back in his chair, his dark eyes flashing with dangerous emotion. "Once a Predator is dead, his body dissolves if placed in water. Like ours does when placed in the ground. Theirs is just a much faster process. And you're not going back to that apartment, so it doesn't matter."

"Well, I sure as hell am not going to Ilyria with you." She took a step toward him to punctuate her comment and walked right into a wall of white flame. She gasped and closed her eyes against the agony. Her skin started stinging like an army of biting insects had been let loose underneath it. She pitched forward with a cry, her fingernails scraping at her neck and arms.

Wyc caught her up in his arms before she had a chance to hit the floor. "Shy! What the hell's going on? Bethany, are you all right?"

Bethany couldn't unclench her teeth to force an answer out.

Shyrana's soft voice floated across her skin, "Side effects. Nothing permanent. It will ease soon. From my experience, the stronger the bloodline, the stronger the reaction."

"Shit." With Bethany in his arms, Wyc strode into the living room. "As far as we know, she's damn near a hundred percent Mystic. That's why she was matched on her first birthday." He sat on the couch, holding her on his lap.

She was having a difficult time focusing. Her cheeks stung like someone had stubbed out lit cigars on them. "It burns," she whispered and twisted in his arms, trying to get her shirt off. Her entire body was being consumed by the inferno.

Wyc put a hand to her face, her hands. "You're as cold as ice, babydoll. Just hang on to me. It'll be over soon."

She tried to writhe out of his embrace. "Let go. My skin is on fire. Like fire ants biting. Crawling around inside. Chewing their way out."

She snatched at her clothes again and Wyc grabbed her hands. She started to shake uncontrollably.

"If this is your cure," she spat, "I'd rather take my chances with the Predators." A fierce shudder racked her body, and she strained against him. Curses flew from her mouth as she jerked against him.

"I swear, Wyc Kilth, if I make it through this, you're a dead man. Or a dead alien. Or panther thing." She gasped and bowed up in his arms. "Oh God. It hurts."

"I'm sorry," he whispered against her hair. "So sorry." He held her firmly to his body and rocked her gently even as she continued to fight and curse him.

Bethany scratched at her skin, leaving long, angry red marks down the inside of her right arm. Wyc pulled her flush to his chest and pinned her hands between their bodies, keeping her from tearing at herself again.

She tried to hold back her tears, pull away from the comfort Wyc offered. Focus on the anger and not the pain. But she hurt. And damn it, she wanted to be held.

* * * * *

Bethany buried her face against his neck and stopped cursing. He felt her hot tears as they fell to his skin. It ripped his heart out and he wished she'd go back to screaming at him. He'd rather have her threaten him to hell and back than cry.

He wished he hadn't been so fast to kill the Predator that drugged her. He should have tortured that bastard. Would have, if he had known this was going to happen. But given the choice, he still would have given her the antidote rather than take the chance of her receiving the second dose that could have put her in the hands of the Sleht.

"I hate this, Wyc."

"I know. I do too." He smoothed a hand over her head and down her back to cup her hip. She felt so good under his hands. He held her close and used all his mental powers to soothe her until her sobs stilled and she sagged against him. She used his shirt to wipe her face.

"It's better. You can let go of me now."

He kissed her ear. "Give me a minute here." Adjusting her body to fit her hip snugly against his groin, he wrapped his arms around her and just held her.

The portal was still weeks from opening. He didn't like the time frame. Any day here rather than tucked away safely in his home was one too many. The Sleht couldn't force an unwilling victim through a portal. No one could. Though at the rate she kept telling him she wasn't going with him, it would make things a hell of a lot easier if he *could* just tie her up and drag her kicking and screaming back to their homeworld.

The only good thing about having to wait for the gateway to open was having a little time to convince her to change her mind. And she would change it. He'd use whatever means he had to make sure that his mate stayed with him. He'd bind her to him physically and emotionally.

There was only the final part of the Matching Ritual left to be completed. The Mating Rite, where she had to accept him willfully as her mate with their rings in place, give verbal assent to their union and take him into her body. And once the Mating Rite was finished, he'd be tied to her mentally as well.

A full telepath like Amdyn would share a direct link with his mate enabling them both to read each other's minds after completing the Matching Ritual. He and Bethany would be able to send and sense each other's specific emotions, but not fully see into each other's minds like his cousin and his mate would. He already had some ability in that area due to his training and the fact that she was his mate. But once they finished the ritual, they would be connected on a much deeper level and Bethany would be able to reach out to his mind as well.

Bethany shifted in his lap, stirring his desire with her movement. She swiped her hand across her face, erasing the last vestige of her tears.

"I'm still hungry," she said.

Wyc smiled and gave her a quick squeeze before setting her on her feet. He was still hungry too, but Bethany needed to eat.

"I can get you something," Shyrana offered. "What are you in the mood for?"

Bethany glanced at him. He nodded. "Go on. The kitchen's fully stocked. I'll check on you later. I need to go with Amdyn and inspect the perimeter we've set."

He watched her walk toward the kitchen with his sister. Shy said something that made Bethany respond with a wobbly smile and glance over her shoulder at him. Emotion plowed into his gut like a wrecking ball.

Much more than the possessiveness or protectiveness of before. More even than the fierce lust that seemed to constantly consume him when she was around. For all the barriers he had put in place around his emotions after his brothers' deaths and friend's betrayal, Bethany had gained access to the very center of his heart.

As much as he hadn't wanted to and had tried to guard against such a crippling emotion, he had fallen in love with his mate.

Chapter Eight

Halfway through Bethany's second sandwich, Shyrana excused herself with a headache and left Bethany to finish her lunch. Bethany was swallowing her last bite when Myrra entered the kitchen with one of the men who had burst into her bath, but who hadn't been present earlier to be introduced with the others. From the pale blond hair and eyes the color of blue ice, she figured he was related to Amdyn and Cirryc, landing in age somewhere between the two. The dazzling smile he offered in greeting failed to thaw the chill in his gaze and had a sensual edge that made her uncomfortable.

"Nice to finally meet the famous, first-to-be-found, Mystic daughter." He sauntered to the table and picked up her hand, bent at the waist and placed a kiss on her knuckles that lingered a moment too long. She jerked her hand out of his grasp and had to choke the final bite of her sandwich down her throat.

His smile set like cement in his face at her reaction. "I'm Kayn, of the First House of Kilth."

"First House of Kilth?" Bethany asked.

Myrra had stopped beside her, her stance closer to "parade rest" than a casual deportment, as if she expected a commanding officer to materialize at any moment and didn't want to be caught off-guard.

"The royal family is split into five houses," she explained, "each descending from one of the original ruling brothers. First House, oldest brother and so on."

Bethany returned Kayn's visual inspection. His face held an arrogance not evident in the other royal heirs she'd met, and he wore his hair shorter than every other man except Jordyn. He pulled out a chair, spun it around and straddled it to face her.

"I'm curious," he said, stacking his arms on the back of the chair, "what do you remember about your sisters?"

"Nothing."

Myrra raised her eyebrows, but didn't comment. Kayn shook his head and propped his clefted chin on his thumb.

"Nothing at all? I find that hard to believe."

"I didn't even know I had sisters until Wyc told me. I'm still not completely convinced I do. This whole situation is a little out of normal for me." That wasn't completely true. She did believe she had sisters. She just wasn't willing to admit it to others. Afraid that if she spoke her hope out loud, it would be crushed under the weight of her own expectations. Just because she was willing to claim sisterhood with strangers didn't mean they'd be willing to do the same.

She twisted the ring around her finger until she could read the lettering embedded in the design.

It was on her right hand. She had always worn it on her left. With a frown, she transferred it back to her left hand. When she looked up, Kayn was watching her movements closely and seemed amused by what she had done.

"You've got to have some memory of something," he said. "Think. It's important."

She glared at him. After having her insides so recently scorched raw by the anti-Predator drug, she was in no mood to entertain an interrogation. She shoved her chair back from the table and stood.

"I know it's important. Don't you think I've racked my brain, trying to come up with even a glimmer of a memory that could help find the other women before the Predators do?" She plowed her fingers through her hair, dislodging her ponytail. With a rough pull, she yanked the rubber band completely out.

Kayn cocked an eyebrow at her. "Perhaps you should try harder."

Bethany bit her tongue, refusing to defend herself to this asshole. Relative to Wyc or not, he had a serious chip on his shoulder. However, she didn't put it there, and it wasn't her responsibility to remove it.

His large body unfolding in a deliberate, unhurried motion, Kayn rose from his chair, turned it around and pushed it under the table. Placing his hands on the top rung of the chair back, he leaned heavily over it, his shoulders hunched. Deep grooves furrowed the sides of his mouth.

"You're only the first of the four sisters we've been looking for. Time is running out. Maybe you should spend more time 'racking your brain'," he repeated her words back to her with a venomous mocking, "and less time fucking."

Bethany's head jerked back as if she had been dealt a physical blow. Myrra bit out a harsh exclamation in a language Bethany didn't recognize.

Kayn straightened and fixed his attention on Wyc's captain. "You of all people should know how distracted Wyc has been since we found her. His decisions are weighted against the entire mission in favor of her safety. The only thing he cares about now is getting between her legs and—"

"Enough!" Myrra's voice echoed off the windows and cabinets. The air crackled around Myrra with the promise of sure and final retribution for transgression, and one look at her would relieve anyone's doubt that she was fully capable of delivering on that promise, well and quickly. Suddenly, Bethany had an instant appreciation for why Wyc had chosen her to captain his personal guard. The woman could be downright frightening. Bethany had met three-hundred-pound biker-bar bouncers less intimidating.

The effect was not lost on Kayn. His eyes flashed in fury, but he clamped his lips together and stalked from the room without another word.

Silence followed his exit, settling like an itchy, wet wool blanket, coarse and heavy against sensitive skin. Myrra turned to face her. The emanation of power that had shimmered around her had dimmed, but was still very much in evidence.

Fleetingly, Bethany wished she had stuck with her karate lessons for longer than a month.

"I make no apologies for Kayn," Myrra stated, her back and expression stiff, "he will have to expiate his own actions. However, it might benefit you to know that his grudge is not personal. Wyc had two younger brothers, twins, who were good friends of Kayn's. He took their deaths hard."

"Wyc's brothers died? What happened?"

Myrra shook her head. "A close friend of Wyc's betrayed them. Kayn holds Wyc guilty by association."

"Was the traitor caught?"

"He died from wounds he received in the trap set for Wyc's brothers. Kayn was the one who found him."

Bethany tried to comprehend losing two brothers, a friend and a family member's trust in one moment. She couldn't. "How do you know Wyc's friend wasn't ambushed as well?"

Myrra's lips pursed slightly, as if Bethany were questioning her ability to interpret a combat situation. "The proof was irrefutable."

"You said, found *him*. Kayn didn't find Wyc's brothers?"

"The Sleht take the bodies of any royal heir back to their capital for desecration before sending the pieces back to the family."

The sandwiches in Bethany's stomach pitched and rolled, making a valiant effort to exit the same way they had entered. "So Kayn automatically hates me because I'm Wyc's mate?"

"The twins were under Wyc's charge when they were murdered. He had left them behind to pursue a lead on your location."

The air Bethany had been struggling to drag into her lungs froze. Sorrow, so sharp she could feel the shards of it pierce her heart, held her immobile in its contracting grip.

"The price paid for your return has been high," Myrra said.

Bethany crossed her arms over her chest and lifted her chin, hurt and defensive, but hoping the gesture appeared defiant. "Not my choice."

"And now?"

"Now what?"

Myrra's voice dropped, and she stepped closer. "How much more sacrifice are you going to demand Wyc pay?"

Bethany's eyebrows winged up toward her hairline. She couldn't have been more surprised if Myrra had told her that she'd turn into a pumpkin at midnight. "I'm not demanding anything."

"You should know, his duty to his people is his life. Everything—and everyone—ranks far below that commitment."

"He explained the Matching Ritual. I know why he had to find me."

"He was duty-bound to search for you. But had you stayed lost, he would have been eventually free to return to Ilyria and take a mate of his own choosing."

The words struck Bethany like a sledgehammer slammed into her gut. "I was under the impression that neither of us had a choice. That the Guardians were permanent."

Myrra frowned. A slight pulling together of perfect brows over perfectly blue eyes. "The time attached to each Guardian varies with the spell. A matched heir is obligated to search for his mate only until one of them is dead, or the Guardian spell ends with the completion of the Matching Ritual or the fulfillment of days."

"And the spell that binds Wyc to me?" Breathe. Steady. Nice and normal. In, out. In, out.

Myrra paused. Looked away. When she brought her eyes back to Bethany's, they glinted like burnished blue steel, hard and unreadable. "Wyc's required time was nearly up when he found you."

"And if he hadn't found me?" Through sheer force of will, Bethany kept her voice level and ignored the panic rapidly expanding within her. "I thought he had to marry a Mystic."

Myrra gave nothing away with her inscrutable expression. She merely blinked and tilted her head to the side. "There are other Mystics on Ilyria. Ones who understand its history, laws and traditions. Ones who would unflinchingly accept the demands and needs of a sovereign."

Bethany narrowed her eyes. "Are you trying to tell me something?"

"No. Not trying. I am telling you. By the rites performed at the Matching Ritual, Wyc is bound by honor to take you as his mate." Her measuring gaze traveled over Bethany in one long, critical sweep. "Be worth it."

* * * * *

"You shouldn't be out here alone."

Wyc's voice coming out of the darkening twilight made Bethany jump. She turned to see him materialize from the shadows and climb the stairs to the back porch.

"Does everyone in your family relish scaring the hell out of me?" She kicked at the planked floor, sending the porch swing into motion.

He crossed the porch to her and stopped the swing. The chains holding it to the porch's rafters screeched in protest and the wooden slats groaned under his weight when he lowered himself to sit beside her.

"Who scared you?"

She shrugged. "Kayn. He did the same melt-from-the-shadows move."

"What did he want?" Wyc asked, his nonchalant tone not fooling her. Not when the muscles at the side of his jaw bunched.

"Not much. We had a misunderstanding earlier, and he wanted to make sure it was all straightened out." That was pretty close to the truth. He had, more or less, apologized for his outburst.

Wyc held her eyes for a beat. "And is it? All straightened out?"

"Yes." She dug in her front pocket and pulled out a small folding knife. "He gave me this." She pushed the silver button in the middle, and the blade popped out. Wyc took it from her and looked it over. Fully extended, the knife was just under eight inches, made of ebony and silver with a mother-of-pearl inlay on one side of the casing.

"He does that. Gives little gifts." He pressed the flattened edge against his palm and snapped the knife closed. "You're not planning on trying to cut out your Guardian again, are you?"

"No." She grabbed it and stuck it back into her pocket.

"So what are you doing, just sitting?" he asked.

"Thinking."

Bethany wrapped her arms around herself. Still early fall, the afternoon air had been crisp and cool. Perfect, if she had cared. But the temperature had dropped since she had been sitting here, thinking about what she had learned from Myrra.

Up until now, she had only considered the situation from her own viewpoint. Too caught up in how her life had changed and what it all meant to her to worry about anyone else. She hadn't once thought what Wyc, or any of the others for that matter, might have surrendered in order to keep their people—and hers—alive.

Wyc started to put his arm around her, but stopped and picked up her hand, staring at her ring.

"I put this on your right hand."

"I moved it."

"It belongs on your right hand."

"I always wore it on my left."

"Not anymore." He started to pull it off her finger, but she curled her fingers into a fist so he couldn't.

"I want it on my left. What difference does it make?"

His eyes narrowed and he pried her fingers open. "You wear the ring on your right hand to show that you belong to me."

The desire for that exact thing flooded her without warning. The need to fit in as old an ache as the number of years she had been bounced around from family to family. She didn't want to deal with that now. She was tired, and her emotions were already strung too tight to think straight.

She tugged her hand away. "A perfectly good reason for me to wear it on my left. I don't belong to anyone."

Shaking her head, she pushed away from him. When his arms wrapped back around her, she glared at him and said, "You don't own me."

Wyc sighed and gently tucked her close to his side. "So what were you thinking about out here all alone?"

She hesitated. Not sure how to ask Wyc about his brothers, the other Mystics he'd soon be free to choose a mate from or whether the sacrifices he had made to find her were worth the price. She didn't know how to ask, or even if she should. She didn't know if she wanted to hear the answers. Shutting down the feelings that reeled in her chest like manic acrobats, she shrugged.

"Nothing," she replied. "And everything."

He lifted her face with a knuckle under her chin to look into her eyes. He searched, but Bethany stared impassively back at him, having closed off any emotion that would give the turmoil in her heart away.

He brushed at the shadows under her eyes. "You should be resting. That antidote put a heavy stress on your body." He ran his fingers through her hair, combing it back from her face. The gentleness of his touch nearly undid her decision to allow him access to her body only, and not her heart.

"I'm fine." She wasn't, but she didn't want to talk. Was tired of thinking. The strain from the emotional intensity she had fought all day screamed for a release. She needed a moment of oblivion. A chance not to think anymore about what could have been or should have been.

She reached for him, pressed against him. The look of surprise in his eyes was quickly engulfed by a heat that made her pussy throb in anticipation.

Angling her head to cover his mouth with hers, she pushed her tongue past his lips and ran her fingers through his hair, scraping her nails over his scalp. Wyc hauled her onto his lap, and she continued to lick and probe the inside of his mouth, humming in pleasure when his tongue battled hers for dominance.

She fought his advances, daring him to push harder. Nipped at his bottom lip when he did. This was what she craved. Heat and lust. Passion that burned away the need to think about anything beyond the moment.

Her hands slid under his jacket, exploring the tightening muscles of his chest and shoulders. His erection hardened against her thigh. Intentionally, she wiggled to rub against it and scored his nipples through his shirt with her fingernails.

A sound of hunger, low and thoroughly male, burst out of his throat when she reached down and squeezed his cock through his jeans. He clamped his hands around her waist and lifted her off his lap to stand in front of him. He stood and backed her against the side of the house.

She wrapped her arms around his neck and hooked a leg around his thigh. Bringing her hips forward, she ground against his swollen cock. He pushed her back enough to give him room to slide his hand between her legs, tracing the center seam of her jeans back and forth over her pussy until he located the distended nub of her clit. She moaned and dug her nails into his upper arms when he moved the seam side to side over that sensitive button.

"I want to fuck you right here," Wyc ground out, his voice hoarse and his breath hot against her ear.

"Yes." She rocked her hips in sync with the strokes of his hand. "Do it."

With a grunt of ultimate frustration, Wyc jerked away and pulled her toward the back door. "I'm not putting on another peep show for my cousins. I want you to myself."

They were halfway through the kitchen when a siren ripped apart the quiet in the house. Suddenly, Wyc was running, dragging Bethany up the stairs and pushing her into the room they shared.

"What is it?" she asked.

"The warning signal. Slayers have been spotted on the property. Keep the door locked and don't come out. I'll come for you when it's safe." Wyc whipped off his shirt.

"But —"

He stopped her words with a glare as he tore out of the rest of his clothes. "I mean it. Stay in this room. I can't protect you if I don't know where you are."

Before she could answer, Wyc, in all his naked, furious glory, was out the door, banging it shut behind him. Bethany yanked it open and saw Wyc change from man to *kyltar*. The deadly black cat turned its head to look at her over its massive shoulder and let out a terrifying, fang-baring snarl.

She slammed the door and locked it. Rooted in place, she stared at the door, at the pile of Wyc's clothes. Wyc hadn't turned on the light when he pulled them inside the room, the gloom broken only by what moonlight managed to slip past the panels of heavy curtains.

From outside the house, a scream, animalistic and enraged, pierced through her fear-induced daze. Unable to stop herself, she moved to the window. There were no trees blocking her view as they had all been cut away, leaving a protected line of sight around the house. But beyond was a thick forest that could shelter not only the perimeter guards, but those that hid from them as well.

A black blur disappeared into the darkness at the edge of the forest. Wyc? She had no way of knowing. Off to the right, Rordyc jumped down from the side of the porch, ran across the yard and vanished into the trees as well. Movement close below caught her eye. Jordyn, crouched down in the deep shadow of the house directly below her window, pulled some sort of small, walkie-talkie from his belt and held it to his mouth.

The siren cut off. Jordyn didn't move. Nothing moved for what seemed like ages. She scanned the length of dark woods, waiting for Rordyc to reemerge. Hoping to see the terrifying form of a black *kyltar* materialize.

Pounding on the bedroom door startled Bethany. She jumped and spun around to face the threat, but didn't move from her spot beside the window.

"Bethany," Myrra's voice commanded, "open the door. We've got to get you out of here."

Bethany walked to within two feet of the door. "I'm supposed to stay right here," she said.

The door rattled. "We're running out of time. Wyc wants you moved. There are more Slayers than he thought. We've got to get you to a safer place."

Bethany opened the door. Myrra reached in and grabbed her by the arm.

"I'm going to show you how to get out of here, and then you're going to have to make a run for it." She led Bethany down the back stairs and through a side door that exited by the garage. It was at this point where the trees grew closest to the house.

"The attack is focused on the other side of the house, so you'll be safe if you hurry."

"Shouldn't I take a car? Where am I supposed to go?"

"The vehicles have all been disabled. Go straight through the woods until you hit a lake. Follow the lake around to the left and you'll come to some cabins closed for the season."

Myrra pressed some folded bills into her hand. "Once past those, you'll eventually come to a town with a bus terminal. Get on the first departing bus. Leave a message for Wyc at the ticket counter to let him know which city you're traveling to. If all goes well, he'll be waiting for you when you get off the bus."

"And if it doesn't go well?"

Myrra let the silence hold for a beat without answering. "Then you'll be free."

Another scream tore at the night like the one that had first drawn her to the window. Though still on the other side of the house, this time it sounded much closer. Myrra shoved her forward, out the door. "Run!"

Bethany needed no further inducement. She ran, jumped, tripped and fell, scrambled to her feet again to keep running until her lungs couldn't draw in air fast enough and her side burned with every labored breath. Branches, twigs, bushes tore at her clothes, face and arms. Roots and rocks snatched at her feet and legs.

She came upon the lake so suddenly, she nearly plunged into it. To her left, she could just make out the silhouette of a house not too far down the shoreline. Staggering onward, she didn't allow herself a moment to rest until she reached the first cabin.

With one hand on the corner of the building, she bent at the waist and took a deep breath. Out of the corner of her eye, she saw movement along the same path she had followed by the lake. She turned and straightened. The animal passed through a patch of moonlight. Large and closing in on her.

For a moment, seeing it move toward her on all four legs, she thought Wyc had come for her. It jumped up on a rocky outcropping, paused and lifted its head to sniff the air.

Bethany's heart stopped. Not Wyc. Not anything she had ever seen before, even in her nightmares. This animal was covered not in silky, dark fur, but a splotchy, rough hide that reminded her of a rhinoceros. There was no elegance to its movement, only compressed evil tightly wound through its powerful frame.

The Slayer flattened it ears against its triangular head, turned and looked in her direction. It snapped its jaws together and Bethany heard the sharp retort of teeth on teeth before it leapt from the boulder and headed in her direction.

Chapter Nine

ഗ

Wyc took the pair of jeans Myrra handed him and yanked them on. He glanced around the kitchen. Rordyc had a gash down his right arm that Shyrana was bandaging, and the back of Amdyn's shirt had been ripped to shreds by a Slayer's claws. Fortunately, the damage was to the fabric and not the skin underneath. Cirryc and Kayn were, as of yet, still unaccounted for. Jordyn and his team were checking the boundaries and resetting the perimeter alarms.

"I got 'em," Jordyn yelled through the backdoor. Wyc pulled the door open and held it as Jordyn and Cirryc carried Kayn into the house between them, his arms flung over their shoulders. The side of Kayn's face was covered in blood, and he kept losing the fight to hold his head up.

"I told you I can fucking walk," he growled.

"Guess that little bump to his head didn't alter his sunny disposition," Rordyc said.

"Fuck you," Kayn responded as Jordyn and Cirryc lowered him to a chair.

"Sorry, my dance card's all filled up." Rordyc winced as Shyrana tugged sharply on the gauze she had used to bandage his wound. She smiled sweetly at him.

"The perimeter's secured," Jordyn said, cutting through the banter, "but I'm missing a man. I have a unit out looking for him."

"Wyc, go check on Bethany," Amdyn said. "Once we're certain everyone's all right, we need to go over this attack. Slayers are sent out in teams of two, not packs. I want to know what the hell is going on here."

Wyc had already been on his way out of the kitchen before Amdyn started talking. As soon as he'd heard the perimeter was intact, his first priority was his mate.

"Bethany?" He flipped the light on in their bedroom. It was empty. "Everything is fine, you can come out now." He checked the bathroom. The closet. Under the bed. Nothing had been disturbed. No sign of forced entry or struggle. Nothing broken or missing. Except Bethany.

But no Slayer had made it past the inner perimeter. None had made it close to the house. Neither Jordyn nor Myrra had reported any security breach.

"Wyc?"

He spun around at Myrra's voice. She was standing in the doorway, a worried look on her face.

"She's not here. She must have gotten frightened and is hiding somewhere else in the house," he said.

She shook her head. "She's gone. I'm sorry. One of Jordyn's team found her footprints by the garage."

Wyc blinked the red fury from his gaze. "They're not hers."

"She's the only one who wears tennis shoes."

Wyc's hands balled into fists. He moved to walk around Myrra, but she stepped into his path. "Move."

She laid a restraining hand on his shoulder. "Bethany knows that her Guardian isn't permanent. That the spell is close to its end."

"She wouldn't leave."

"Really? And what's given you that impression?"

Wyc was surprised at the bitterness in his captain's voice. She rarely showed emotion at all, and never anger. The worse a situation, the calmer her response.

"Because," Myrra continued, "I've been under the impression that she's fighting you at every turn. Has she once said she wants to go to Ilyria? Told you that she's willing to accept you as her mate?"

Wyc ground his back teeth together. No. Just this afternoon, while fighting the antidote, Bethany had sworn she would never go to Ilyria with him. He had thought she was speaking out of her pain, that she had come to accept, at least in part, who she was and what that meant.

"She doesn't belong in Ilyria, Wyc."

"She belongs to me," he growled.

Myrra's fingertips grazed the dragon tattoo. "Not for long."

He knocked her hand away. "With me. Wherever I am. Guardian or no Guardian, Bethany is mine. Now get out of my way."

She took a step back. "There are others who would gladly serve you and Ilyria by taking you as their mate. Others who truly love you."

Wyc stopped and turned back to her. "Captain Lansyr, there is no one else *I* will take as *my* mate. Is that understood?"

Myrra immediately stiffened and focused on empty space over his shoulder. "Yes, sir. I was out of line to suggest otherwise."

The edge of his anger diminished fractionally. Myrra had been with him for years. He could trust her with his life. He had. Any overstep on her part was out of her care for him. She wasn't the first to imply that he was operating a little left of center since Bethany had been found.

And, he understood the personal emotion at the core of her concern.

"Myrra." He waited until she met his gaze. "Never did I allow your sister to think I would take her as my mate. Under any circumstance. Never."

A tense moment passed as they held eye contact, weighing the truth that stood between them. Myrra nodded. Acceptance settling on her features.

"She headed toward the lake. Do you want me to go with you?" she asked.

"No. After the last dozen years, tracking her down with less than an hour's lead will be a piece of cake." He left Myrra standing in the room and headed back to the kitchen. He wanted to talk to Jordyn's patrol.

The tension in the kitchen was thick as Mississippi mud when he entered. Jordyn, Cirryc and Shyrana were gone, and Amdyn's expression was set hard as granite.

"How's Bethany?" he asked.

"She'll be fine once I catch up to her."

"She's not here?" Amdyn's sharp question set an alarm off in Wyc.

"What's wrong?"

"A Slayer is missing. We took down eight, but Jordyn's team could only find seven."

"Shit!" Wyc rushed from the kitchen, tore off his jeans, and with a roar of fury that echoed through the mountains, relinquished complete control to the beast within.

* * * * *

Bethany tried the cabin's door. Locked tight. Ran to the next cabin. This one was locked as well, but the door rattled loosely in its frame when she hit it. She battered against it with her shoulder and wood splintered.

Glancing backwards, she could no longer locate the Slayer, lost in the shadows of the night. But she could feel its approach. Sixth sense, Mystic intuition—whatever you wanted to call it, it was working overtime to deliver the countdown of her impending death.

She slammed her shoulder into the door again, and this time, the wood gave. The door popped open, and she fell into the tiny cabin. Bethany shoved the door closed, but found she had broken the only lock. Refusing herself the time to indulge a cry of despair, she looked around for something to fortify the door with.

The choices were few. Set up in the design of a honeymoon cottage, there was only the large, rustic log bed, a small dinette set and a loveseat in the corner.

Opting for the loveseat, she dragged it across the floor and, putting all her weight into it, jammed it against the door. Once the barricade was in place, she scanned the room for a possible weapon.

Suddenly the door shuddered with a loud bang as the Slayer crashed into it, forcing the sofa back and opening the door several inches. Claws reached in and scraped the inside of the wall before she was able to push the loveseat back and get the door closed.

Bethany angled her body to use as a lever with her feet planted against the footboard of the bed and her shoulder wedged against the loveseat. Closing her eyes, she took a deep breath and shifted to better cushion her shoulder for the next onslaught.

This time, when the Slayer attacked the door, it didn't budge.

She needed something to defend herself with. Nothing was in reach, and she couldn't leave her wedged-in position without risking the chance of the Slayer getting through the door.

The knife Kayn had given her. It was still in her pocket. She dug it out and turned it in her hand to find the button that would release the blade.

The window over the dinette set exploded. Bethany screamed and instinctively jerked away from the blast of shattering glass. The knife dropped from her hand and spun under the couch.

Snarling and swiping, the Slayer burst through the pane amid the rain of glass. It landed less than a foot from her and went into an uncontrolled skid over the broken glass until it collided with the wall next to the door.

The only alternative to trying to get past the Slayer was the bathroom. Bethany half crawled, half ran into the tiny room, closing the hollow plywood door behind her. She flipped the light on to discover that there was no lock whatsoever on this door.

She boosted herself up onto the sink, braced her shoulders against the mirror and her feet against the door. Wiping her hand across her face, it came away wet. Tears she'd cried but been too scared to notice.

There was a gentle scratching along the edge of the door, moving from the top to the bottom. Then a sniffing at the crack between the floor and the door, followed by a low, grating purr.

Abruptly, a huge paw broke through the center of the door, right between her feet. Particle board fractured, and splintered slivers cannoned at her chest and face. She shrieked and kicked at the seeking paw with one foot while trying to keep the door shut with the other.

The paw withdrew. Then returned with another crash, widening the hole. A claw snagged on her tennis shoe. For one terrifying second, her foot was yanked through the hole to the other side, and her desperate grip on the sink slipped as she was pulled forward.

Bethany wrenched her foot back through the door, minus her shoe. The momentum of her action threw her off balance. She fell off the sink and landed on her side across the toilet.

The door snapped open, and the Slayer's body pitched into the tiny room. It lunged at Bethany but the paw it had pushed back through the door caught on the jagged wood and brought it up short.

Flinging herself into the tub, Bethany twisted to slide the plastic shower door along its track until it slammed shut. She hunkered down in the rust-stained porcelain and jammed her hands against the flimsy metal handle to keep the door in place.

The Slayer rose up on its hind legs, but the ceiling was low and it couldn't get more than a paw or its snout over the shower door. It clawed at the handle, but the curved design precluded purchase by anything other than fingers hooked around it.

Bethany's shoulders shook with her sobs as the Slayer began a relentless, steady pounding at the door. Throwing its weight behind every thrust, the animal began to make progress in weakening her final stronghold. The plastic held, but the metal frame started to bend.

The constant, brutal thud of malevolent animal against such a flimsy wall of defense tore at her sanity. The frosted white shower enclosure blurred reality and sharpened the imagination every time the massive beast lunged against it. The terror of shadow and sound consumed Bethany's senses.

With a loud crack, the door broke from its frame and Bethany was crushed beneath the weight of the Slayer, less than a quarter inch of plastic between them. Her screams echoed loud in her own ears, equaled only by the snarling fury of the animal on top of her. It clawed at the edges of the door, trying to reach her trapped beneath the sheet of plastic.

Abruptly, the animal let out a horrific, ear-splitting scream and disappeared. The weight, the noise, the shadow — gone. Bethany didn't move. Didn't breathe. One moment it was crushing her into the cold bottom of the chipped and stained bathtub, and the next it had vanished.

Her body demanded air and she sucked it in as quietly as she could, slowly becoming aware of the ringing in her ears. As the bell tone faded away, scuffling noises close by sent a new wave of fear crashing over her. Before she could react, the saving sheet of cheap plastic covering her was ripped away.

* * * * *

Wyc looked down at Bethany. Her auburn hair pooled around her head like dried blood, her eyes were wide and glassy with fright, her skin had a sickly, fish-belly paleness to it and her body was curled into a tight fetal ball. He had never seen a more welcome sight than the rapid pulse at the base of her neck.

He squatted down, and she pushed herself to a sitting position.

"Where's the, the animal?" she asked. Her voice was shaky, and her eyes kept darting around him.

"Dead." He ran his hands over her arms, torso and legs. "Are you hurt?"

She looked down at her hands, flexed them, bent her knees. "No." With one hand on the side of the tub and the other on the wall, she stood. When she released her support, her hands visibly trembled.

The relief at finding her alive was replaced by undulating waves of anger that grew with each passing second that proved she was truly alive and unharmed. Images, both real and imagined, streamed through his mind, feeding his fury. Bethany, with her head thrown back, crying his name in ecstasy. Swearing at him that she'd never go to Ilyria and then pitching forward in agony. Reaching for him on the porch. The broken window in the cabin. The broken bathroom door, snarls and scraping noises coming from within, her tennis shoe lying on its side, torn and muddy.

The *kyltar* had been given its full release to scent and track Bethany. It hadn't been hard. Her trail had been fresh, but the overlaying trail of the Slayer had been stronger. Having the two of them mixed spurred the hunt as nothing else could do. Slayers didn't waste time playing with their prey. They tracked to kill, and killed immediately.

Deep inside the *kyltar*, Wyc had automatically logged the scents, sights and sounds that came through the beast's senses. A streaming blur of information. The sharp scent of pine, the flash of moonlight on the lake, the startled flurry of a bird's wings. The smell of Bethany's fear close to the cabin, the few jagged points of a shattered pane still stuck in the window frame, demoniac snarls ricocheting off the tiny bathroom's vinyl walls.

Each impression passed through without thought until the *kyltar*'s eyes locked on the size six, white sneaker abandoned in the middle of the cabin's destruction. The sight didn't cause even a momentary break in the *kyltar*'s momentum. It cleared the debris and entered the bathroom with a single leap, sank its teeth and claws into the back and neck of the Slayer, rolled with it out of the bathroom and finished what one of his team members had started.

The small tennis shoe might not have stopped the *kyltar*, but it had nearly stopped the human heart that beat deep inside it.

"Is she okay?" Jordyn's voice rumbled from behind him.

Wyc didn't turn around. "Yes."

"Shyrana's out here. Do you want her to check for shock or injury?"

"No. I've checked. Have your men remove the carcass and clear the house." There was a brief moment of tense silence when no one moved. A second later, he heard Jordyn turn and issue a couple of curt commands. He didn't take his eyes from Bethany, and she shifted nervously in front of him.

Shyrana's voice floated through the doorway over the sounds of scuffling and of the dead Slayer being dragged across the floor. Jordyn's clipped response told him that the man was still standing in front of the bathroom door, faced away. There was the sound of glass being brushed up and exiting footsteps.

"It's clear," Jordyn stated and then left. The clean-up process over in a few, brief minutes.

Bethany glanced around. Pulled her bottom lip between her teeth. He almost had regained enough control to trust himself to touch her. She released her bottom lip and dragged her tongue over it. His lust spiked at the movement.

"Is it safe for me to leave?" she asked.

"Safe." He repeated, the rush of anger returning. His jaw clenched, and his next words ground out. "To leave." And suddenly something inside him snapped.

Grabbing her by the front of her sweatshirt, he pulled her toward him. Her feet stumbled over the side of the tub to keep up with her upper body being hauled against his chest. "It will never be safe for you to leave me, Bethany. Ever."

With both her wrists manacled together in one of his, he dragged her out of the bathroom and over to the bed. When he turned to face her, she opened her mouth to speak.

"Don't," he warned. "Not a word." He picked her up and tossed her onto the bed. She bounced once, rolled to her side and immediately started to scramble toward the opposite side. Before she could reach the edge of the bed, he was on her, pinning her facedown beneath him.

"Still trying to run?" he asked. "That's turned into a bad habit for you." He leaned back enough to jerk her sweatshirt up and over her head, leaving her arms tangled in it. His fingers wrapped around the thin straps and lace of her bra next. It gave quickly and he tossed the resulting scraps to the floor. She was still struggling against the twisted fabric of her shirt as he shoved a hand underneath her body to unfasten her jeans. "But I bet that's a habit I can break."

Going up on his knees, he straddled her legs and grabbed the waistband of her jeans. He yanked it down to her knees, leaving her ass covered only in a tiny pair of silky black panties.

She twisted her head around to look at him. "Wyc...I was going—"

His hand landed with a smack on the right cheek of her ass. Hard enough to sting, not hard enough to really hurt. Bethany let out a startled gasp.

"I told you, not a word." He pulled her panties down to her knees, revealing the bright red imprint of his hand. Quickly, he finished stripping her and tossed her clothes to the floor. With one hand to the center of her back, he kept her pressed into the mattress when he leaned over her to tug a pillowcase off its pillow. He put one end in his mouth and ripped it down the seam.

Bethany's head came up off the bed. "What're you—"

His hand landed on her other ass cheek. She stiffened and sucked in her breath. He smoothed his palm over the swell of her bottom.

"Babydoll, I told you once that I would never hurt you, and I meant that. But I have no problem spanking this pretty little ass until you learn I mean what I say. Understand?"

Bethany nodded.

"Good, because I want your full attention." He used the strips of pillowcase to tie her hands to the headboard. "And if I have to tie you to a bed to keep you from running—" he gave his makeshift bindings a test yank, " —I will."

Slowly, he ran his hands down her arms, splayed his fingers when he reached her shoulders and then followed the line of her spine with his thumbs. When he reached the curve of her waist, he saw the beginnings of a nasty bruise that wrapped over the top of her right hip. That wasn't there this morning.

Anger and agony flashed through him. It wouldn't be there tonight if Bethany had stayed put like he told her to.

He lowered himself over her body, aligning his with hers, but keeping the majority of his weight supported on his forearms. His chest pressed against her back, and his groin pressed up against her butt. He rocked until his erection was nestled between her ass cheeks.

She tensed underneath him, her muscles tightening and inadvertently squeezing his cock. He dropped his head to the mattress beside hers and groaned. Damn, she felt good underneath him. That she had come so close to ripping his life apart by nearly getting herself killed tonight only intensified his determination to keep her with him, no matter what he had to do. He needed her underneath him, in his bed, every night of his life.

He swept her hair back from the side of her face and kissed the top curve of her cheek. "There are some things we need to get straightened out," he said. He felt her tremble beneath him.

"First, with or without the Guardian, you are my mate. Mine. Eventually, you will take me as yours.

"Second, never run from me again." Bethany's eyes widened and cut up sharply to look at him, but she didn't say a word. Progress.

* * * * *

Bethany tried to make sense of what was happening. She had been so relieved to see Wyc standing over her after the Slayer's attack, she could have wept. But the look in his eyes had thrown her. He had been furious.

The hands he had swept over her body, checking for injury, had been cold and impersonal. He hadn't helped her to stand, but had blocked her from leaving. And when she asked if it was safe, the hard edge in his eyes darkened and his face had sharpened into a mask of barely contained rage.

She had never truly feared for her life in his presence until that moment. When he dragged her to him, her heart stopped, skipped a beat and then thudded in double time. It hadn't slowed down yet.

His anger made no sense. She had followed his instructions. But when she tried to explain, to ask what was the matter, he refused to let her utter a word. Had stripped her and tied her to the bed. And then he had gentled and kissed her. She didn't know what to think.

What had happened to make him believe she was running away from him? She hadn't run from him. She had run from the attack. Like her mother.

Oh God. Just like her mother. Did he think he was going to lose her like they had lost her mother all those years ago? He had just claimed that she was his, even without the Guardian. That sparked alive a hope she had been trying to snuff out since her conversation with Myrra.

He stroked the corner of her mouth with two fingers. She was suffused with a sudden craving to taste him. To connect to him. Bridge the gap of whatever misunderstanding had happened. Even if it was only temporary, she needed him.

Her tongue darted out and flicked over the tip of one of his fingers. His nostrils flared and his eyes narrowed. Slowly, he pushed his finger between her lips, into her mouth. She closed her eyes and gently sucked.

Yes.

A low sound vibrated out of his chest and he pushed his finger in deeper. She sucked harder. Swirled her tongue around it.

"Do you know how helpless I felt when I knew you weren't where I could protect you?" he whispered. He pulled his finger partially out, pushed it in again. Repeated the action. She continued to suck. "When I found out that you had a Slayer after you, and I might not reach you in time?"

He pulled his hand away to flatten it on the bed and push himself off her back. His knees moved between her legs, pushing them apart. He thrust his hips back and forth, rubbing his thick cock along the crevice of her bottom.

"At that moment, I would have given anything to make certain you were safe." He pressed her legs further apart so that his balls hit her pussy every time he rocked forward. "But there wasn't anything I could do."

The anger she could hear vibrating in his voice didn't stop the need for him from building within her. She pressed her stomach into the bed to tilt her ass up and expose her pussy more fully to the gentle slap of his testicles.

He immediately pushed himself up to his knees.

"You want to put your ass in the air for me? Then let's do it right."

She didn't have the maneuverability to accomplish it on her own, not with her arms stretched in front of her and tied to the bed and her legs spread by his knees. In fact, she was completely at his mercy. The thought of being so vulnerable to Wyc and what he might do to her had her burying her face against the quilt to stifle a moan of pure sexual anticipation.

He lifted her hips and her knees slid into place under them. His hands roamed down the outside of her thighs and up the back of them. He cupped the twin curves of her ass and squeezed.

"You have a gorgeous ass, babydoll." He massaged it, working his thumbs closer and closer to her sex. "Arch your back. Show me that pussy of yours."

She did, and slid her knees further apart, putting herself on full display.

"Good girl." He spread her cheeks. "Goddamn. What a sight. Sitting there so pink and pretty, just waiting for a good fucking."

Bethany whimpered, and her cunt clenched around emptiness.

Wyc leaned over her, his cock sliding between her legs. The scalding friction against her clit sent a burst of sensation through her body. He rotated his hips, and his cock moved against her clit again, making her shudder and sharpening her need. "I'm going to fuck you, Bethany," he whispered next to her ear. "Hard and deep. Fuck you until you'll never think about leaving me again."

Sliding a hand between her legs, he rubbed his fingers over her pussy until she was sure her cream was dripping off them. Moving his hand up between her ass cheeks, he circled her anus with his wet fingers. When he pushed one blunt fingertip in up to the first knuckle, she gasped, her muscles tensing in alarm and anticipation.

"And one of these days," he said, "I'm going to fuck this tight little hole of yours as well."

At his words, heat flashed over her body and she forced herself to swallow a whimper. His erotic promise both frightened her and fired her desire to give herself to him in any way he wanted. He worked his finger back and forth until it was deep inside her. The pinching sensation only drove her need higher, and her clit throbbed with the hot rush of lust. Just when she was on the edge of begging, he removed his finger and began the slow thrust of his cock between her legs again.

"But first," he ground out in a jagged voice, "I'm going to show you what it feels like to be powerless to get what you so desperately want."

This time, she couldn't keep her soft cry of need from escaping.

Chapter Ten

ဆာ

Wyc thrust against Bethany several times, enjoying the feel of her hot cream slicking his cock. He was about to the point of just ramming inside her when he forced himself to pull back. Not yet. First, she had a lesson to learn.

Reaching down, he put pressure on the base of his cock until the blinding need dulled to a constant ache. A quick tug on her ankles had Bethany once again flat on the bed. If he left her ass so provocatively propped up for him, he'd never be able to withstand the temptation. He'd been fantasizing about fucking her in that position too long. As it was, her unexpected but highly sensual reaction to him probing her ass had already nearly made him sacrifice his goal in favor of seeing just how far she'd let him go. Sitting up on his knees, he took his time looking over her body. Her pretty little feet, the curve of her calves and softness of her thighs. The sweetest ass. The narrowing of her waist and gentle line of her spine. The perfect proportion of shoulders and hips. Hair that, against her alabaster skin, appeared nearly black in the darkened room. Slender arms stretched and tied above her head.

He leaned over her and laid down a long, slow line of kisses along her spine, stopping to swirl his tongue over her skin with each new inch covered. Near the small of her back and again at the top of the cleft in her ass she was extremely sensitive. When he licked and teased her there, she wiggled and tried to follow his tongue with her body when he moved away. But tied down as she was, her ability was limited.

Next he explored the backs of her legs. Licking and nipping his way down first one leg and then the other. Her entire upper body jerked off the bed when he sucked at the back of her knees. By the time he was finished, she was whimpering his name.

As he placed a kiss on her shoulder, he slid his hand between her legs. When he cupped her mound she pressed against his hand.

"Don't get in a hurry," he said. "I've only just begun."

She closed her eyes and groaned low in her throat. Squeezed her thighs together. Kept them tight on his hand.

"Pull your legs back apart," he instructed. She hesitated, then separated them a fraction. "More," he bit out when she stopped. She complied. "That's good. Real good."

He slid two fingers between her pussy lips. "You're so wet. Slick and creamy." He stroked the center of her heat, letting her juices cover his fingers.

"Is your cunt starting to ache yet?" He stroked her pussy faster. Added a third finger and swirled them over and around the soaked folds of her sex. "Do you need my cock inside you, Bethany?"

Her back arched, and she strained at the bindings on her wrists, trying to give herself more slack to bear down on his hand.

"I could finger-fuck you to orgasm right now." He flicked her clit once with his middle finger and her body bucked. He pulled his hand away. "I could. But I'm not."

The muscles in her thighs flexed as she started to pull them together. He clamped his hands on them, pushed them wider than they had been before. "No. I want to see your need. Want to see that cunt pulse and weep for what I have to give it."

Bethany released a frustrated groan and lifted her head to look back at him. He raised his hand over her ass.

"Do you have something to say?"

She glared at him for a long moment, and then dropped her head back to the bed and took a deep breath.

He flipped her over. Began kissing and nipping at the front of her body with the same care he had covered the back. Taking his time with her neck and breasts. Loving the way she writhed and gasped at his attentions. He sucked her nipples until she cried out. Pinched and tugged at them until she moaned and threw her legs around him, trying to force his cock to enter her. With one hand, he held her hips down while his mouth moved down her belly and his other hand continued to fondle her breasts.

She gasped and twisted. Planted her feet to thrust her body against his. The scent of her desire was so strong it made his cock hurt with the demand to be inside her greedy cunt. Her pussy pressed against his stomach and her wet heat nearly undid him.

He pushed her legs wide, still bent at the knees with her feet flat on the bed. "I want you to keep your legs just like that for me. Understand?"

Her eyes were dark with need. Her mouth opened as her breath panted in and out. She nodded.

He scooted down the bed until his head was between her thighs. Past the point of gentle touches, he wanted her to need him. To be out of control with her desire for him. To be completely unable to withhold anything. To feel utterly helpless in her lust.

With a savage intent, he attacked her pussy with his mouth. He licked deep inside her cunt, stabbing in again and again until he felt her tightening toward release.

Then he withdrew and she let out a strangled shriek of frustration. Clamped her thighs around his head. He pressed her legs nearly flat to the bed, spreading her out completely and changed his mode of assault. Started working her clit. Immediately her body started racing toward climax again. Denying her yet again, he moved to nip the inside of her thigh. She screamed and bucked.

Dragging his teeth over the inside of her other thigh, he began a campaign of long licks from her opening to the top of her slit. Slowly at first, then building in pressure and speed until the muscles of her abdomen started to contract with the intensity of her need. Her body shook, begged for him.

The tip of his tongue circled her entrance over and over. She was taking great sobbing breaths. He dipped his tongue inside. A fast, shallow dunk. She gasped, and a hard shudder racked her body.

He raised himself over her. Placed his cock at her entrance.

Bethany went completely still. Looked at him with a mixture of harsh need, hope and disbelief. Her cheeks were bright with color, damp hair clinging to the sides of her face in ringlets. At some point, tears had started falling from the corners of her eyes. She had bitten her bottom lip until it was red and swollen, and her entire body was slick with sweat from being brought so close to the peak again and again.

He held her hips in place and pushed inside her. A quick shallow movement that allowed nothing more than the head of his cock entry before he pulled out. Again and again. Each time only teasing little plunges that withheld far more sensation than they delivered. Her cunt gripped at him, covered him with thick, dripping pussy juice. She whimpered, tossed her head from side to side. Pushed her hips against his restrictive hands. Pushed against the force of his will to make her understand.

"What do you want, Bethany?" He thrust in a fraction deeper. Pulled out. Stopped. Held her trembling body in place with his hands. "Tell me what you want."

She blinked. Swallowed. Sucked in a breath. "You."

His heart constricted around hope. "What else?"

"Nothing else." She shook her head. "Just you."

With a noise that sounded harsh even in his own ears, he pulled out of her, rolled her back onto her stomach and yanked her hips up. In one hard thrust, he impaled her on his cock to the hilt. Filling her and slamming so deep inside her, he felt the tip of his shaft hit her cervix.

Bethany screamed and clawed at the ties around her wrists as her body convulsed around his in the climax she had so desperately needed. Her cunt gripped and milked him hard.

He rode out her storm, teeth clenched against the beautiful torture. He wasn't going to let her get off that easily. With a final whimper, her body relaxed and would have slumped to the bed if he hadn't been holding on to her.

Deliberately, he pulled out and pushed in again. One long, slow stroke that made his intent clear. She shuddered and looked over her shoulder at him.

"I don't think I can."

His smile was strained. "Yes. You will." With even, measured thrusts, he pushed her need back up. When she started rocking her ass back against him to counter his thrusts, he reached around with one hand and stroked her clit.

"Oh God." She moaned. Rocked back faster. "God, Wyc. So good. Oh God!" Again her body shuddered, her muscles tensed. And then her breath burst out and her inner muscles performed their erotic massage around his cock once more.

Bright spots exploded in front of his eyes as he struggled to keep his own release at bay. "Again," he demanded, voice harsh and hard.

She pressed her forehead to the bed. Shook her head. "I can't."

Leaning forward, he splayed his hand between her shoulder blades and pushed until her shoulders and breasts were pressed into the mattress. Her knees slid further apart and her back arched sharply, changing the angle of his penetration. He started fucking her fast and deep. "Again."

With each thrust, his cock moved hard against the front of her vagina. He shifted slightly with each plunge until he found the exact position that hit the cluster of nerves that made her mewl with intense pleasure every time his cock dragged over it.

"Wyc!"

Up until this point, he had blocked his mental connection to her. Knew he would never have made it this long without release if he even brushed her mind. But when she called his name, keening it out as she drowned in ecstasy, he cast off his control. Mental and physical.

The room filled with his shout, and he fucked her like a man possessed. Possessed by need and love. And he was. For her. Only for her.

* * * * *

Bethany had given up on breathing. It was too much effort. After what seemed like hours of sexual teasing that left her body cramping in desperate need for release, Wyc had driven her to an explosive climax. And another one.

And then, with every muscle, every nerve still fighting an excess of ecstasy, he forced her body into another dimension of mind-blowing pleasure. Even if she ever wanted to fuck someone else, he had probably ruined her for any other man.

Wyc's final shout rang in her ears. Deep inside her, the pulsing of his cock slowed, her cunt filled with his flesh and his seed. His big hands continued to hold her in place even when the last aftershocks had passed. He groaned, a low tortured sound, and slowly rotated his hips.

"Bethany. Oh God, babydoll." He slid his hands up her sides and over her arms until he reached her wrists. His weight pressed her down as he untied the bindings.

He shifted off her, lay pressed full length against the side of her body and massaged her arms. With gentle fingers, he worked the stiffness out of them, paying special attention to her wrists. She pulled her arms out of his grasp and wrapped them around his neck. Pressing her face into his neck, she cuddled against his chest.

"You okay?" he asked. His hands stroked her shoulders and back.

Okay? If she had any muscles in her body that still worked, she would have giggled. Instead, she snuggled closer. "No."

His hands stopped. "No?"

She pressed her cheek to him and let out a soft sigh. "Not even close to okay."

He pulled back and tilted her chin up. His eyes were worried as he searched her face.

She placed her palm against his cheek. "I'm far, far better than okay." His concern melted into a look of pure male arrogance. A small smile tugged at the corners of her mouth. With a sexy, half-lidded look, she said, "I think three consecutive orgasms qualify somewhere closer to 'stupendous'."

"Just stupendous?"

"It's the best I can come up with until the haze of sexual ecstasy clears."

He chuckled and ran a hand down her back.

She closed her eyes and inhaled. Slowly. Deeply. The air was heavy with the musk of their sex. The sharp smell of pine trees and wind off water wafted in through the broken window.

The thought of the broken window reminded her of tonight's events and she shivered.

"Cold?" he asked.

She shook her head and pressed close to his body. He stopped rubbing her back and wrapped his arms around her. Hard and tight. He dropped a quick kiss on her hair, and then tucked her head under his chin.

"Don't ever run from me again, Bethany. Ever."

Inwardly, she cringed at the bite of his words, the remoteness of his tone. She tried to reconcile those with the look she had seen in his eyes the moment he had lifted the shower door off her. A look stark with fear and desperation.

But it had been almost instantly replaced with a cold rage. The same icy quality had been in his answer when she asked if it was safe to leave.

"I wasn't running from you, Wyc. I was trying to get to safety. Exactly like you told me to."

"I told you to stay in our room." Angry tension vibrated from every inch of his body.

"And I did. Until the attack got so bad, it was unsafe for me to stay."

He pulled back, looked down at her. "Bethany, not a single Slayer got past the second perimeter. You were safe until you left the house."

God she was tired, and this conversation was going in circles. Her mind and emotions were on overload and her body passed exhausted a long time ago. She closed her eyes, hoping she wouldn't be required to open them for days. "Can we please talk about this tomorrow?"

"Answer me. Why did you leave?"

"I was following your instructions." She yawned and stretched her legs. Curling back up against him, she said, "Just like Myrra told me to."

Her head was swimming with fatigue. Every single cell of her body felt wrung out and hung up to dry. She started to fall to the seductive draw of unconsciousness as sleep's silky fingers began to wrap around her mind. The image of Wyc's face looking at her tonight right before he fucked her floated through the swirling pictures pulling her toward sleep.

He had asked her what she wanted, his heart shining in his eyes. At that moment, she saw a deep need, a desperate hope he had never shown her before. The flash of relief when she said she wanted him. The almost instant doubt, and then the feral victory that shimmered around a core of love when she repeated herself. A sigh of contentment slipped past her lips. Wyc might not realize it yet, but he was falling in love with her.

She covered his heart with her hand. Kissed his chest and rested her head against him. She'd be happy sleeping next to this man for the rest of her life. It might have taken two Predators and a Slayer attack to bring her here, but this was where she belonged. She was more certain of that than of the sun coming up tomorrow morning.

"I love you, Wyc Kilth," she whispered.

Wyc twisted away from her with a curse and sat up. Her eyes flew open to find him staring down at her in horrified shock. Before she could say anything, he rolled off the bed, picked her clothes off the floor and tossed them to her.

"Get dressed. We need to get back."

Bethany stared at her clothes. Hurt. Angry. And completely mortified that she had just told the world's biggest jerk she was in love with him. Whatever the emotion had been in his eyes earlier, she had obviously and grossly misunderstood it.

Damn him. Couldn't he give her even ten minutes to bask in all the good feelings that were supposed to accompany earth-moving, soul-shattering sex?

She reached for her clothes and yanked them on. Maybe she should have her own eyes checked. Maybe she was going crazy. Seeing things that weren't there. Or maybe she was simply delusional. Hell, maybe insanity was a hallmark of the Mystic bloodline.

She looked around for her other shoe. She hadn't seen it since it had been ripped off her foot by the Slayer. Scanning the room, she found it in Wyc's hand. She reached for it, but he shook his head and knelt down in front of her to slide it on her foot. Once it was on, he held her foot and the shoe in his hand for a long moment, just staring at them. Like he was memorizing her shoe size or something.

Abruptly he stood and headed out the door. She followed, stopping to pick up her pocketknife, fold the blade down and stuff it into her jeans' pocket. Wyc was on the porch, putting on the clothes that someone had left in a neatly folded pile outside the door.

When he was finished, he gestured for her to move out ahead of him. The severe lines and planes of his face weren't softened in the moonlight. His expression could have been cut from marble.

As she clambered down the steps, she paused only long enough to throw him an angry glare. "You really, *really* suck at the whole afterglow thing. I'm beginning to have serious doubts you even know what the damn word means."

* * * * *

A long line of virulent curses streamed through Wyc's mind. There were more important things than afterglow, and the foremost was keeping his mate safe no matter how she interpreted his motives.

When Bethany told him that Myrra had given her instructions to leave the safety of the house, razor-sharp rage sliced through his gut, the frozen shards of betrayal cutting deep. Demons from his past rose up to crush him with their arsenal of hate, grief and blind rage.

His first reaction had been instant denial. He wanted Bethany to be lying. Some part of him hoped she was. Because if she wasn't, Myrra had betrayed him and sent Bethany into danger.

If Myrra had turned on them, a lot of the recent "coincidences" would make sense. His captain moved within the inner circles of Ilyrian nobility easily enough to meet Rordyc's suspicions of a highly placed traitor.

He needed to confront his captain, but first, he needed to catch up with his mate.

Bethany was pissed. Really, *really* pissed. He didn't need to touch her mind to know she was working up a mad of hurricane force. Each step away from the cabin seemed to fuel her anger. She was literally stomping along the lakeshore back toward the house with her back stiff, shoulders thrown back, and her hands swinging in tight fists by her side. And all because he hadn't held her long enough after fucking her to near oblivion.

He knew what afterglow was, damn it. Knew it was important to a woman, and he'd like nothing more than to lay with her for hours after making love, whisper things against her skin that made her sigh. Stroke her body until she was soothed to sleep...or demanding to be made love to again.

His eyes dropped to her ass. Even her mad-as-hell walk didn't detract from the sexy way she moved. She hadn't even asked him for an explanation of why he had pulled away so abruptly. Not that he would have told her anything—yet. But it bothered him that she might think he was the kind of asshole who used women for sex without another thought. He'd never do that to her.

Yes, he'd done that in the past to other women. But he'd always been up front with them. They all knew he was matched and with everyone but his mate, sex was sex, nothing more. No expectations other than mutual pleasure—and he'd always made damn sure it was mutual—no commitments and no emotional attachments. The only one who hadn't taken what he said at face value was Myrra's sister. As soon as he realized that, he'd broken things off immediately. And still it had been too late.

In front of him, Bethany stumbled over a rock. His hand shot out to steady her, but she had already jerked herself up and was moving on. She was too tired to be making the trek back to the house. It wasn't far, less than three miles, but she was exhausted.

He would offer to carry her, but had a feeling that would only get him another scathing remark. Her anger was hot enough to get her the rest of the way back under her own steam. And if she kept up this pace, they'd arrive sooner than anyone would expect.

That was good. He needed to catch his team unaware. Especially his captain.

Bethany cursed as her foot caught on a root. They had turned away from the lake now and were following the path deep through the woods that ended close to the garage.

She yanked her foot back, but the shoelace tangled on the root and she lost her balance. She went down, landing on one arm and her hip. With another vicious curse, she tried to kick her foot free.

Wyc bent down and unhooked her shoelace. He reached for her hand to help her up. She ignored him and pushed herself up.

Brushing at her jeans and her arm, she kept her eyes averted. "If you really want to help me," she said, "you can keep your damn hands to yourself."

Turning her back on him, she continued down the path at a near run.

"Bethany, slow down." At least by the lake the moonlight had shed some illumination to see by. But here under the trees, it was too dark to move quickly without taking a chance on getting hurt.

She didn't answer him. Instead, she broke into a flat-out run. He took off after her, getting whacked up the side of his head by a low-lying limb for his trouble.

"Damn it, Bethany. You're going to fall and break your neck."

"Good. Then I won't have to deal with you anymore, and you can go back to wherever you came from and find someone else to fuck over."

She didn't slow, even when the sleeve of her sweatshirt snagged on a bush. With a fierce tug, her shirt ripped but she pulled free.

He had been within an arm's length of reaching her when he heard the fabric tear. The bush that had caught Bethany snapped back and hit him in the face and chest, its thorns digging into his own shirt and skin. With a growl, he yanked the branch away, too mad to care about the barbs biting into his hands.

Bethany had just broken into the clearing when he was finally able to put his hands on her. He grabbed her by the arm and roughly swung her around to face him. She glared up at him, fury snapping in her eyes even as she frantically blinked back tears. Heated words died in his throat, and his anger left in a whoosh. His shoulders sagged and his grip eased.

"Well, shit," he sighed in disgust. He couldn't argue against her tears. Couldn't even remember what he was about to yell at her for. His only thought was how to keep those tears from falling. If even one tracked down her cheek, it would kill him. He already felt guilty as hell for the way he had treated her earlier when he had believed that she had tried to escape him. If she started to cry, she'd totally undo him.

The only warning he got was a sudden narrowing of her eyes. He was able to turn just enough to keep her knee from connecting with his groin, though it hit high and hard on the inside of his thigh.

"I told you to keep your damn hands to yourself," she hissed and twisted out of his hold. She turned and fled around the garage and into the house.

He started to go after her, but was stopped when Amdyn stepped into his path.

"Get out of my fucking way," Wyc said, not waiting for him to move before attempting to go around him.

"That can wait," Amdyn replied. He adjusted his position to block Wyc's advance.

"The hell it can." Wyc felt fury build in him again and welcomed its rise. His muscles tensed and his shoulders hunched aggressively, ready to beat the shit out of his oldest cousin. He sure as hell needed to beat the shit out of someone.

Rordyc stepped from the shadows and stood beside Amdyn. "We have a problem," he said.

"Take a number."

"Jordyn found his missing man," Amdyn said. "He's dead."

Wyc let his aggression cool slightly. "When?"

"He was found less than an hour ago," Amdyn said. "We were on our way to get you. Evidence suggests he was the one who disabled the alarm and then was killed by a Slayer."

"Evidence suggests?" Wyc kept his voice low enough to float no further than the distance between him and his cousins.

"That's what I said." Amdyn's voice was flat. Serious.

Wyc looked from Amdyn to Rordyc. Both wore the distant and hard expression of a soldier in full warrior mode. Giving away nothing except the willing intensity to fight to the death and making damn sure that death was the death of their enemy.

He knew his cousins well. The simple absence of emotion revealed all he needed to understand that his problems with Bethany would have to wait.

Rordyc and Amdyn knew the importance of a mate. Of finding and keeping your mate. Of getting her to the place of willingly completing the Matching Ritual. The only thing that would trump that was ensuring your mate's safety.

For whatever reason, neither one of them believed the evidence regarding Jordyn's team member. This wasn't the place to discuss it. Not here in the open, where they might be overheard. He had some evidence himself he wanted to put on the table.

"Where's Myrra?" he asked.

"Perimeter patrol," Rordyc answered.

Wyc gave a curt nod and headed inside. "Contact her. I want her here. Now."

Chapter Eleven

ဆ

"You don't think a Slayer killed him. Why?" Wyc asked. After making sure Bethany was safe in their room and charging Shy with keeping an eye on her, he had joined Rordyc and Amdyn.

They had taken seats in what would have been termed the library if a realtor had been giving prospective buyers a tour. But since Rordyc had furnished the room, there wasn't a book in sight. Leather couches, leather chairs, leather ottomans and a miniature refrigerator holding bottles of his favorite beer and several types of cola took up most of the space in the large room. A big screen, wall-mounted plasma TV, DVD player, stereo, several game systems and built-in shelves stocked with movies and video games filled one entire wall. Rordyc got bored easily.

"You've seen a Slayer attack before?" Amdyn asked.

Wyc nodded. Slayer attacks were brutal, vicious. The carnage left behind was sickening and, once seen, could not be forgotten.

Cirryc and Shy had found the missing man a half mile from his post, his flesh torn and slashed into a nearly unrecognizable mass.

"Have you ever known a Slayer to stay with a body after it's killed it just to mangle it? Especially when that body's not the prime target?"

Wyc raised his eyebrows. Rordyc picked up where Amdyn left off.

"It's impossible to tell exactly which injury was the killing blow, but one thing is certain, whatever—or whoever—killed him continued tearing him to shreds long after Tunyn was dead."

"And," Amdyn said, "he was half buried."

"What?" Wyc sat forward, rested his elbows on his knees. If he stretched what he knew about Slayers, there might be a small chance, a very small chance, he could believe that the animal had torn the man to pieces in a blood frenzy after delivering the killing blow. But to stay and bury its victim? No.

A Slayer was given a scent and pursued that scent to the death. It would destroy anything that got in its way, but it wouldn't stay and try to bury the evidence of the attack when the hunt was still on.

"Are you sure?"

Amdyn nodded. Rordyc looked insulted that he had even asked.

"Who else suspects it wasn't a Slayer killing?"

"No one." Rordyc leaned back and spread his arms over the back of the couch he was sitting in the middle of. "Shy and Cirryc brought Tunyn back. The condition of his body and the timing of the attack left no doubt in anyone else's mind. Except perhaps Myrra's," he added as an afterthought.

Electricity skittered over Wyc's skin. "Why Myrra?"

Rordyc shrugged, but the intensity in his eyes told Wyc he wasn't taking anything for granted. "Nothing she said. Actually, probably more of what wasn't said."

"Explain."

His sharp command increased the already nerve-snapping tension in the room. Amdyn crossed his arms over his chest and focused a hostile glare on him.

"Is there something you need to tell us?" Amdyn asked.

Wyc ignored him, kept his gaze on Rordyc. "Why do you think Myrra knew Tunyn wasn't killed by a Slayer?"

"She didn't ask any questions when Cirryc and Shy brought him in. Just stood in the background and listened. Watched."

"It was Jordyn's man. His job to deal with the details of the death," Wyc said.

"True. But she wasn't listening as a friend to the deceased or as a fellow soldier. She was listening as Captain Lansyr. Watching everyone's reaction. And she traded out with Cirryc to run the patrol tonight."

A sharp knock sounded at the door.

"Come in," Wyc answered before Amdyn could ask his question again. Both his cousins knew more was up than he was telling them. But there were things even they didn't come between.

Myrra stepped into the room, but stopped when she saw all three men. Then her gaze settled on Wyc. Her clear blue eyes bleak, but determined.

Without a word, she walked into the room and stopped at the coffee table before him. Pushing her right sleeve up, she unclipped the thin gold dagger bound to the underside of her forearm. She placed it on the table and took a step back, body rigid and head held high.

Neither one of his two cousins could stop the shock her actions gave them from momentarily showing on their faces.

"Amdyn, Rordyc, I'd like you to leave us."

Though clearly unhappy with his request, both left without protest.

Once the door had closed behind his cousins, Wyc said, "You're resigning your command?"

"I sent her away." Emotion flashed in her eyes. "But I swear, Wyc, on my blood as a Keeper, it was only after the report had come in that every Slayer had been killed."

Wyc's fingers dug into the leather arms of the chair. Apart from a very few individuals, Myrra was closer to him than anyone. Closer even than most of his family.

"Why?"

"Your Guardian is nearly expired. She didn't want what you offered her. Nor does she understand our country, care about our people or the importance of our mission. She didn't deserve you." She drew in a long, deliberate breath, before releasing it with her next statement. "She still doesn't."

Anger roiled in Wyc's gut. Never in a thousand years would he have thought his captain would betray him. If he hadn't been here to witness her confession, he would never have believed it.

"Your life has been your duty to your country," she said. "I have always respected that. Understood it.

"When Bethany was finally found, you were so close to being released from the Matching obligation placed on you by the Elders and Prophets. I wanted you to have a chance at real happiness with a mate of your choosing, and I knew you wouldn't if she stayed."

Though Myrra's stiff posture had held through her declaration of guilt, she had stared straight ahead at an indeterminate spot over his left shoulder. Had not once met his gaze after resigning her commission. An automatic admission when an officer voluntarily relinquished his *qauntar*, the traditional—and deadly—dagger presented by a royal at the formal recognition ceremony. He had presented Myrra's to her seven years ago.

He let the silence stand between them for a long moment before he asked, "Is that all?"

She inclined her head. Looked him in the eyes. Did not attempt to hide the regret there. "I would never have intentionally put Bethany in harm's way. I made a mistake out of my devotion to you. But, it was a mistake. One I will never forgive myself for."

His eyes narrowed to mere slits. Hours ago, he would have trusted this woman with his life. Now he didn't know what to believe. "Did you attempt to get rid of Bethany because I rejected your sister?" That the question even had to be asked cut through him like a knife.

Myrra's eyes widened. "No. After everything…" she let her words trail off. Shook her head. "I only wanted to see you happy. For once. But when you went after her, I realized how wrong I had been." Pain etched deep furrows between her eyes. "The one person you have a chance of loving, I had sent away.

"Bethany is your choice. As a soldier or civilian, I will defend her with my life. I would have protected her against the Sleht regardless."

The remorse she felt at her actions was evident in her voice, her expression. He almost believed she was sincere. "Tell me about the Slayer attack."

Immediately, Myrra snapped into Captain Lansyr and full military mode. With clipped, authoritative words, she said, "I don't believe it was a Slayer that killed Tunyn. Nor do I believe Tunyn disabled the perimeter alarm, though I can't prove it at the present time. I was investigating a hunch when I was called in."

"What is it that you believe then?"

Myrra's eyes held a wary edge. She had a long, hard history with him, but her actions had nearly cost him his mate's life. She had lied and gone against orders. She was probably wondering why he was even bothering to ask her opinion of the attack. Suspecting that he held her guilty of far more than misguided loyalty.

"I believe Tunyn's killer is Ilyrian."

Wyc was impressed. Not many men would have the balls to make such a declaration after having made a career-altering error. Especially when that declaration would have moved them to the top of the suspect list.

"Go on."

"I also believe that the killer is someone close to you."

Something he had considered, but when spoken aloud, the possibility cut deeper than he would have guessed. His next question would be cruel, but he needed to see her reaction.

"How long have you been working for the Sleht, Myrra?"

Myrra's face went white. She grabbed the knife off the low table, and in one smooth motion, flipped it in her palm to point toward herself. The blade sliced through the air on its way her heart.

"No." Wyc's sharp command forbade her from finishing the ritual suicide that, to his knowledge, hadn't been performed for hundreds of years. When an officer stood accused of treason, he had the opportunity to refute the indictment by plunging the *quantar* into his heart. From the moment the dagger was picked up, the Royal making the accusation had the option of stopping the act's execution. If he did, the Royal was legally abrogating the indictment. If not, the charge stood, but the officer was allowed an honorable burial.

Myrra reacted without hesitation. Goddamn, her response had been so swift, he'd barely had time to get out the word to stop her. If the table hadn't been low enough to extend her action, his captain would be dead.

Even now, her movement had been halted, but her white-knuckled grip on the handle hadn't lessened, the tip snagging the front of her shirt. She stood frozen as she stared down at the dagger.

Wyc leaned over the table, wrapped his hand around hers and pulled the knife away from her chest. "No."

The *quantar* clattered to the tabletop. He released her hand and she took a step back.

"Bethany is more important to me than my own life, Myrra."

She held his gaze, accepting the truth.

"Treat her as such."

She nodded, the vow unspoken but absolute.

Wyc nodded. "That's all. You may leave."

Myrra took several steps toward the door before he said her name. She turned, waiting.

"You forgot something."

She frowned. He tilted his head toward the dagger on the table.

"It was surrendered."

"It was not accepted." When she didn't make a move to pick it up, he crossed his arms over his chest and growled. "Don't waste my time. I'm not in the mood to argue. Find Amdyn and Rordyc and send them back in."

Her internal struggle still raging in her eyes, Myrra retrieved her dagger and, with several deft movements, secured it once again to the underside of her arm.

Her hand had grasped the doorknob before he asked, "Do you know who the traitor is?"

The pause before her negative answer spoke volumes. She had strong suspicions, but would not reveal them without proof. That meant her suspicions lay not only with an Ilyrian, but one connected to a royal house. She would not bring accusations against nobility without irrefutable evidence.

Myrra was a good soldier. He was relieved that, even without being in Rordyc's information loop, she had surmised the same threat. Relieved, but angry that the suspicions were being confirmed rather than denied at every turn.

Rordyc and Amdyn hadn't gone far. Rordyc was propped against the opposite wall in the lazy, careless posture of the class troublemaker waiting outside the principal's office. He raised his eyebrows at Myrra's exit and indolently rolled his shoulders off the wall. Amdyn stood like a bull ready to charge, the stormy expression on his face clearly indicating his legendary patience was nearing its end.

Myrra nodded deferentially to them and moved out of the way.

Wyc caught the look on her face as she turned to move down the hall. Yesterday, she would have been included in the discussion with Amdyn and Rordyc. She understood what had not been said during their conversation. Her position remained, but his personal trust in her had been damaged. Perhaps irrevocably.

Amdyn closed the door behind them. "Now is there something you need to tell us?" His anger set as sharply on his face as his cheekbones.

"Myrra's suspicions center on a traitor as well, but as of yet, she has been unable to obtain proof."

His answer wasn't to the true question Amdyn had asked, and all three knew it. Wyc's unspoken message was received and they moved to the next topic.

"We have some possibilities to look into," Amdyn said, "including Shyrana's recent headaches. She's been unable to connect to either one of her normal contacts in Ilyria for two days." He looked at Rordyc. "Has she said anything to you tonight?"

Rordyc shook his head.

"Why wasn't I informed of Shy's problems?" Wyc couldn't help his older brother syndrome. Shy hated it, but had no choice but to live with it.

He didn't want her here. For all its problems, life was still safer and more easily protected in Ilyria. But intra-world telepaths were rare, and an intra-world telepath he'd trust with the lives of his team and now his mate's? Shy hadn't been his best choice; she'd been his only choice. Without her, they'd have no communication to their homeworld during the long months between portal openings.

"She asked us not to tell you until she was sure it wasn't just the flu or something. And you've had other concerns," Rordyc remarked dryly. "One, especially, that is becoming increasingly difficult to keep safe."

Amdyn leaned forward. "You need to get her out of here, Wyc. We don't know where the danger is coming from, but two Predators and a Slayer attack in less than five days? Slayers are released by twos, not in packs of eight."

"And they had her scent," Wyc said. "Not a chance in hell did they break into her apartment to get it, and then follow her here, hundreds of miles she crossed in a car."

Silence ruled for a moment as none of the three wanted to put their damning thoughts into words. Rordyc let out a disgusted breath. "Shit. The scent has to be fairly fresh, which means someone with access to the house and your room, took something of hers to give them. Is she missing anything?"

The thought of someone else entering the room he shared with his mate and touching, taking anything of hers had fury rising like a tidal wave through his veins. Wyc forced it back. Refused to let emotion cloud his thoughts. "I'll have her check. And I want to know how the hell portals are being opened at will."

All three of the cousins knew there were ways, but few others would. The methods were costly both in lives and to the stability of their homeworld. For those reasons, among others, those secrets had been buried for centuries in the literature of the ancients few had access to. But like the secret to the drug, *Yes Master*, the Predators were now using, those secrets had been discovered by someone and sold to the Sleht.

There were too many possibilities and at the same time, impossibilities. And working the problem from two worlds was enough to drive the strongest mind insane. But one thing was certain—if they didn't find their mates soon, and the prophecy was left unfulfilled, Ilyria faced a dark age it might never recover from.

"I'm working on it," Rordyc said. "But Amdyn's right. You need to get your mate out of here. I have an option, if you want to take it."

One of Rordyc's jobs was to secure safe houses and living quarters for the teams that worked the retrieval detail. Initially, Amdyn had been responsible for that detail, but Rordyc had complained once too often about the Spartan accommodations and Amdyn had shoved the task into his lap. Turned out, he had the uncanny ability to find the most out-of-the-way places that were easily defended and, more often than not, met his high standards for hedonistic pleasure. Everyone was happier, though Amdyn would never admit it.

"Who knows about it?" Wyc asked.

"No one. I was saving it for my mate. In case she needed some convincing to complete the final rite of the Matching Ritual." Rordyc's grin highlighted his lecherous intent. Though two years younger than Wyc, he had been matched to Bethany's older sister, Eavyn.

"Find anything new on her location?" Wyc asked.

Rordyc shrugged. "Nothing to speak of."

For the first time all night, Wyc smiled. His cousin's laid-back attitude could fool everybody except him. The last time Rordyc had been with Eavyn, she was a tiny slip of a three-year-old child, yet had still managed to push him into the river when he tried to kiss her cheek in the customary greeting. Not something his cousin was likely to forget or let go unreciprocated.

Rordyc had something, he'd bet on it. But with the recent attacks, his best friend would probably be mated and have Eavyn back in Ilyria with their first child well on the way before he got around to telling anyone. Rordyc had been in a library in Des Moines four days ago, yet the last lead he had mentioned to anyone but Wyc was in Madrid. And even then, his comments were made days after the lead had turned into a dead end.

Though none would question his loyalty, most assumed Rordyc wasn't too interested in finding Eavyn. But the uncharacteristic advances in the Sleht strikes put Rordyc's taciturn nature regarding his mate's search in a new light. Wyc wondered just how long Rordyc had suspected a traitor among their ranks.

"Think you can get Bethany out of the house without her feeling the need to knee your balls into your throat?" Rordyc asked.

Wyc's response regarding Rordyc's family jewels jolted a bark of laughter from his cousin before they all got down to the business of moving Bethany to a new location.

* * * * *

Bethany woke in a different room from the one she fell asleep in. The hurt and anger that had propelled her out of Wyc's grip and into the house had evaporated by the time she reached the bedroom. Too tired to maintain that level of emotion, she had fallen face-first and fully clothed onto the bed. Her last coherent thought as she turned her head to the side to breathe had been that if she kicked Wyc in her sleep, at least with her shoes still on, he'd be sure to feel it.

She had a dreamlike memory of being carried down the stairs and laid in the backseat of an SUV. The bumpy ride had her head bouncing on Wyc's thigh. Too tired to care about appearing as cranky as a crotchety old lady with her support hose in a knot, she grumped her way back to sleep each time the uneven road woke her up. She was pretty sure she heard Rordyc laugh once or twice, but for the most part, she remembered Wyc's patient, soothing voice as he rubbed her head and she slept. Until the next bump.

She stretched and let her limbs slide along the softest, silkiest sheets she had ever slept between. Since she was laying here in just her panties, Wyc had obviously taken more time to undress her before putting her to bed than she had done for herself earlier. Her duffel was on a chair close to the bed, and she retrieved a clean pair of jeans and long-sleeved, v-necked T-shirt and got dressed.

Pulling open one of the shuttered French doors to see where she was, she was momentarily blinded by the searing light of day. She slapped her palm over her eyes to block the sun. Much more cautious the second time, she slit two fingers open and peeped through her hand.

And then let it fall to her side. "Wow," she whispered, her eyes rounding in awe at the view in front of her. The house seemed to be located at the top of a low mountain, surrounded by aspen trees, their bright golden leaves shining like tiny burnished shields against the perfectly clear blue sky.

"There's lunch waiting for you on the front porch," Wyc said from behind her.

She turned to face him, finding him dressed in dark cargo pants and a black thermal crew that emphasized his broad shoulders and thick, dark hair.

"Lunch?"

"You slept through breakfast."

His gaze dropped to the front of her shirt. She hadn't bothered with a bra yet, and now her nipples tightened and pushed against the thin material under the heat of his stare.

She was fighting the urge to cross her arms over her breasts when a confident, extremely arrogant grin spread across his face. The jerk. Fine. This was a game two could play. She propped her hands on her hips and stuck out her chest.

"Great. So, if you're done ogling, I'm going to go eat now." She pushed past him and only taken three steps down the short hall before coming to a dead stop.

"Oh my God." It looked like something straight out of a decorating magazine. The comfortable but sparse modern decor, accented with light wood and a cream and blue color scheme made it feel like you were truly sitting in the sky. The river rock fireplace reached to the ceiling and had a thick fur rug in front of it.

The front wall was dominated by a huge picture window, unbroken by seams or panes. If possible, the view out the front outshone the back like the sun did the moon.

Bethany rushed out the front door, stood at the edge of the porch and looked down into a valley studded with stands of pines among more fall-kissed aspens. Not far from the house stood a gorgeous mountain lake that mirrored the sky and forest around it in startling detail. Regal, snow-capped mountains rose in the distance to frame the entire vista.

"Where are we? This place is amazing."

"You can thank Rordyc the next time you see him. Meanwhile—" he took her by the arm and guided her to the small table on the porch set up with sandwiches and iced tea, "—you need to eat."

Bethany looked at the table. The chairs were too close together. The table was too small. She didn't want to be that near to Wyc. It was one thing for him to complicate her life, but her heart could only take so much. If the only way to protect it was to maintain an emotional distance, then that's what she would do.

Easier said than done she found out as the afternoon wore on. For some reason, no matter what she did, he was determined to be charming. And thoughtful. And witty. And he did sexy just by breathing, damn it.

He kept talking to her. Asking questions. Acting interested in her answers. Telling her about Ilyria and the place reserved for her among their people. Filling in what he knew of her family. When he brought up the classes she was taking in college and told her about the types of similar schools on their homeworld, she actually got excited about the possibilities.

He smiled at her enthusiasm, encouragement shining in his eyes, and she laughed. Her heart expanded with happiness. Unthinkingly, she reached for him. And froze. Oh God. One stupid conversation and she was ready to crawl up his body. Again.

She excused herself to get a drink in the kitchen. And refined her plan. She obviously needed physical as well as emotional distance, so she would simply avoid him.

When he entered a room, she left. He followed. Her wanderings took her through the house, poking her nose in several closets and finding Rordyc's hedonistic tendencies didn't stop at sheets. The pantry was stocked with nonperishable delicacies such as caviar and expensive wines, the bathroom cabinets revealed a selection of lotions, oils, bath salts and extra-large, kitten-scruff-soft plush towels.

Her exploration ended in the bedroom when she opened the armoire and found herself staring at an impressive array of sex toys and accoutrements. She was standing there, trying to decide what the heck some of the odder-looking items were used for, when she felt the heat of Wyc's body radiating against her back. She sucked in her breath and tried not to imagine exploring the possibilities this chest offered with the sex god behind her.

"Rordyc keeps quite a toy chest," she commented, hoping her sarcasm would cover the signs of her nervous arousal.

Wyc reached around her, his chest bumping her shoulder, and brushed his fingers over a set of black velvet cuffs. His warm breath tickled her ear when he whispered, "Want to play?"

Her heart immediately tried to thump out of her chest, drumming a resounding *yes* through every drop of blood in her body. Before the demand could override her previous no-sex, no-attachment resolution, she slammed the cupboard shut, barely giving Wyc enough time to yank his hand out of the way.

"I'm going to take a walk." Ignoring his quiet laughter, she headed outside and down to the lake. He went with her. Taking out some of her aggravation on an old stump sticking out of the water a good fifty feet from the shore, she hurled rock after rock at it.

"You're letting go of the rock too soon. Hang on to it just a bit longer," Wyc advised from the post he had taken next to a boulder several feet away.

She glared at him, picked up another rock and flung it at the stump. It hit it dead on. She picked up another one, looked at him while she threw it, again hitting the target's center.

"Or maybe," he said, "you were hitting everything you aimed at."

"I was going to go to college on a softball scholarship." Another rock thumped against the water-logged wood with a solid *thwump*. "Until an ankle injury knocked me out at the start of the season my senior year." *Thwump. Thwump.*

"So you were missing the stump on purpose?"

She dropped the rock she had just picked up. Turned and headed back to the cabin. "I was knocking off the sticks on its sides."

He grabbed her hand as she stalked by him. Pulled her to him until she stood close enough for him to loosely hold her in the circle of his embrace. She crossed her arms over her chest, ensuring the space between them.

"I'm sorry your plans didn't work out."

"Thanks. But it wasn't a big deal." It had been, but she didn't want to get into it. Besides, if he wanted a list of the plans that hadn't worked out in her life, they'd need more than an afternoon to cover it. "I managed."

Something akin to regret flashed through his eyes. "I know."

By the time they returned to the cabin, she was drained from constantly resisting the magnetic pull Wyc had on her.

A nap would help. Would have helped, if he hadn't joined her. As soon as the bed sunk under his weight, heat rushed down and swirled through her pussy. She jumped up like her butt had been rocket-launched off the mattress.

The man was driving her crazy. If having an extra shadow hadn't been bad enough, throughout the day he kept finding reasons to touch her. Brushing a strand of hair off her face. Resting a hand on her arm or waist. Standing close enough to graze up against her. Dropping a kiss on her forehead.

Every time he touched her, her body reacted. She wanted to lean into him. Ask for more. Demand more. But after last night, she knew she wasn't able to keep sex with Wyc separate from her feelings. And since her heart wasn't listening to reason and falling back out of love as fast as it fell into love with him, the least she could do was not to fling it out there for him to stomp on again.

* * * * *

Bethany was weakening. He could tell.

"Talk to me," he prompted, joining her on the couch. He had unsuccessfully tried to initiate conversation throughout dinner, but only received one- or two-word answers on her part.

She crossed her arms and stared into the fire he had started in the fireplace. Her nervous action of running her hand through her hair had left it mussed and curling around her shoulders in sexy waves. Her lower lip was red and slightly swollen from being dragged through her teeth. She was turning him on with her anxious little mannerisms. He wanted to suck that pouty lower lip into his mouth, smooth back the glossy strands of auburn hair and bare the lovely curve of her neck.

He knew if he pressed, she'd fall to the passion between them. It was too damn strong for either of them to resist when it flamed at full force. But he was determined to draw her out emotionally as well. Not simply overwhelm her with desire.

After the Slayer attack, he had allowed his fear and fury at nearly losing her to take control of his lust. Though he had been harsh and unyielding to her cries, she had whispered that she loved him. He still couldn't believe it.

He hadn't deserved that kind of gift after how he had treated her. And hearing those most treasured words after he had accused her of betraying him and then refusing to give her a chance to defend herself was more than he could take. The second after she had spoken, he had despised himself and couldn't bear to allow her to lie next to him so soft and giving.

Once he got his head out of his ass, however, the truth hit him square in the heart. It didn't matter whether he deserved her love or not, he wanted it. Hell, he needed it. And each minute that passed with her trying to keep it from him, he died a little more.

He was determined to hear those words from her again. Only this time, he would hold her and love her until her fear and insecurity was less than a distant memory. All day he had been working on her, taking every opportunity to touch her. To tell her, *show* her the possibilities of what their life could be like once they returned to Ilyria.

"Bethany?"

"What?" she snapped.

He smiled. Even grumpy, she was adorable. "Talk to me," he repeated.

Her eyebrows dove down over her eyes. "I don't want to talk to you. Did you ever think that maybe you bore me?"

Wyc burst out laughing and pulled her against his side. "You're right. We've done enough talking for a while."

"You are the most arrogant b—"

Wyc stopped her rant with a kiss. She twisted against him. He held her gently, allowed her to turn her face away. And rained soft kisses down the length of her neck exposed by her movement.

The hands that had been pushing against his chest slid up to cup his shoulders. He scraped his teeth across the sensitive skin behind her ear. Settled his mouth there to kiss and tease until he felt her start to melt in his arms. Moved down and opened his mouth over the pulse point at the base of her neck.

He circled the erratic heartbeat with his tongue and soared when it kicked up, fast and hard.

Her fingers pressed into his shoulders and he shifted to kiss her mouth. Just a light kiss, lips brushing lips, before he pulled back to look at her face. Cupping her cheek with his palm, he surveyed the beauty he held. Her green eyes, glittering like jewels, were heavy-lidded with passion. His thumb swept over the curve of her cheek and down to the corner of her mouth.

"Wyc?"

He hated that her voice sounded uncertain. He threaded his fingers through her hair. Relished the heavy silk sliding across his palm as it slipped free from his grasp. Pushed his hand in further to tangle in the dark mass.

His gaze returned to hers, watching every flicker of emotion that skittered through her eyes. Desire, fear, nervousness. Love. *Yes.* There it was. What he needed to breathe.

His eyes narrowed, and his nostrils flared. His hand tightened to a fist in her hair as the intensity of his emotion crashed through him. Then she looked away. Closed her eyes. Strangling his breath in his throat.

"Look at me," he whispered. Slowly, she opened her eyes. With his fingertips, he followed the line of her jaw from under her ear to the tip of her chin. "I want to make love to you, Bethany."

"I can't...I mean I don't...I—"

He covered her lips with his fingers. "Let me?"

Chapter Twelve

ରେ

Let me? He was asking? Holy shit, she was in trouble. And not just because that emotion releasing her stomach on a freefall to her feet wasn't the panic or anger she expected. Not the panic or anger she needed to be strong enough to pull away.

All day, she had been fighting. Determined to outlast his charm and the pull he had on her. At least for this one day. And she would have. Was all set to be bad-tempered and argumentative clear up to the end.

Before he made the fire. And laughed. And kissed her. And looked at her the same way he had last night right before he flipped her over and gave her the first of three screaming orgasms.

And now he was asking to make love to her? Oh shit. Her stomach flopped around in the bottom of her feet. She trembled.

He gathered her against his chest, nuzzled her hair. "Please let me touch you, babydoll."

"Yes." The word was out before she even knew she was going to say it. She wanted him. She wanted the emotion she saw in his eyes to be real. To be truly for her. Only for her.

Her fingers dug into his muscles and she arched her body into his embrace. One strong arm banded around her back. His other hand smoothed down the side of her body to rest lightly on her hip. He tilted her backwards over his arm, searching her face.

Whatever he was looking for so intently, he must have found. An incredible tenderness lit his eyes and was joined by a slow, sexy smile. That lethal combination struck the final deathblow to her determination to keep Wyc out of her heart.

He sealed his coup with a kiss so sweet her surrender seemed more victory than defeat.

A quiet sigh of protest left her lips as he pulled away. Stood. Helped her to her feet.

"Stay right here," he said.

She watched him extinguish lights and light candles, leaving only their soft, flickering flames and the fire glowing. He walked back to the bedroom, and then went into the kitchen, returning with two glasses, a bottle of wine and a black satin bag. After dropping the bag on the floor beside the rug, he set the glasses and wine beside the fireplace before opening a cabinet and turning on the stereo. Low music drifted around her from hidden speakers set throughout the room. She didn't recognize the song, but the man's voice—low, strong and smooth—was wrapped in the primitive, jagged edge of ruthless sensuality that had her blood smoldering with the need to be touched.

Her eyes closed and her head dropped back. There was no doubt the music came with the cabin. It fit too perfectly. God, she was sorry for whomever Rordyc had gone to all this trouble for. The woman was in for the fight of her life if she intended to resist his seduction.

A small smile played about her lips. Right now, she didn't care about Rordyc or whatever plans he may have for his future.

Strong arms encircled her, drawing her close to a muscled chest. She kept her eyes closed as her smile widened. Wyc nuzzled her neck.

"I like that smile," he said. The smoky timbre of his voice sent shivers across her skin, tightening her nipples and weakening her knees. "Want to tell me what it's about?"

"Uh-uh," she said, sighing as his lips made their way down her neck to her collarbone. "I'd have to think." She lifted her head to meet his gaze. "And I'm done with thinking today."

His brows drew together slightly. "That bad?"

She closed her eyes again and nodded. "Oh yeah. That bad."

His mouth settled firmly over hers. She opened eagerly and welcomed the easy slide of his tongue over hers. With languid strokes, he delved and tasted. She took her own sweet time exploring his mouth, running the tip of her tongue over the edges of his teeth, letting him hold it between his lips and suck.

With a soft moan, she pushed herself up to her toes and pressed her hips to his. His hands slid down and seized her bottom, kneading it in his big hands.

He pulled his head back, though he kept his hands in place, ensuring their lower bodies maintained contact. "Do you know how crazy you've been driving me all day? Running around without a bra—"

"I'm dressed perfectly modestly," she said.

"And every time you got a little chilly or caught me looking at you," he said, bringing one hand up to cup her breast, "these beauties stood up and saluted."

His thumb flicked back and forth over her nipple until it peaked underneath the stretchy material. "I think you left your bra off on purpose."

She hummed, neither denying nor confirming. He bent and covered her nipple with his mouth. Laving it through the shirt until the material clung to her flesh.

He stepped back and looked at his handiwork. Heat flared in his eyes. "You have too many clothes on," he said, the rasp of his voice causing her other nipple to tighten in anticipation. Lifting her shirt by the hem, he slowly peeled it up and off her body.

"Much better," he said. And then said nothing for a very long time. The systematic attention he lavished on her breasts had her whimpering long before he showed signs of finishing.

When her knees started to buckle, she tried to pull away. He wrapped his arm around her waist and lowered her to the thick alpaca fur rug in front of the fireplace. She was surprised at the softness of the rug, not just the silky curls of the pelt, but the thickness of the padding underneath it. Definitely designed with laying on it in mind rather than walking on it.

Wyc stretched out beside her, raising himself up on one elbow to continue his concentrated devotion to her breasts.

His hair seemed to absorb rather than reflect the shimmering light from the fire and candles. Its darkness stark against the white of her breasts. As she watched, he moved his head again and a puckered nipple peeked out from between ebony strands. So incredibly erotic.

He sucked hard on her opposite breast and she moaned. Rubbed her thighs together to try to alleviate the ache between them. Slid her fingers through his hair and tangled them in place.

"Oh God, Wyc," she whispered.

Shifting, he covered each breast with one of his hands. "I've been waiting to get my hands on these all day," he said, squeezing them to emphasize his point.

"And my mouth." He pressed his face to her chest and kissed the valley between her breasts. And then took as much of her left breast into his mouth as possible, sucking hard.

Bethany gasped and cradled his head. Her hips rose off the floor.

Wyc sat up and whipped off his shirt. His skin glowed in the firelight, warm and golden over sculpted shoulders, defined pecs and a set of abs that rippled as he moved back to her.

He held her gaze as he lowered himself. His eyes glittered with emotion and she reached for him. Splayed her hands over his chest and slid them up to his neck as his chest neared hers. As soon as the tips of her breasts came in contact with his skin, she closed her eyes and whispered his name. Overwhelmed by the intensity of his touch.

He rocked side to side and back and forth, rasping her nipples against his chest in slow, tortuous circles. When she opened her eyes, he was still leaning on his elbows, still watching her face. She wanted him closer, wanted to feel his weight on her. The sensation of only having their skin touch at the places where he allowed her nipples to drag across his skin was making her wild.

"Wyc!" She tightened her arms around his neck, arched up into him.

He responded to her demand and crushed her beneath him. Hot, hard body above, soft, deep-pile fur beneath. Her breasts flattened against his chest and the thick ridge of his erection prodded her thigh. He took her mouth in a steamy, tongue-thrusting kiss until she was breathless and grinding her hips against his.

Damn. They both still had too many clothes on. All their clothes, for that matter, below the waist. She pushed her fingers into his front pockets and tugged. His pants didn't move. Since that didn't work, she tried to pry her hands between their bodies to get to his zipper.

Wyc slid down her body, taking his pants out of her reach. She was about to voice a protest when his hand slid between her legs and pressed. Her protest came out as a moan of pleasure.

He kissed his way to the top of her jeans, making the muscles in her stomach jump. She reached for her own zipper and he pushed her hands away. God, she couldn't take much more of this. Her jeans had to be wet through by now. When his tongue traced from one side to the other just under her waistband, her toes curled tight inside her shoes.

Pressing the side of his face to her belly, he whispered, "Your skin is so soft. And you have the most amazing body. Perfect."

Bethany's automatic response was to think of a self-depreciating comment to throw back at him. To laugh at the reverence in his voice, especially since he had made such a ridiculous statement. Her? Have a perfect body? But the sincerity of his words and the worship-like veneration of his touch left her in awe and speechless.

No one had ever shown her so much tenderness or affection. She wasn't sure what to do with the feelings he continually evoked. Once already, she had fooled herself into thinking about love and even saying it out loud.

That had been a mistake. Big, big mistake. Whopper. He hadn't been able to get away from her fast enough. She might not be the next Einstein, but she did learn from her errors. No way was she going to confuse lovemaking with love again.

There was clearly emotion running between them; she'd accept that. But for all she knew, it could be a residual effect of the Guardian spell. If Myrra told her the truth, that enchantment was nearing its end. Whatever tenderness Wyc felt toward her could disappear with the spell's termination.

Bethany closed her eyes against the gray weight of hopelessness that bore down on her at that idea. She put the thought out of her mind. No matter what her future held, at least she had more answers to her past now. She'd had a mother who loved her and tried to protect her. She hadn't been purposely abandoned as a child and might still have family living.

And she had the sexiest man on the planet unzipping her pants. If he didn't love her, he at least seemed to care for her. For now. And that was something. More than she'd ever been given before.

She wiggled her hips and helped him get the rest of her clothes off. He pushed to his feet to remove his pants and boots. The room was just cool enough to make her miss the heat of his body, but as he undressed, she gladly relinquished a little warmth for the sight of the man in front of her. From top to bottom, Wyc Kilth was lust molded into perfected, human form.

Once he had removed the last of his clothes, he stood motionless above her, looking down. Held suspended in the moment, she caressed him as intimately with her eyes as he did her. The fire crackled quietly behind her. The constantly altering flames danced light and shadow across his form. Lovingly, she catalogued as many nuances of his body as she could, tucking the memories away for a time when they'd be all she had.

On her pass back up his body, her gaze collided with his frown. He knelt beside her and pulled her into his arms. His kiss was firm and giving. But there was an edge of desperateness to it she didn't understand. She took it, returned it. Until she was twisting against him, demanding more.

He laid her down on her back and joined her, reclining on his side next to her, propped up on his forearm. She started to roll toward him, but with a hand on her hip, he gently guided her to lay back. He skimmed a rough hand down her outer thigh to her knee, hooked it and drew it to the side, opening her legs.

The air was cool against the wet heat that had been building at the apex of her thighs. His hand moved up her inner thigh. He didn't pause when he reached her pussy, but slid a finger deep inside her cunt.

Not sure what she had been expecting, she knew it hadn't been that. Her eyes locked on his in surprise. His finger began a leisurely rhythm of retreat and advance.

She opened her mouth to say something. His finger plunged deeper. A sound of grating ecstasy overrode her words. Her head pressed into the rug and her neck arched. The desire to touch him was enormous, but her fingernails had dug into the thick, silky fleece of the rug and refused to let go.

"Come for me, Bethany," Wyc said. Her eyes opened to see him watching her face, intensity sharpening his features.

A second finger joined the first and she swallowed a sob of need. The heel of his hand pressed down on the top of her cleft, leaving the tip of her clitoris to chafe against the calluses on his palm as he ground his hand on her sex.

Heart hammering, Bethany felt the pull of her impending climax tug every nerve ending taut as it coiled tighter and tighter with each move of his hand.

"I love to watch you come, Bethany," he whispered. "Your eyes go wide. Blind with your pleasure. Your skin turns the prettiest pink. The little sounds you make deep in your throat make me so goddamn hard.

"And listen to that." He stabbed his fingers in and out of her again. The liquid suction of her cunt on his finger sounded in the room along with her harsh breaths. "So wet for me. Showing me how much you want me."

She let out a hiss of agreement as her body jerked, his erotic words pushing her over the top. The coil that had been winding so tightly in her lower abdomen sprung apart, releasing frantic wings of sensation to beat against the cage of her skin.

Suddenly Wyc removed his hand, and in the next instant, lodged his cock inside her, deep and filling. She cried out and clutched at him. Her hands caught his hips, her fingernails digging tiny half moons into his skin. Her cunt bore down on his thick erection as another contraction took her.

Holding himself above her with straight arms, he ground his hips in a slow circle. She wanted his weight on her, wanted to feel him move hard and fast inside her. Wanted him as mindless and saturated in pleasure as she was.

"God, Wyc," she pleaded, her voice strained as another, lesser, contraction fluttered through her, "fuck me."

"I am, babydoll. I am." A light sheen of perspiration sat on his forehead. His body was rigid as he continued the slow, grinding circles, letting her climax play completely out in ever-decreasing shudders.

When her body had quit convulsing, he lowered himself to his elbows, framed her face with his hands and kissed her lightly.

"Do you have any idea what you do to me? How incredible it feels to be inside of you?"

Her hands smoothed up his back. "Can't feel as good as it does to have you inside of me."

He chuckled and nipped her chin, moving against her in a shallow thrust. She tightened her inner muscles around his cock.

"You keep doing that, and I might not let you get any sleep at all tonight."

She lifted her knees, brought her thighs high around his hips and allowed him to slide deeper inside. He groaned and kissed her again. Wrapping her legs around his waist, she locked her ankles behind his back and pressed her pussy hard against him.

He lifted his head, closed his eyes. A quick shudder raced down his body. When he opened his eyes and looked at her, they were dark with sensual promise. Her cunt seized around him in response.

His eyelids lowered and he slowly pulled out, the drag of his cock over her sensitive pussy flaring need through her. Her body tried to hold on to him. Gripping his cock to keep it deep inside. The friction of her inner fight only heightened the sensation each time he withdrew.

Suddenly he slammed back into her. One hard push and he was in to the hilt, the head of his cock butting against the opening to her womb. Her thighs clamped around him and she cried out. He repeated the process, never giving her a warning when he was going to ram back into her. Again and again, he would come excruciatingly close to pulling completely out of her, and she shook with need until he filled her again. Tormenting her by prolonging the withdrawal of his cock for different lengths of time, he kept her off balance, unable to control any part of their lovemaking.

"Please, Wyc. I can't take this anymore. Please quit teasing me."

"I'm not teasing you, Bethany. I'm very, very serious about this." He had pulled back, and this time when he slid back in, he did so slowly. Inch by inch. Letting her absorb each little twinge of her body as it stretched to accommodate him.

Her hands slid up the flexing muscles of his back to hold onto his shoulders. He lowered his mouth to her neck and swirled his tongue over the spot beneath her ear that seemed to have a direct line to her pussy. She moaned and turned her head to the side, granting him full access and herself full pleasure.

Rocking against him, she let herself fall into the moment. When he held her like this, it was easy to believe that all was right with the world. With her head turned away from the fire, she faced the large wall of glass that fronted the cabin. Thousands of stars glittered like pinpricks of light splattered against the velvet black of night.

But it wasn't the innumerable stars shining in through the top of the window that caught her attention, but the reflected image at the bottom of the pane. Two bodies moving together, clothed only in firelight. Wyc's skin a dark, burnished gold, her fairer skin appearing more the color of champagne.

She lowered her right leg to see the length of him in the glass. His face was buried against her neck, biceps bunched as he held himself on his elbows to keep from crushing her. Her hand followed the strong line of his back down to his hip. She watched the muscles in his ass and thigh flex and relax with each measured stroke of his cock. Fascinated by the shallow hollow in the side of his buttock, she splayed her fingers over the spot, caressing it in honest wonder.

He steadied the rhythm of his thrusts. Building her anticipation slowly. God, he was so big. So hot and hard. Completely filling her, she could feel it all the way to her heart.

Seeing Wyc make love to her like this started an avalanche of emotion she was helpless to stop. She turned her face from their reflection. Closed her eyes to hold back the unexpected tears. One escaped before she could stop it. Left a cold trail from the corner of her eye into her hair.

Wyc shifted over her, his breath warm across her lips. She couldn't bring herself to open her eyes and look at him. Was afraid if she did, more tears would fall.

With a gentle touch, he traced the path left by the errant tear. "Bethany?"

Damn.

Chapter Thirteen

❧

Wyc repeated her name. Bethany still didn't open her eyes.

No. She would not shut him out like this. Not when he was still embedded in her body. Not when he was so close to getting what he needed.

Since this morning, he had been keeping close tabs on the emotions that ebbed and flowed over her face. Watched her wrestle with her feelings every time she felt vulnerable. Pushing herself into anger or indifference where he was concerned. Throughout the day, he had regularly brushed her mind to gauge her resistance and let him know when to push and when to let up.

But he wasn't going to back off tonight. Wouldn't allow her to withdraw and insulate herself from him. Already her emotions were starting to recede under her layers of self-protection.

Determination steeled within him. She would not hide from him. Not tonight. He'd pulled out her emotions through her body's reaction before. And he'd do it again and again until he was so deep in her heart she had no choice but to take him as her mate.

He kissed her hard and deep. Thrusting his tongue into her mouth in time to the thrusts of his cock. Bethany's passionate response made his heart leap.

She wound her arms around his neck and bucked underneath him to meet his thrusts. He wrapped his arms around her shoulders and held her tightly to his body, crushing her breasts to his chest. His hips rocked fast and steady.

Bethany twisted her face away and dragged in a ragged breath. It rushed out when he plowed into her wet heat again.

Her cunt gripped him with soft undulations as the exquisite tension rose between them.

Her soft gasp told him she was near her climax.

"Look at me Bethany," he said. "Kiss me while you come."

Lifting her head to meet his lips, she squeezed him with her entire body—arms, legs, pussy. She trembled as her climax swept over her, and those sexy little purring sounds at the back of her throat filtered into his mouth. Damn he loved it when she did that.

He inhaled her breath and pounded into her until he exploded, shooting hot streams of cum into her cunt. The world disappeared in a flash as he was totally consumed by the feel and smell of his mate. He rode out the conflagration that had become his body, fully absorbed in the complete ecstasy he had only ever experienced with Bethany. For what seemed an eternity, he allowed himself to drift in the stunning waves of pleasure she always led him to.

Two fingers poked his shoulder. "You're kinda heavy."

Wyc lifted his head and looked down at Bethany. He had collapsed on top of her when his orgasm short-circuited his brain. It was scary how easily this woman could completely undo him.

He rolled over and off her, taking her with him. She ended up sprawled over the top of him. He held her head and kissed her soundly.

When he let her go, she had a dazed look in her eyes. He speared his fingers through her hair, rubbed his thumbs over her cheekbones.

"Wyc, I..." Bethany started. Stuttered to a halt. Closed her eyes and tilted her head sideways to press into his right hand. Licked her lips.

"Yes?" Hopeful anticipation clutched suddenly around his heart for what he wanted, needed to hear.

She shook her head slightly. "Never mind. It's not important."

Wyc growled low in frustration. "It is important."

With a sigh, she slid off his body. He didn't let her go far. "Tell me."

She relaxed into his side. "I've decided to go back to Ilyria with you." The words were rushed, as if she was afraid they wouldn't all get out if she didn't hurry.

Her decision to return to Ilyria wasn't the declaration he had wanted, but at least she was headed in the right direction.

She frowned up at him. "I can come back, right? I mean, if it doesn't work out? If I don't fit in with the culture or if the people hate me?"

Wyc swallowed his first response. Forced back the immediate, vehement rejection that rose like acidic bile from his gut at the thought of her even thinking of leaving him again. Either here or in Ilyria. She wouldn't. He'd never let that happen. He'd follow her through a thousand worlds to keep her.

Inside, he winced at remembered late nights and too much drinking with his cousins. They had all taken their turns bragging about how they'd find their mates, fuck their brains out and bring them back to their homeworld.

He always finished his boast by saying he hoped his mate was practical enough not to expect anything more from him than an Ilyrian royal title and the opportunity to bear his children. And then he'd gone on to outline just how he'd keep her in Ilyria, on her back and well-fucked, until she had given him several sons. Then he'd magnanimously release her from her vow made during the Mating Rite. Once he had what he wanted, she'd be free to choose either to go or stay. It wouldn't matter to him.

He'd been such a fucking, arrogant bastard.

He would never have what he wanted unless he had her. She *was* what he wanted. Everything he wanted.

"So?" she asked. She propped her head up on her hand and looked down at him. "I can get back, right?"

"Portals work both ways," he said.

Before she could ask another question he'd refuse to answer—or answer with the truth and start an argument—he rolled her underneath him.

Her eyes widened in surprise. "So I can leave at—"

He cut her question off with a hard kiss meant to steal her thoughts. When her lips softened against his, he switched to a deep, leisurely exploration of her mouth. By the time he lifted his head, her eyes were glazed with a new wave of lust.

He nipped her bottom lip and reached for the black bag. Inside, he had hidden several sex toys from Rordyc's arsenal. When the satin rustled, Bethany turned her head to see what he was doing.

"What's in there?" she asked.

Palming the objects he was searching for, he gave her a wicked grin. "You'll soon find out."

When she started to protest, he covered her mouth with his and drew her into a prolonged, tongue-tangling kiss until she arched under him, pressing her luscious curves against him. He released her mouth to kiss his way down her neck before lightly scrubbing his whiskers over the sensitive peaks of her breasts. Bethany's soft exclamations of pleasure filled him with a deep, surprising satisfaction as he continued laying a trail of kisses down her abdomen.

He dropped the items from the bag out of Bethany's line of sight and splayed his hands over her hips, holding her firmly in place. A quick glance told him she was paying close attention to his every move, desire and curiosity clear in her green eyes. From underneath half-closed lids, he watched her as he drew his tongue in one long swipe across the tender skin just above her curls.

Her lips parted, but she didn't say a word. He repeated the action, this time with more pressure. Her breasts rose on a sharply indrawn breath, her hips pressed up against his hands and she tried to widen her thighs. With a smile, he licked her again. The scent of her arousal, warm and beckoning, spiraled up to wreathe seductively around him. He lowered his head again, this time to open his mouth over her skin and suck.

Every time he made love to this woman, he found another spot that demanded his indulgence. The soft dip below her belly and above her mound was surprisingly sensitive, the texture smooth and creamy against his tongue. With her scent so close, her curls brushing his chin and the taste of her warm skin pulling against his teeth, he could spend hours occupying himself right here. But from Bethany's increasingly impatient writhing, he knew her desire needed more, and soon.

With a soft pop, he broke the suction and looked at the mark he had left on her. A bright red oval that would stay for days, certain proof of where his mouth had been on her body. He had a sudden urge to place hickeys on her everywhere. Her quiet moan and restless toss of her head changed his mind.

Sitting up on his knees, he grabbed two pillows off the couch, positioned them on the floor and then rolled Bethany onto her stomach on top of them. He adjusted her placement until her thighs were spread wide and her ass was propped up just right.

Bethany started to push herself up on her hands, but he stopped her with a gentle pressure on her back. She looked over her shoulder at him.

"Wyc? What are you doing?"

"You'll see. Relax."

She frowned at him.

"Fold your arms under your head," he instructed, "and rest your forehead on them."

She hesitated.

"Trust me," he said. "I would never do anything to harm this gorgeous ass of yours." He ran his hands up the back of her thighs, over her butt and down her back. Slow, massaging strokes he repeated until she did as he had said. He continued running his hands over her in long sweeps, feeling the tension in her muscles slowly ebb at his attentions.

When she was limp and pliant under his hands, he began to brush closer and closer to the cleft in her ass and her exposed pussy. His continual movements soon had his fingers sliding between her buttocks, lightly grazing her anus before continuing down to rub over her swollen folds. With each pass back up, he spread her slick cream over that puckered hole he intended loosen up some more tonight. She was too tight to take his cock yet, but eventually she'd be able to.

The thought of sinking into her ass sent a flickering sensation batting at the base of his spine like fiery butterfly wings. His balls started drawing up and his cock jerked. Drops of sweat rolled down the side of his face and he looked down to see pre-cum beading on the head of his cock. Hell, if just the thought of fucking her ass had him this close to the edge, he was going to make damn sure she was ready when he actually did take her like that. Otherwise, the chance of injuring her was too great, and he never wanted her to associate their lovemaking with hurting. The type of pain that brought pleasure, absolutely — and they'd have all their lives to learn each other's preferences, moods and fantasies — but the pain of injury due to his lack of care? No.

With that in mind, he reached for the small tube on the rug. Keeping one hand moving over her body, he used his teeth to unscrew the cap. As his hand moved over her ass again, he squirted some of the lube over his fingers and then rubbed it over her pussy lips. He wanted her to experience the warming lotion in an area she was familiar with his fingers working before moving on into more skittish territory.

Bethany jolted and her head snapped up.

"It's cold going on, but give it a minute. It'll heat up."

"What is it?" Her voice was husky, thick with slow-building desire.

"A warming lotion." He squeezed some more onto his fingers and inserted them deep into her cunt, scissoring them and twisting his wrist until he had coated her inside and out.

"From that little black bag?" Her pleasure-laden voice purred out like a kitten having its ears rubbed.

"Yes." He spread the lube up between her ass cheeks. Adding more when she began to rock backwards.

"Oh God. I hope you're going to fuck me soon, because that stuff is amazing."

The air rushed out of Wyc's lungs with the punch of lust that hit him right in the gut with her statement. Her desire licked at him with an urgency that nearly flattened him. He continued to massage her ass, but looked away and concentrated on counting the stones that covered the fireplace. When he was able to draw a steady breath again, he laid the lotion tube on the floor and deliberately spread the cheeks of her butt.

"Remember when I promised you I would fuck this tight little hole of yours?" His voice rasped out, low and dark. Bethany instantly froze. He traced the puckered opening with the tip of a finger. A shudder worked its way over her suddenly rigid body, leaving goose bumps in its trail.

"Now?" The word was breathy. Frightened. Excited.

He squeezed the firm curve of her left buttock. "No. You're too tight." And he didn't think she was mentally ready to be fully ass-fucked. He had a lot of plans for her, and none of them included scaring her off from any form of pleasure he could bring her.

Her breath rushed out and she sagged back into the pillows. Leaning over her, he pressed his heated skin to hers, sliding his cock suggestively against her ass.

"But we are going to stretch that snug channel, because eventually, I'm going to push my cock so far up your ass, you'll feel it in your throat."

* * * * *

"Oh God," Bethany moaned.

She couldn't think. Couldn't move. Couldn't do anything but grip the rug and wait. She was so freaking turned on it felt like a wildfire was burning through her cunt and traveling under her skin until she was sure sparks had to be shooting out of the tips of her fingers and toes.

The way Wyc settled over her, he covered her, surrounded her. The slide of his hard, sweat-slicked body over hers only increased her awareness of his incredible strength, his massive size. Surprised, she realized that instead of intimidating her, his position emanated protection, safety.

Wyc thrust his cock between her buttocks again. A forceful reminder of his promise that drenched her pussy with liquid lust.

"Mmm..." Wyc's low rumble of appreciation vibrated against her back. "The thought of my cock up your ass excites you, doesn't it?" He smoothed his hand over her hip and down around to cup her mound. "You crave me—I can sense the hunger in your mind, feel your arousal. And it's not just down here." He patted her pussy and she shot toward the peak of orgasm.

God, she was so close to climax! One more pat and she'd be there. Please, please, right there. Just one more time. She would have begged if she still possessed the ability to string together words in a coherent group. In an attempt to rock against his hand, she settled his cock in tighter between her buttocks.

"Oh, yeah, babydoll. Soon."

She moaned, a pleading fuck-me-now moan she was too desperate to try and muzzle.

He dragged his teeth over her neck. It wasn't a gentle gesture, scraping her skin sharply before he sucked in a loud breath and jerked straight up. Denied the cocooning warmth he had wrapped her in, she pressed the back of her thighs into firmer contact with his, inadvertently shoving her swollen, slick pussy against his cock.

"Goddamn, woman," Wyc ground out, "you drive me fucking crazy."

Her skin felt cold without his covering, but before she could complain, his large hands were on her again, rubbing, kneading, forcing her back into the pillows. And then he was pulling at her ass, separating her cheeks. Every muscle down her back stiffened.

"Don't tense up now," he said, circling her anus over and over with his lube-slick fingers. "You need to breathe. It will be easier if you're relaxed."

"Easier?" Her voice squeaked.

"Deep breaths, Bethany. Put your head back on your arms and concentrate on breathing."

Bethany pressed her forehead into the crook of her elbow and drew in a lungful of air. When he did no more than continue the gentle circling, her heart slowed to as close to normal as possible in her supercharged horny state. Until she felt something push into her asshole.

Her head snapped up, wrenching shoulders back. A big hand splayed over the middle of her back, slowing pushing her down again.

"Calm down, it's just the lube." As if to prove his point, he squeezed it into her.

She gasped as her ass filled with the cold, melted-jelly substance that immediately started to heat. There wasn't time for her to assimilate the sensation before Wyc had withdrawn the little nozzle and was rubbing the warming lotion over and inside her cunt again. Unable to hold still, she began to roll her hips and press into his hand.

While one set of fingers returned to massaging her anus, the other set played with her clit, flicking it, tapping it, tugging on it. Her muscles were coiling tighter and tighter, readying for an explosion. She slid her knees further apart and arched her back hard until her breasts were mashed into the rug.

"Feeling good?" he murmured.

Her affirmative answer came out as a muffled mewl. She was so close, she could see the match striking to light the truckload of fireworks set to go off in her body.

A slight pinching sensation in her butt dampened the impending display. It was quick—a brief stretching of her sphincter muscle before it constricted again. Only there was definitely part of an object inside her now, and her puckered hole gripped around something about the width of Wyc's finger. With even, small tugs and pushes on the object, he moved it up and down in her ass, sending licks of fire straight to her cunt.

Combined with the lotion and his fingers working her clit, her nerve endings immediately started to unravel. "What is that?" she rasped.

"Something that's going to prepare you to take me up your ass." He pushed slightly harder and she felt that same muscle stretch, the pinch a little more pronounced as a larger—bump?—was inserted inside her. With the two fingers he slid into her cunt simultaneously, the pinch was overridden by the novel pleasure of being twice filled and stretched.

Two fingers pulled out of her, then three fingers thrust in, spreading and flexing against the inner walls of her vagina. Another, larger bulge slid past her constricting muscle and her anus started to burn with the stretch. She gasped, tried to take a deep breath, settled for quick pants.

"You're doing great, babydoll."

Bethany had never heard Wyc's voice so ragged. So harsh with want. The knowledge that she could bring this dangerous, indomitable, absolute *man* to a state of desperate need—for her, for what she could give him—sent a shiver of utter satisfaction through her. She knew if she asked, he'd stop now. Even as far as they'd come, he'd stop.

She didn't want him to. Not just for him, but for her. He had been right. She did crave him. Wanted him every way she could have him.

Forcing herself to relax, she pushed back against him, offering.

Wyc cursed softly, shifted and then rammed his cock into her cunt, grinding it in to the hilt. Bethany screamed, tried to claw her way forward off the pillows. With one hard hand on her hip, he held her in place as he started to drive into her with a slow, steady rhythm.

Several great gulping breaths later and Bethany still hovered on the edge of madness. A sweet, enthralling madness that she reached for with every fiber of her body.

The fire in the fireplace crackled and flamed like the fire building in her lower body. Droplets of perspiration trickled down her back and over her shoulders, doing nothing to cool the blaze raging through her. Wyc's cock was solid heat without the warming lotion. With it, each thrust scalded ruthlessly. When he started twisting whatever the hell he had stuck up her butt, her brain stopped trying to understand the battering of sensation and simply gave over to the experience. Out of the depths of her soul came a long, low keening of desperate supplication.

Whether he was reading her emotions or her body, Wyc responded. He began to fuck her hard and fast. Her body gripped him, caressing and milking him through each long thrust until the unrelenting pressure of her approaching climax had every last nerve taut in excruciating expectation. Gasping, trying to find an anchor in the violent sensual storm, she looked back at Wyc and lost her breath at the sight.

She should be used to the power and virility that radiated from this man intent on making her his. He was beautiful. Thick waves of ebony silk for hair. Eyes, deep as the night outside the cabin and the color of darkest sapphire. His nose, straight and perfect, above a mouth that belonged on an angel but had the devil's own talent. Shoulders, arms, torso and thighs all delineated muscle and sinew. His body every inch stark planes and sharp angles. Not a single soft edge anywhere to blunt the effect of his appearance. Exertion and the cost of restraint had sweat glistening and running in rivulets down his chest. His fingers dug into her hip. The look in his eyes slammed into her with demand. She knew the moment he reached out and brushed her mind with his. Suddenly, what was happening to her body was nothing compared to the emotion he swamped her with. Then he twisted the plug in her ass, popped a fourth and even larger knob into her restrictive channel and banged into her cunt deep and hard, coming with a hoarse shout and scorching streams of cum.

It was the end of what her body could stand. She was filled beyond what she had thought possible, burning with pleasure and caught in the middle of an unbelievable climax of phenomenal force. She screamed. Writhed. Twisted and thrashed under his hold until her body simply collapsed. With muscles still trembling in aftershock as blackness crowded in, she slipped over the brink into welcomed unconsciousness.

* * * * *

Breath bellowed in and out of Wyc's lungs as he tried to adjust from the mind-numbing crush of absolute nirvana to the glaring reality of fucking a mate senseless.

"Bethany?" He pulled out of her, grimacing. The slide of his sensitive dick out of her still-throbbing cunt bordered on pain.

She didn't answer. Didn't show any sign of having heard him. Carefully, he removed the knobbed butt plug he had used and rolled her off the pillows. She flopped with dead weight onto the rug.

"Bethany?" The idea had been to distract her from the thought of leaving him, not to send her into a dead faint. He brushed her damp hair off her face and cupped her cheek. Finally, her eyes fluttered open. For a moment.

Just as quickly, they closed.

"Babydoll? Talk to me. How do you feel?"

"Tired," she mumbled. "Cold." Curling up in a ball, she scooted toward him, seeking warmth.

Wyc smiled and grabbed a folded blanket from cubbyhole next to the fireplace. Spreading it over them, he gathered her close.

He was exhausted. Elated. If someone had told him that making love to his mate would be a remarkably different, breath-stealing experience every time, he would have laughed in their face. Sex was good, occasionally great, but it was only sex.

Until Bethany. She was amazing. Each time he reached for her, it was like embarking on a journey to a new world. He knew her, but she always surprised him. When had she looked back at him over her shoulder tonight, her eyes glowing with demand and the same harsh need that was driving him, she once again ripped the reins of control out of his hands and made it possible for him only to ride with her through the storm. The lust that raged through him met and matched by her own.

She sighed and shifted closer. He looked down at the vision in his arms. Her head pillowed by his shoulder, her hair a dark cloud around her pale face. The black sweep of her lashes created shadowed half moons against the smooth skin of her cheeks. Her lips parted slightly on deep, even breaths. When she had moved closer, she reached her arm across her breasts so her hand could rest on his chest. A possessive gesture made in sleep that was too telling for her to make when she was awake.

He had known the second she had given in to the craving hunger she had for him. For what lie between them. She had made a choice tonight and had offered her body in acknowledgment. Seeing it for what it was, he had seized the opportunity. Using it to bind her another step irrevocably closer to where she belonged. With him. To him.

They should be mated by now. Each day that passed without the final rite being completed was like a fresh scourge on his soul. It burned with chilling portent inside him for reasons he couldn't explain. The threat of Predators and traitors exacerbated the feeling, they didn't instigate it. The soul-deep fear that, for some reason, Bethany would ultimately refuse to claim him as her mate. That once found, she'd be lost to him again.

Instinctively, he pulled her tightly against him until she murmured a sleepy protest.

He would not let her go. He would not lose her. He would not.

* * * * *

Something was tickling her ear. She scrunched her shoulder up. Burrowed deeper into the warm body next to her. The tickling stopped. Started again on her neck. She swatted at it with her hand. It brushed her fingers.

"Bethany, wake up." Wyc's voice was rough with sleep.

"No." Hers was rougher.

The tickling was back. Her cheek this time. She tried to roll away. A strong arm wrapped around her back and held her in place.

"I want you to see something."

"I saw it last night."

He chuckled. A rather jarring sensation against her chest. She squeezed her eyes shut harder until the skin gathered at the corners like a child's fold-up fan created out of a piece of art paper. If she ended up with early crow's feet, she was blaming Wyc.

"Not what I'm talking about." He pressed his impressive morning erection against her stomach. "Though we'll get there. Now open your eyes."

"I'm sleeping, damn it."

He tweaked her nipple.

She jolted. Cracked one eye open just enough to glare at him. "You are seriously pissing me off. And," she said with a sniff, "I don't even smell coffee."

He bracketed her jaw with one hand and turned her head to look over her shoulder.

Her other eye cracked open. The next second, they both flew wide. She flopped over and propped herself up to a half sitting position.

The view through the living room windows was beyond breathtaking. The cabin faced east, and the sun was just about to top the mountains in the distance. From their position on the floor, the sky took up all but the bottom fourth of the window, flooding the vista with the extravagance of color that could only be experienced firsthand at Mother Nature's generous bequest.

Rich, deep cobalt bled into lighter, softer blues that were little by little relinquishing their place to ever-increasing vibrant pinks until a fuchsia, bright enough to be gaudy on any canvas but the heavens, kissed the bottom of the horizon.

Bethany found herself holding her breath as fuchsia turned electric orange, heralding a thin glowing line of searing yellow that highlighted the uppermost peaks of the surrounding mountains. The brilliance increased, intensified between the two tallest mountains, centered in the panorama. Suddenly, golden rays engraved the sky in proclamation of the sun's arrival, and the drama of the previous act was outshined by the entrance of the main attraction.

She turned back to Wyc, the exclamation of amazement dying on her lips at the look in his eyes. He wasn't watching the sunrise as she expected. His penetrating gaze was zeroed in one hundred percent on her.

He took advantage of her lowered defenses and dived into her emotions, still raw from yesterday's constant struggle. She hadn't been awake long enough to fortify her mental barriers, and the breathtaking early morning show left her wide open for his probing regard.

The touch of his mind to hers snapped her out of the moment and she twisted away from him. Rattled at feeling so exposed—did she have to be naked as well?—she gestured toward the window with one hand and grabbed her shirt with the other.

"That was beautiful. Thank you."

Wyc was silent behind her. His only response, the calloused warmth of his palm sliding down her arm. The lingering intimacy of the moment continued to settle around them despite her uneasiness with it.

"I haven't seen a sunrise like that since I was twelve. Maybe I was thirteen. It was at a summer camp," she rambled, nervously tugging the T-shirt on over her head. It would help matters if Wyc got dressed too. Having his naked sexiness spread out beside her in all its aroused glory was making it extremely difficult not to abandon her efforts at detachment and simply throw herself on his body.

She looked around for her panties, gave up and reached for her jeans. "My newest set of foster parents was taking their kids to Disney World and said they couldn't afford to take me as well. So they dumped me at this low-budget nature camp in the middle of nowhere and—oh my God!" She dropped the jeans and spun around to look at Wyc.

"I remember something!"

Wyc's gaze snapped up from the, as of yet, still unclothed lower part of her body.

"It was at the camp. One of the counselors I met was young. Had just graduated high school. Her name was Elle…Ellen…Ella…something like that. She basically took me under her wing for the week I was there. Asked me a lot of questions and kept telling me how special I was. At the time, I just thought she was being nice."

She paused to catch her breath. Wyc waited, still reclining back on his elbows with one knee pulled up, but his rising tension was evidenced in the grooves of concentration etched between his eyes.

"The point is, once, when she leaned over to give me a hug, a ring she was wearing on a chain around her neck fell out of her shirt. It looked so similar to the one I had lost the year before, I grabbed it to take a closer look.

"When I asked her about it, she just shrugged it off, said it was a souvenir from a place she had been. The next time I saw her, she had taken it off. I'd forgotten all about it until now."

Wyc leaned up and tucked a curl behind her ear. "Do you remember what she looked like?"

Bethany nodded. "Short, spiky hair. Dark like mine, but she had put purple streaks in it. And her eyes were deep green and always seemed so serious. She had this way of looking at me when I talked to her that made me feel like everything I said was really important to her." She shrugged. "A novel experience for me at the time."

"Do you remember her last name?"

"We didn't call the counselors by their last names. But it was on their nametags." Bethany closed her eyes in an effort to remember. She could picture the teenager in her mind and tried to concentrate on the badge the workers were required to wear. A hazy memory was the best she could do. She opened her eyes and sighed.

"It began with a 'B'. Baily maybe? Brady? I'm pretty sure it ended with a "Y" because I remember thinking it looked a little like my first name."

Embarrassed, she turned her face back to the beauty outside the cabin. "It sounds silly now, but then, I took it as a sign we were supposed to meet. Helped with the whole not-good-enough-for-Disney-World incident."

Wyc brought her face around to his and the expression in his eyes would have melted her heart, if it wasn't already a puddle of mush from last night. He placed a soft kiss on her lips.

"I promise, I'll take you to Disney World as soon as it's safe enough to do so."

His hand slid around to the back of her neck and drew her back down to the rug with him.

"Do you think she could be one of my missing sisters? We did sort of look alike."

"Don't get your hopes up, Bethany. The age fits for your oldest sister, Ellyna, but we've run into a lot of coincidences in the two and a half decades of this search. We won't know for sure until we find her. *If* we find her."

Silent for a moment, she traced the outline of his Guardian tattoo. When she was finished, she looked up at him. "What was my name in Ilyria?"

"Eiyian."

Her nose wrinkled. "I think I'll stick with Bethany."

"Okay." He picked up her hand and started twisting the ring around her finger. "You can call yourself anything you want as long as you remember that you're mine."

It was too early to argue, so she ignored his last comment and watched him play with her ring. "You never told me how you got this," she said, wiggling the finger with the ring on it.

He brought her hand up to kiss her fingers. "A couple of years ago, we had tracked you to that little town outside of Denver where you had been living with the foster parents whose house burned down. Rordyc actually got your ring back."

"Where was it? I had always kept it with me, but I don't remember much about that night. I was in the hospital for days and when I got out, the state shipped me off to another family in a different city. It wasn't in the stuff they returned to me."

"A stripper was wearing it when Rordyc found it."

Bethany rolled her eyes. Wyc grinned.

"I'd be willing to bet you still had it on you when you were checked into the hospital. The stripper said she had gotten it from one of her mom's boyfriends who had worked there. Rordyc talked her into selling it."

"I bet he did."

Wyc laughed and reached for her shirt. She stopped him. "Don't we need to tell someone about what I remembered?"

"Yes," he said. Her shirt came off. "Later."

He pulled her down on top of him. She wasn't ready to let the subject drop. Was about to voice another protest when he took her mouth in a scorching kiss.

Leaning over on one arm enough to lift herself slightly up, she skimmed a hand down his chest to his erection. Hard, hot and ready. Just like the man. It had been over twelve years since she'd been at that camp. Waiting another hour or so to relay the information wasn't going to hurt anything.

Wrapping her hand around the base of his cock, she squeezed gently. Slowly, she slid her hand up to the top, squeezed again and circled the sensitive head with her thumb.

Wyc broke from the kiss, dropped his head back and groaned. "Make that much later."

Bethany smiled at Wyc's uninhibited response to the pleasure she gave him and determined to press her lead.

Keeping the leisurely sliding up, squeezing, sliding down, squeezing, rhythm on his cock with her hand, she kissed the underside of his chin. He grabbed her butt and began kneading, one ass cheek in each hand. His unshaven skin pricked her lips and she switched to scraping nips with her teeth over his jawline up to the sharp angle where it connected just under his ear. She bit his earlobe hard enough to sting, and his retort was a playful slap on her ass.

"So," she purred in his ear, "you don't appreciate my mouth up here." With a quick, soothing flick over the teeth marks she had made, she scooted backwards, dusting light kisses down the center of his body. "Maybe," she said, lightly circling the flared ridge of his cock with the tip of her tongue, "you'll appreciate what it does down here."

Wyc's cock jerked in response. Bethany grinned. "That's better."

"I agree." His words were tight, strained.

Suddenly Bethany dipped her head and took the entire head of his cock into her mouth, sucking hard and rubbing the flat of her tongue over the tip. Wyc bucked underneath her.

"Shit, woman! You need to warn a man before you do something like that."

Swirling her tongue over the hot head, she tasted the pre-cum beading out of the little slit. She glanced up, caught his narrowed gaze. Forcefully sucked on him. Wrapped both hands firmly around his thickness and slid them up from the base of his shaft to her lips.

She smacked her lips and released him. "Is that a complaint?" she asked, giving his erection a harder squeeze with her hands. Wyc's remarkable chest expanded on a deeply indrawn breath. Bethany suppressed a grin at the struggle working across his features. She laved the top of his cock. "Well?" She couldn't keep the teasing, singsong smugness out of her voice.

His head fell back as his breath rushed out. "Hell, no."

"I thought not."

* * * * *

He was a dead man.

The unrestrained exploration of her mouth and tongue was truly paradise. She kept testing out different strokes with her tongue that made it a struggle of pure agonizing delight to hold back his orgasm just to see what she'd try next. He almost lost the fight when she flattened her tongue near his base and dragged it all the way up in one long, firm lick, and then finished it off with quick, darting licks around his slit like a greedy kitten with its milk. Another time, he'd tell her which techniques he preferred, but right now he was more than content to let her experiment and learn him in her own way.

Once he was sure he had a modicum of control again, he lifted himself on his elbows to watch Bethany work his cock. Seeing his dick disappear into his mate's mouth was the most erotic thing he had ever witnessed. Pink lips stretched in a perfect "O" around his width. Her dark hair brushing his thighs. Her tongue lapping at him eagerly as she sucked him into a hot, wet heaven. And the look on her face. Dear God.

She was enjoying going down on him.

Definitely a dead man.

She released one hand and used it to cup his balls. Her fingers so gentle as they stroked his soft sacs. He bent his knees, drew them up and widened the space between his thighs to give her more room to work.

Bethany licked her way down his cock and over the seam that separated his balls. He groaned low in his throat when she traced that sensitive line down and around, nearly coming out of his skin when she flicked at his perineum.

Her head popped up, a concerned look on her face. "Did that hurt?"

He shook his head. Leaned forward and ran his fingers through her hair. "No. Oh no. It feels fantastic. Totally, completely, amazing."

She smiled and took him back into her mouth.

Propping himself back on his elbows, he hissed through his teeth. "That is so good, so good."

Turning her head to the side, she took more of him into her mouth. And then even more. A shallow thrust of his hips and he went in even deeper.

"That's it, babydoll. Take me in. As much as you can handle. Eat me up."

He tried to not move, to let Bethany take him in at her own pace, but the fantasy fuck she was giving him made it impossible. He wanted to see her swallow all of him. He started to thrust into her mouth. Shallow, slow movements.

She glanced up at him, a wicked gleam in her eyes. Wyc stilled.

That look made him nervous as hell. Especially with his dick in such a vulnerable position. It wasn't the first time he wished he knew what was going through her head, but it damn sure was the strongest.

Bethany closed her eyes. Shifted to sit up on her knees. Her tongue and mouth relaxed. Slowly, goddamn fucking slowly, she lowered her head. When her lips reached the hand she still had wrapped around him, she took a deep breath, moved her hand and continued swallowing him.

Her teeth scraped the sides of his cock as she took him deeper. *Fuck.* Her tongue massaged the underside of his cock as she convulsively swallowed around him. *Goddamn fuck.* The restriction of her mouth eased around the head of his cock as it passed into the space behind her tongue. *Fuck. Goddamn fuck.* Tightened almost painfully around his sensitive head as she kept sliding down, pushing him deep into the narrow channel of her throat until she had all of him in her mouth. *Fuck! Goddamn fucking fuck!*

A dark, dangerous lust rose inside him. Primitive in its ferocity. Unheeding of civilized restraints. Simply needing. Demanding. A harsh sound tore its way out of his chest and Bethany's eyes opened to dart a quick look up at him. For a startling second, her stunned gaze froze on his face, on the primal being she had released reflected there.

"Hmmm…" she hummed while she raised her head, the sound reverberating like a shockwave through his cock as her lips dragged up his entire throbbing length. "I'm starting to feel more appreciated."

Without a word, he jerked up. Grabbed her by the hips. Twisting, he lay back on the rug with her knees on either side of his head, her thighs spread and her pussy open and ready over his face.

Bethany yelped in surprise, but quickly regained her balance. The soft press of her breasts into his stomach as she shifted more comfortably in place had him growling in pleasure. Her inner thighs were slick where her pussy juice had dripped, and her cunt had darkened to a beautiful deep pink. He reached around her back with both hands, grabbed her ass and pressed her down to his mouth.

Refusing to dampen the wildness she had unchained, he took her cunt without any preliminaries. Just hot mouth to hotter cunt, working her ruthlessly. Once he had her securely in place, his tongue swirling between her folds and over her clit, he reached for the little black bag from last night. Pulled the small metal object out and held it tightly in his fist to warm as he tongue-fucked his woman.

Bethany had wrapped her lips around his cock again. The harder he ate at her pussy, the faster she sucked and licked. Every time he squeezed her ass with his free hand, she pushed backwards and purred in enjoyment, her whimpers and moans of ecstasy vibrating from his cock through his entire body like an electric current.

Gently, he skimmed his fingers into her crevice and over her anus. The shudder that skated down her spine let him know she was aware of what he was doing. But he only brushed the puckered opening. He wouldn't probe or stretch it this morning. It was probably still tender from last night. Pulling his fingers away, he gave her buttock another hard squeeze.

Her cream smeared his face as he ground his mouth against her. Its earthy, womanly scent unique to his mate. He loved the smell and taste of her arousal. Loved the proof of what he did to her.

Her thighs shook against the sides of his head as she built toward climax. He thrust his tongue deep inside her and her cunt pulsed with the early tremors of release.

Quickly, he turned the little vibrating egg he held in his hand on high and shoved it deep into her cunt. Then he fastened his opened mouth over her pussy, sucking hard and rubbing her swollen clit with his tongue.

Bethany immediately released his dick. Screamed. Bucked hard against him. He held her clamped to his face with his hands pressed hard into the sweet flesh of her ass.

Heat flooded her pussy, scorching his tongue. Fresh, hot cream flowed from her opening. Her thighs pressed and released, pressed and released with the contractions of her climax. Writhing and rearing up, she rode his face like a wild woman on the back of an untamed animal. Still he held her locked to him. Forced her to accept every moment of bliss.

When the quaking of her body faded to a light shivering, Wyc pulled the vibrating egg out of her vagina, turned it off and dropped it on the rug. He continued to lick the cream from her pussy and thighs as she lay on top of his body, a boneless mass of sated woman. Her head rested on his inner thigh, her rough breaths blowing hot over his engorged cock.

After a minute, he felt the swipe of her tongue over his shaft. His teeth snapped together with an audible click as the effects of that single action blasted through his nervous system to explode behind his eyes in a fiery finale.

Bethany pushed to her hands and knees, straddling his body with her cunt hovering over him still wet and red from her recent climax. She took him in one hand, bent down, her hard little nipples branding his abdomen, and closed her mouth over him. He groaned and reached for her breasts.

It soon became evident that she had been paying attention earlier. Again and again she sucked hard on the head, followed by one firm, continual lick down and back up his entire length before covering his tip with lightning-fast flicks.

In his hands, her breasts swelled and her nipples chafed his palms. Over him, her pussy swayed back and forth just inches from his face. No way in hell was he going to last very long with this show going on. Another long sweep of her tongue down his cock and her pussy rocked forward, gifting him with the sight of the tight little hole he planned on fucking.

This time, when she reached the base of his shaft, her tongue swirled over his balls. The muscles in his back clenched, his hands tightened on her breasts and he broke out into feverish sweat. By the time she licked her way back up to the head of his cock, he was set to detonate.

The moment he felt her mouth open around his cock, his hips surged up, pushing himself deep inside.

Bethany didn't balk. Bracing herself with both hands on the floor, she held herself steady for his thrusts. At first he tried to hold back, to make sure this was what Bethany wanted because it sure as hell was answering his most fervent prayers at the moment. She moved her tongue side to side in her mouth against his shaft and hummed her encouragement.

Wyc's balls drew up tight and his hips bucked involuntarily. In his mind, he remembered how it looked for her to swallow his entire dick, her hair falling in a silky curtain around her face, lips stretched taut, eyes closed with concentration as she loved him. Above him, her labia began to swell again, the little nub between them poking out with pouty insistence. A drop of pussy juice slid from her cunt and down her thigh. She was getting turned on by eating him.

Fuck!

Every thread of control he had left snapped clean off. His hips came off the ground and stayed off the ground as they pistoned hard and fast. The head of his cock butted against the back of her throat and then down it. His climax tore through him with blinding speed as ecstasy gripped him and ripped his release out of him in pulsing, fiery streams.

His neck arched, tendons straining. His stubbled chin scraped Bethany's pussy and she jolted as he matched the roar of his blood with a roar that echoed through the cabin.

Bethany released his cock and rolled off him. For long moments, they lay beside each other, breathing hard and staring at the ceiling. When he was able, he lifted his hand and rested it on the top of her thigh.

"Did you come when my chin scraped against you?" he asked, still fighting his labored breathing.

"Yes," she whispered. Her breathing sounded no better.

"Good."

Silence ruled again as neither had the energy to speak, let alone move. If he had his way, he'd keep Bethany naked and on this rug for weeks. He wouldn't let her up until she took him as her mate. Hell, even then he'd keep her naked as long as she'd let him.

Every time they came together she simply and totally undid him. Until he found Bethany, he'd resigned himself to a bleak life of duty to responsibilities as a royal heir. But in his mate, he found a sweetness and vibrancy to life he'd thought he'd lost forever. The woman made him lose his control, act like a raging lunatic and often made his life a living hell. But every time she gifted him with another piece of herself and reached out to trust him, it was worth it.

Soon, she'd trust him enough to fully accept him as her mate. Soon.

But not soon enough. Not with the threat to her life still out there.

He glanced out the window. The sun was fully up now, warm beams of light streaming through the windows. Outside, birds chattered, and the wind occasionally rustled the aspens flanking the house, making soft shushing noises when the branches brushed the log siding. Nearly indiscernible over the heavy scent of sex that permeated the room was the smell of burned candles and the barely smoldering fire.

He needed food and Bethany needed coffee. Next time, he'd remember to set the timer on the coffeepot and put emergency rations within arm's length. He thought about moving again. His body didn't respond. The only thing that changed position was his eyelids. They closed.

"Goddamn, woman. One of these days you're going to fucking kill me."

"It's only fair," she replied, languid amusement coloring her voice. "Since you're trying to kill me with fucking."

* * * * *

For at least the hundredth time that afternoon, Bethany circled through the house. Replaying the conversation she had with Wyc right before he left.

"Stay in the house until I get back," he said. "I'm not going far and shouldn't be gone long."

"Don't worry. I'll be fine."

"Stay in the house," he repeated.

"I heard you the first time."

"I'm not questioning your hearing. I'm questioning your doing."

Okay, so her track record hadn't been the best in following through with what he asked her to do. But not all of it had been her fault. And besides, being hunted was a brand-new experience for her. The closest she had ever come to playing the part of prey was when an overeager frat boy had followed her home. But just the threat of a face full of pepper spray had him off to search for a quick lay in a more amenable field.

Bethany looked down at the light wooden floor polished to a high sheen and considered counting the slats. God, she was losing it. Bored, bored, bored. If there had only been a TV in the house it would have helped. But unless it was hidden behind a secret panel, she was out of luck.

After stretching her shower out to the longest in her life, she dressed in jeans and a clean blouse, remembering to put on a bra this time. She prowled through the house, looking for something to do, something to read. But she gave up on Rordyc's choice of reading material after thumbing through a copy of the *Kama Sutra*, *The Joy of Sex*, a volume detailing Tantric sex and a sex toy manual that cleared up the mystery to several of the items in the bedroom's armoire.

There were plenty of other options, including an entire shelf of erotic fiction, but she didn't need any help with horniness at the moment, thank you very much. Especially since Wyc was taking so damn long to return.

At one point, she had found herself in the kitchen staring at the flour jar with the thought of passing the time baking a mouthwatering treat from scratch. But ten minutes of trying to come up with what one added to flour besides chocolate chips to make cookies cured that absurd idea.

She even tried to whittle a stick with the knife Kayn had given her, but for the life of her couldn't see the point to making a small stick smaller. She had ended up flicking the blade open and shut for close to an hour like some jaded ex-con from a B-movie sitting on a run-down stoop, waiting for life to give him a break.

Cabin fever sucked. Stir crazy from being so bored, she refused to consider she was actually missing Wyc. He had only been gone, what? Five, six hours? And he had called to check on her. Once.

God. What the hell was she going to do when he walked out of her life for good?

She couldn't go there. Not after spending the night and morning in his arms. Not when his whisker burn was freshly faded from her inner thighs and breasts.

He had said he wasn't going far, but he had sure been gone a long time for someone sticking close. She looked out the bedroom window and then walked into the living room for another lap around the couch.

She had wanted to go with him to talk to Rordyc, but didn't argue when he refused to take her. She agreed that she needed to stay hidden until they discovered how she was being tracked, especially since the first Predator to have found her was still out there. The thought of ever coming face-to-face with Enath again sent a cold chill down her spine. She hugged her arms close around her body, the beautiful house suddenly feeling too big and too empty. Damn. Where was Wyc?

Footsteps crossing the planked porch kicked her heartbeat into high gear. She ran across the living room and yanked the door open.

"It took you—"

In less time than it took to blink, the world froze around Bethany. The heart that been racing in expectation crashed into her ribs and came to a sudden stop.

Enath stood framed in the doorway, a sneer stretching over his loathsome features. "Miss me?"

Bethany was running before she even realized she had turned away from him. Heading toward the French doors in the bedroom. Blood roared in her ears with the fear pounding through her veins.

The Predator wasn't slowed by his bulk. She hadn't gotten past the couch when his hard hands clamped into her flesh. His fingers dug into her arms and he yanked her back against his body.

"You're mine now, bitch."

Chapter Fourteen

∽

Bethany's emotional terror ripped through Wyc's mind. Like being body-slammed against a brick wall, the effect was brutally crushing. For a moment that passed like a century, fear held his feet to the ground, froze his breath in his lungs and took every coherent thought captive.

And then he was running. Transforming. Not taking the time to strip in order to completely alter his state. Concentrating solely on reaching Bethany. Taking a giant leap off two feet and landing on four. The distance disappeared beneath him, but it wasn't fast enough.

He was too far from her to have heard a scream with his ears, but the intensity of her distress howled through the connection he held to her. Her terror and panic sliced through every emotion he had, leaving his soul in shreds.

Fuck it! If he had made her complete the Mating Rite, he would have felt her danger long before her very life force cried out in mortal fear. He would know exactly where she was, would be drawn directly to her. Instead, if she wasn't where he told her to be, he might not find her in time. Just once, please, all deities in all the heavens, let Bethany be where he had told her to stay.

* * * * *

Bethany screamed and thrashed against Enath. Kicked back with her heels, connecting several times. It made no difference as Enath dragged her out the front door of the cabin.

He forced her around the side of the house, her heels leaving deep grooves in the ground as her fight to get free escalated alongside her panic. She stared in disbelief when she saw where he was taking her. A shimmering circle hung in the air halfway down the path to the lake.

"You can't take me through a portal. I won't step through of my own free will."

"You have no idea how persuasive I can be." The amusement in his voice infuriated her beyond her fear.

With a volatile hiss, she wrenched an arm free. Clawed at the hand still holding her. Enath cursed and jerked her nearly off her feet. When she stumbled, he grabbed her arm again and twisted it up behind her until she cried out. Not once had he stopped moving toward the portal.

"You should know," he said close to her ear, sending spittle flying across her shoulder, "I enjoy finding exactly what it takes to make a woman beg me to take her through the portal just so I'll stop playing with her, even for a moment." His hand snaked around her waist and up to her breast. He fondled it roughly and then pinched her nipple until she gasped from the pain.

He released her breast and slid his hand between her legs. "We're going to have a lot of fun."

She let out a snarl of outrage and bucked against him.

"That's good," he crooned. "Fight me. It ruins the challenge if you break right away."

His hips ground against her backside and Bethany fought down the nausea making her stomach lurch wildly. What had Wyc told her about Predators? Their two areas of vulnerability — their throat and the very center of their chest. Neither of which she could reach the way he held her. Damn it. Where was Wyc?

He had been able to touch her mind. Could she reach his?

She tried to concentrate. Focus on Wyc. Find a connection.

Nothing. Save her own mounting panic as Enath continued to heave her closer and closer to the portal. The arm he had twisted behind her back began to throb and her nostrils filled with the scent of her own terror.

Giving up on trying to reach Wyc through a mental bond she had no idea if she could even use, she tipped her head back and screamed. A piercing, desperate cry that echoed through the mountains, carrying the sound of her fury and despair through the clear mountain air.

Enath's jaw clapped shut with an audible, sharp click and the deep warning sound of a deranged beast spiraled out of his chest. Bethany strained against his hold and screamed again.

The Predator shook her with a force that had her head snapping back and forth. "Shut up, bitch. Quit making that noise."

She took a deep breath and prepared to let loose the loudest, shrillest scream of her life.

He released the grip he had on her pussy and slapped his hand over her mouth. His move freed the arm that had been trapped against her side.

Shoving her hand in her pocket, she slid her fingers around the cold, comforting shape of the switchblade Kayn had given her.

Enath shifted his hold again. With one hand still over her mouth, his other arm wrapped completely around her upper torso, flattening her breasts with his forearm and pinning her back to his chest.

He spun her toward the portal and she saw it flicker. Shrink. Enath's movements became tinged with urgency as he shoved her forward.

She yanked the knife out of her pocket, pressed the blade open and stabbed it into the arm vised around her chest.

Blood spurted and soaked into her shirt. He howled in pain. Released her to pull the knife out of his arm.

Bethany dropped to the ground. He lunged at her, slashing the knife before him. She rolled away from the wild swing of the blade.

Her feet tangled in his as he turned to lash out at her again. He tripped, tumbled toward the fading portal. Bethany drew back her legs, and with the full force of her fury marshaled for attack, hit him with a kick powerful enough to shove him directly into the portal.

Enath let loose a vicious shout of rage as he was sucked from this world. The gateway undulated like a puddle disturbed by a stone as it swallowed the Predator.

Bethany scrambled to her feet and backed away from the spot where the portal flickered erratically for several seconds before disappearing completely. She stood, shaking, too afraid to blink, watching the air and waiting for it to shimmer again and release the monster back to her. Her chest heaved on a sob of relief and shock when Enath failed to reappear. Her head spun with the dizzy elation of being awarded life in the face of certain death. Wrapping her arms around her middle with viselike force, she concentrated on stopping the racking shudders convulsing her body.

Suddenly, from behind her, something large moved over the ground straight toward her.

A cry of battered outrage nearly choked her as she spun to confront the new threat.

* * * * *

Wyc cleared a fallen tree and landed in time to see Enath stumble backwards and disappear through a dimming portal. The Predator's shout of rage followed him out of this world, fading as the shimmering gateway shrunk into oblivion.

Shit. Since when were the Sleht able to start activating unsupported portals? They couldn't. Unsupported portals only opened by the free will of a Keeper and were held in place with royal blood. More evidence that Rordyc's fear of treachery within the Ilyrian nobility was more on target than he would have believed.

Wyc jerked to his feet, barely having time to return to his natural form before Bethany spun around, fear and rage stamped on her face and in her straining muscles and fisted hands. She blinked, registered his presence and threw herself at him. Her hands clutched his shirt, and her body shook in his arms.

"I stayed where you told me to," her voice wobbled over the words. "I didn't leave. I wanted to, I was so bored, but I didn't—"

"I know, babydoll. I know." He brushed his lips across the top of her head. "Shhh."

Too relieved she was alive, he could do no more than hold her, rocking her close to his chest. Trapping her tightly against him, he tried to quench the desperate need to reassure himself that she was all right. Not taken, not injured, not dead.

When her trembling subsided, he pulled back enough to see her face. It was pale, her eyes wide with shock and blood smeared across her cheek.

Fear scraped its icy nails down the inside of his skin as he realized there was also blood staining one side of her shirt. Gently, he lowered her to the ground and then ripped her blouse open with a savage movement that popped buttons off to land lost in the grass.

"Where are you hurt, Bethany? What did that bastard do to you?" Wyc felt the cold sweep of panic as he took in the amount of blood but couldn't find the wound. If he didn't get the bleeding stopped soon, he could still lose her. She was trying to tell him something, but he couldn't hear over the roar of his own breath rushing in and out of his lungs.

Bethany closed her hands over his and stopped his frantic movements. "I'm not hurt. It's Enath's blood."

He inhaled the scent of the crimson stain. Not Bethany's. Enath's. He should have recognized the smell immediately. But seeing Bethany covered in blood froze everything in his mind except the lashing fear that his life had just ended.

"I'm fine." She gave him a reassuring smile that wasn't reassuring at all given her face had as much color as a corpse and her eyes were still glazed and dilated from the horror of what she had just lived through.

"Well, I'm sure the hell not," he growled and tore the shirt from her body. He had no patience for tender expressions of love and gratitude. She was alive. Unhurt. And he needed her. Now. Needed to have her body wrapped around his, letting him know for certain that she was unharmed. That she was whole. That he was whole. Because without her, he would not be complete. Would never be again.

"Wyc, I—" Bethany froze, her terrified gaze fixed on a spot above his right shoulder. At the same moment, he heard a shuffling step on the grass behind him.

Instinctively, Wyc pushed away from her and kicked back in the direction her eyes had focused. His foot connected with solid flesh, and as he rolled to his feet, he watched Enath stumble backwards into a tree. He heard Bethany scurry away to a safe distance, and with that knowledge, allowed his concentration to laser onto the menace facing him.

The Predator snarled, his lips curling away from his teeth. Bright red scratches slashed across his cheek and down his neck. Blood ran in thin rivulets down his left arm and dripped from his fingers. His flat, beady eyes narrowed, and he crouched to spring.

Wyc had never welcomed a chance to take out a Predator so much in his life. The sharp, consuming anguish of almost losing Bethany coalesced into one solid mass of hate for the creature before him. The need to avenge his brothers' deaths paled in the face of the fury of nearly having his woman taken from him. Simply for touching her, Enath would die.

Suddenly, a rock zinged past his head and hit Enath hard on the temple. If Enath hadn't jerked out of the way at the last minute, it would have nailed him right in the middle of the forehead.

For less than an instant, Enath's eyes flicked over to Bethany, unrestrained violence blackening his gaze. He lifted the arm that had a long, ragged gash in it and shook drops of blood into the grass.

Wyc realized that whatever had happened between Enath and Bethany before he arrived, Enath was now taking this retrieval personally. Anger had submerged the Predator's strictly trained responses. A low, furious hum vibrated from the Sleht's throat and the edges of his eyes twitched erratically.

"First, I'm going to kill you," Enath hissed, sending spittle flying from the side of his mouth, "and then I'm going to make that bitch of yours suffer in ways she's never begun to imagine." He swiped at the thin trail of blood trickling into his eye from the wound the rock had inflicted.

Wyc almost smiled. Bethany. He had never asked her what position she played on her softball team. His bet would be pitcher. Two more large rocks whizzed through the air following Enath's declaration. One slammed into the Predator's shoulder and the other hit just below his ear. Enath let out a deafening bellow and charged.

Wyc twisted out of the way as Enath surged toward him. Enath lunged sideways as he fell, snagging Wyc's leg and tumbling them both down together. They rolled over the rough ground, each grappling for the dominant position.

Enath was fighting out of emotion, clawing and reaching for Wyc with reckless fury. Wyc thrust a knee into the Predator's chest, of one of the two soft spots on his body, and clubbed him in the head in the same place Bethany's first rock had landed.

Howling in rage and pain, Enath began swinging wildly, groping for a hold. Wyc took advantage of the blood slicking Enath's hands and slid easily out of the Predator's grip.

They rolled again, and Enath landed with the force of a tank on top of Wyc, forcing the air from his lungs. Before Enath could benefit from his position, another well-aimed rock cracked him above his eye, snapping his head back.

Wyc surged up, dislodging the Predator's weight. He twisted and let his opponent's own unbalanced momentum carry him down. His fist plowed into the middle of Enath's face, slamming the back of his head into the rocky ground.

He pinned him down and shoved his hand under the Predator's chin, seeking the only vulnerable, irreparable organ in his enemy's body. Enath tore at Wyc's hands and arms, but Wyc forced his fingers in deeper, piercing through the tough skin. Ignoring the desperate clutching and the jawbone grinding against the bones of the back of his hands, Wyc pushed further into the soft, slick tissue of Enath's throat.

With a final thrust, his fingers pushed past the surrounding muscle to the breathing passage that was the key to the Predator's death. Wyc found the small tube, and with the move he had practiced from the first day of his military training, wrapped his hand around it and crushed it.

Enath began to writhe in his death frenzy. Unfortunately for Wyc, the crushing of the Sleht's breathing passage had no effect on his ability to speak. Even as the tube began to fuse together under his hands, Enath cursed Wyc, Bethany and any resulting progeny in the vilest and most creative manner he had ever heard.

Suddenly, Enath quit bucking underneath him and a smug, grim smile stretched the corners of his mouth even as his eyes began to gray in death.

"Are you wondering how I found your mate, Ilyrian? For once, I didn't have to waste precious time tracking you." His tongue, already reverting to its natural black, forked state, darted out to lick lips swollen and bloody. "And your brothers? Ever think about why their bodies were never found? Or returned in the manner favored by my people?" His grotesque grin faltered briefly as pain flashed through his eyes. "And Kilth? You haven't avenged your brothers' deaths by killing me. They didn't have the honor of dying by my hand."

Before Wyc could process his words, the Predator's eyes glazed from gray to white. He was dead, and any explanation to the taunts were confined to a realm Wyc's limited powers were useless to reach.

The reference to his brothers touched a spot in his heart he had closed off years ago. A small corner harboring the hope that the message of their deaths and the witnesses he had interrogated afterwards had all been wrong.

He slid his hands from around Enath's neck. He would not be drawn away from his mate to hunt down the possible truth to the vicious last words of a hated enemy. Even for another lead regarding his brothers' murders. There would be a time when his vengeance would be satisfied, but it wasn't now.

He pushed the final ramblings of the Predator out of his mind. He had a mate to protect and return to their homeworld. A mate who had nearly been taken from him.

Unless they had told someone else, only Rordyc and Amdyn knew where he had taken Bethany. But if the Predator didn't track them here—and with all the precautions in place, there was little, if any, chance he could have—that left only one other answer.

Betrayal. Again.

One of the few he had trusted with his life, and even more importantly, that of his mate's, was a traitor.

He heaved Enath over his shoulder and crossed the short distance to the shoreline. Walking into the water up to his thighs, he tossed the Predator's body toward the center of the lake. With vicious swipes, he used the water to rub dirt and blood from his face and arms. The least he could do before taking his mate.

It was past time for them to finish the final step in the Matching Ritual. Bethany was his, and he would be damned if she wasn't going to take him as hers. Now.

Chapter Fifteen

80

Bethany watched as Wyc ran his hands through his hair, pushing the wet strands away from his face. With fingers clenched into his palms, he stalked out of the lake. She wanted to run to him and throw herself into his arms. She wanted to feel the hardness of his chest against her hands, press her face into his neck and inhale his masculine, virile and very *alive* scent.

But pure, simple elemental fear stopped her. The hands she burned to have caress her had just destroyed a trained killer by brutally crushing his throat. Not exactly the stuff love songs were made of. As if he had ever mentioned love in the first place.

The one time she had voiced her true feelings for him, he had yanked himself from her like she had jabbed a red-hot poker into his gut. No, throwing herself at him was not an option.

Stepping onto the bank, he pulled off his tattered shirt and used it to scrub away the remaining dirt on his upper body. His mouth hardened in a grim line and cuts and bruises tattooed his body. Harsh triumph blazed in his eyes. Primeval power radiated out from him to wash over her in indomitable waves. Crashing over her will and leaving submission her only recourse.

Wyc dropped his shirt and searched the deepening shadows. Express and stark possessiveness marked his features as he scanned the trees looking for her. Crouched next to a large oak with her arms wrapped around her, Bethany felt the force of his gaze the instant he found her.

"Come here, Bethany."

She didn't move. Couldn't. Her eyes locked onto his hands as he unbuckled his belt. Every fluid movement completed with a mesmerizing rhythm and force. Even as a man, he conveyed the same dangerous grace and deadly power of the animal he became when attacked.

"Come here," he repeated, harsher.

She shook her head.

He removed his belt. His voice lowered to a velvet threat. "Do you really want me to come and get you?"

She shook her head again.

"Then come here." A command. Sharp. Hard.

She took a step forward and he unsnapped his jeans with a flick of his wrist. She froze again. He finished unfastening his pants.

"Babydoll, you're starting to try my patience." He stripped out of the rest of his clothes and closed the distance between them.

"It's time, Bethany. There's no going back. Even if you could, I wouldn't let you. You're mine, and it's time you took me as yours."

Stunned by his words, she didn't resist when he knelt before her and unlaced her tennis shoes. She had to lean forward and hold onto his shoulders to keep herself upright. His skin was hot to the touch. From her position, she could see the play of muscles down his back and arms. His hair, a fall of thick black silk over his shoulders.

He lifted her feet to gently tug first one and then the other shoe off. It was such a humble action, yet Wyc performed it with forceful dignity.

Visceral strength shimmered off him. She pressed her fingers into the corded muscles of his shoulders. Felt his strength under her hands as surely as she felt it in her heart.

Strength to fight and conquer. Strength to protect and shelter. Strength to love.

The sheer potency of all that Wyc Kilth was overwhelmed her. Crumbling her final defiance against the destiny he had been goading her toward. Only now he wasn't pushing, pulling or persuading. He was insisting. He was her destiny.

He raised his head and reached for the snap on her jeans.

"Wyc," Bethany whispered, suddenly afraid of a future shrouded in the mist of a world foreign and frightening. With a frantic surge of fear, she tried to push his hands away.

He flicked her efforts away with an impatient gesture and finished undoing her zipper. Smoothing his hands over her hips, he soothed her with a tender kiss below her navel and then pressed his cheek against her stomach, holding her tight and secure until her rush of fear receded and she was breathing again.

Bethany sank her teeth into her bottom lip when he relaxed his hold and slipped his fingers under the waistband of her panties to push them down with her jeans. He stopped at her ankles, waiting for her to lift her feet and step free from her clothes.

She hesitated a brief moment before obeying his unspoken command. He tossed her clothes aside and straightened. Reaching around her back, he unsnapped her bra. Instinctively, she brought her arms up to keep it from falling from her body. Without taking his unwavering gaze from her eyes, he passed his hands from her shoulders to her wrists, gently unbending her arms and removing her last remaining item of clothing.

Wyc took her left hand and removed the Ilyrian ring she wore. Raising her right hand, he slid the ring onto her middle finger. He held her right hand flat against his left so that their rings touched. An electric jolt speared through her, and she tried to pull her hand away. He intertwined his fingers with hers and refused to let her go.

"What do you want from me?" she whispered.

"I told you."

She shook her head. "Take you as mine? I don't know what that means."

He splayed his free hand over her back and slowly drew her to him until their bodies met in a binding crush from thigh to chest. His erection, hard and hot, pressed into her stomach. She had to tilt her head up to see his face. The fire she felt from her own need was echoed in his eyes. He kept a tight grip on her hand with the ring on it.

"You are mine, Bethany Mitchell. Now. Forever. Body, heart and soul. Kept for and by me, free to live completed in my love."

Bethany's mouth dropped open. Wyc's mouth turned up in a contemplative, sexy smile.

"What? You thought you were the only one in love here?"

"I just…I mean, you never… Yes. That's what I thought."

For a split second, anger flared in the dark depths of his eyes, and he tightened his hold on her. Then he lowered his mouth to hers in a fierce, quick kiss.

"You were wrong. Now it's your turn."

She blinked hard and swallowed. Her whole being cried out to possess him, to take him. On the same primal level of needing her next breath, she needed Wyc. Wanted him. Yet even as she stood on the edge of her desire, she was unsure.

"Bethany." His voice rumbled deep in command and impatient entreaty.

Letting out a stuttered breath, she raised her eyes to his. And saw the promise there. The absolute, unconditional offering of love. Her world shifted, and each unsettled piece of her heart slammed into place.

She raised her free hand and cupped his cheek in her palm. A long moment passed as she ran her thumb over his bottom lip and tried to absorb every facet of his face. Intensity lived there, at home in the sharp lines and striking planes. A hard-lined mouth that could tenderly but ruthlessly tease her toward oblivion. Dark brows slashed over hot, night-blue eyes half hidden under lowered lids. Waiting for her answer. Hoping.

"You are mine, Wyc Kilth." Her words, faint at first, grew stronger with each syllable. "Now. Forever. Body, heart and soul. Kept for me and by me, free to live complete in my love."

She paused. Frowned. "Did I get it right?"

"It's not the words that make the vow." He brushed a kiss into her palm. "It's the intent of the heart."

He curved a hand around her head and held her to his chest. She could hear the thunder of his heartbeat under her ear as he pressed a soft kiss into her hair. "Yes. You did it right."

He skimmed his other hand up her back and then down to grasp the curve of her bottom and squeeze. "About damn time."

She pulled back slightly and smiled up at him. "So? Are we married? At least according to Ilyrian laws?"

"We're much more than married, Bethany. There is no breaking or voiding our vows, because I won't ever release you. I'm yours for eternity, through this life and beyond."

He framed her face between both his hands. "And you are mine. Understand?"

Pure emotion hit Bethany like rising ocean waves of hurricane force. Yes. She understood. Beyond what her mind was capable of catching and comprehending, she understood and responded the only way she could.

Reaching up, she speared her fingers through his hair, fisted them there and tugged his face down to hers. She slanted her mouth against his and thrust her tongue inside. She tasted, defied his natural dominance and plunged deeper.

He growled and pulled her closer, but she pushed at his arms, broke the kiss and ran her tongue down his neck to his chest. Her hands swept over his muscled abdomen, down his hips and back up. She sunk her teeth into the muscle above his nipple, then, licked where she had placed her love bite. She smiled at his harsh intake of breath, at his hands reflexively contracting around her shoulders.

With purpose, she angled her body so as not to touch his jutting cock and continued to lavish attention on his chest. She took her time laving his nipples, scraping her teeth over them and sucking them in turn. She loved the firmness of his muscle against her teeth, the heat against her lips and the way her tongue made his nipples pull tight. The textures and tastes changed some as she worked her way across his chest, but everywhere he was hot, slightly salty with a hint of spice and utterly, blatantly, primal male.

She closed her eyes and released a soft moan as she let the essence of Wyc infuse her senses and build her need for him. Her breasts grew heavy and ached to be touched, teased by his hands and mouth. Her skin constricted around every nerve ending until the faintest breeze felt like a firebrand against her flesh. She could feel blood pulsing through her pussy at every heartbeat, making her sex swell and cream. The more she took Wyc in, the more she wanted him.

While her mouth was busily devoted to his chest, she let her hands slide over his stomach, thighs and butt with whisper-soft caresses. Feathering her fingertips across his skin, she followed a path that drew intricate designs over his ass and around to the front of his legs. Lightly, she raked her nails through the silky hair at the inside of his thighs, coming close, but never touching any part of his hard and straining cock.

Wyc hissed out a curse and started to reach for her. She nipped his chest in warning and took hold of his wrists, placing them back at his sides. He released a low rumble of frustration. When she was sure he was going to cooperate, she let go and resumed plundering his body.

Her mouth trailed down toward his navel. Her splayed hands skimmed softly over his skin. Her fingertips sensitive to every texture, every shift of muscle and ripple of need as it coursed through his body.

His scent was sharp, wild—arousing in its utter maleness after his fight. Tinged with the metallic smell of blood and the musk of spent fury. She kissed her way back up to his Guardian tattoo, circled it lightly with the tip of her tongue and then placed a soft kiss on it.

A hard shudder racked his body and his big hands clamped on her ass, forcing her flush against him. Wyc rocked into her, his erection a hot steel rod pressing into her belly. She pushed at his chest, and after a moment, he released her enough for her to slide down his body. She leaned back until his hands dropped free and curled into fists at his sides.

She settled herself on her knees and watched his face, his gaze locked on her hands as they glided over his abs, his hips, his upper thighs. His eyes narrowed when her hands stopped within a hairsbreadth of his cock. It jerked and an ominous rumble rose from deep in his chest.

Bethany smiled. Leaned in. Licked her lips. Waited.

He growled her name. "Quit teasing. I need to fuck you. Now."

He started to pull her up, but she resisted, glaring up at him, angry at being distracted.

"Damn it, Wyc. You're the one who was so insistent about having me take you. Now let me do it." She shoved his hands away again, and began laying down a trail of wet, openmouthed kisses over his waist and left hip. Pulling back enough to watch his face, she tongued small circles along the crease that joined hip to thigh, moving ever closer to his fully hardened erection. On her cheek, she could feel the heat emanating off his cock and wanted it deep inside her.

Soon, she promised herself. But first, she wanted to taste him.

She remembered the first time Wyc had made her come with his mouth. The fantasy he had made her weave as his tongue danced and swirled everywhere but where she had desperately needed it. The look on his face when he finally licked her dripping pussy. An expression so severe, so stark with such dangerous need and emotion she couldn't understand at the time.

She did now. Her desire to taste Wyc, to take him fully into her mouth, was not built of the curiosity she had felt this morning, but a craving to know his very essence. To claim him in every way a man could be claimed. As was her right.

Caught in an undertow of emotion, she *needed* Wyc. That need broke the final restraints holding her back from truly bonding with her mate. She felt her soul tearing free and launching into him until she wasn't simply stroking his golden skin on the outside, she was caressing the man from the inside out as well.

She had no words for this experience. Every other time they had made love, she had felt him like this within her, as if he were merging with her soul as he merged with her body. This time, she was not only on the receiving end, but the giving end.

Mine, she whispered with her heart. *You are mine.* The words flew through her, into Wyc. Branding them both within a union beyond words or a physical joining.

Dark with passion, his eyes locked on hers. She saw his response in his gaze an instant before it rolled through her with the force of a full-body shockwave.

Yes.

And suddenly his presence was moving through her, melding to her as she was to him. Both a part of the other, both complete as they lost themselves to each other. She soared in the freedom of his control. Safe, loved, whole.

As gentle as one would hold a newborn child, Wyc slipped his fingers through her hair to cradle her head. A gesture made all the more tender for the fierce firestorm of emotion she felt spurring his actions.

Bethany dipped her head, breathing in the intoxicating scent of Wyc, aroused and fully hers. She pressed her palms into his buttocks, felt him tense in anticipation as she let her opened mouth hover above the tip of his cock. His face was taut with barely restrained savagery as his fingers curled and tangled in her hair. His breath soughed in and out of his lungs.

She was panting herself, and her nails dug into his ass. And still she taunted him. Slowly ran her tongue over her top lip. His eyes narrowed, and a dangerous sound of warning rolled at the back of his throat.

"Bethany." It was a command. A plea. It was all she needed.

With a hum of pleasure, she took him deep and fast into her mouth, alternately sucking hard enough to draw in her cheeks and stroking with her tongue. He was thick and long and there wasn't a hope in hell she could take him fully inside in this position.

Wyc's hips immediately jerked forward and he grabbed the sides of her head to hold her in place.

"Jesus, woman." He closed his eyes and his head fell back. After releasing a long, deep breath, he loosened his hold slightly. Bethany pulled back and circled the ridge at the head of his cock with her tongue before flicking it back and forth over the tiny slit in the top. His fingers dug into her skull again.

"Enough." His voice grated out the hoarse demand. He pulled her away, ignoring her protest, and lowered them both to the ground.

"But I wanted—"

"Another time." He smoothed her hair back from her face. "To seal the Mating Rite, I have to come inside you the first time after the vows are completed."

When he pushed her thighs apart and started to sink into her, she pushed at his shoulder until he rolled over onto his back.

Filled with a determination that surprised even her, she straddled his hips. "Fine. But you're still mine to take."

* * * * *

Wyc started to tell her she was more than welcome to take him as much and as often as she wanted, but she leaned forward and bit his bottom lip, cutting him off before a full word fell from his mouth. Emotion, sharper than pleasure and deeper than desire, flared within him.

He ran his hands down her sides and let his head drop to the ground. At this minute, there was nothing in either this world or in Ilyria that could make him look away from his woman who had suddenly become unyielding in her lust for her mate after speaking her vow. Yet another matching myth proved true.

With a smile of victory and a wicked gleam in her eyes, Bethany lowered herself until his cock was nestled against her pussy. She slid slowly up the length of his shaft, helped along by the juices flowing out of her cunt. She shuddered and threw her head back, whipping her hair up and off her face. She thrust out her breasts, let out a cry of driven ecstasy and spread her thighs wider to rub her clit against him harder and faster.

Wyc had never seen anything so beautiful in his life as the picture of pure passion and wild release Bethany presented above him. Her breasts, hard-tipped and plumped to round, lush mounds, bounced and swayed in sensual counterpoint to the cadence her hips set. Her eyes were closed, her face strained with the pursuit of her climax. The smell of her arousal as she continued to spread her cream up and down his cock stirred the dark side of his lust.

The feral animal within him tore at the human will restraining it from rising up and fucking his mate, ramming into her body until this savage need was sated to his satisfaction. He dug his fingers into her thighs, stopping her fervid motion.

"Now, Bethany. Let me inside now."

Her eyes flew open, and he was pleased to see the same desperation that was coursing through his veins reflected in her eyes.

She rose up on her knees and grabbed his cock with both hands. He fought not to black out with the effort it took to keep from unloading the second she wrapped her sweet hands around his erection. Sensitive to the point of pain, his cock throbbed from holding back on his release.

Bethany rocked back and forth, rubbing the head of his penis around her opening until Wyc was shaking with the need to be inside her. Suddenly, she blinked and focused on his eyes, her own wide and bright. She positioned him to enter her, sunk down enough to hold him in place and then leaned forward, planting her hands on his chest.

Wyc reeled from the sensation of her tight, wet pussy contracting around the head of his cock. God, how could one small woman make him so weak? So needy? He was ready to beg if she'd just lower that sweet cunt of hers and take him all in.

Her eyes blazed, her fingers dug into his muscles. "Mine," she whispered roughly, right before slamming her mouth and her body down on his. And he was lost.

She was in him, with him. A part of him. They were completely matched and no barriers remained to keep him from her, body, mind or soul. Before, he could go to her. Now, she could come to him.

Her emotions, so clear he could almost read the thoughts that went with them, floated through his mind. He felt her touch his heart and stroke his soul. Fear still slithered around her unanswered questions, but she refused to submit to it. Her acceptance and trust of him rose in force. He drank it in, reveled in it, but it wasn't enough.

"Love me," he said against her mouth.

She moved on his body, taking him deeper into her. "Yes."

His animal instinct thrashed against the limits of his control. Wanting Bethany. Wanting to consume her in his lust.

Panic shot through him at the thought of her encountering the full force of the beast that had been created within him for her protection. He only allowed the animal loose during Predator attacks. Never with a woman. But no woman had ever touched him deep enough to rouse the beast when he hadn't called for it.

Bethany's hands slid over his shoulders and chest, grasping and flexing. Writhing her body against his, her cunt gripped his cock as her climax crashed over her.

He felt the rush of power and ecstasy burst through her. With a curse hissed through clenched teeth, he thrust up into her, his hips flexing hard and fast.

His frenzy ignited her own. She didn't balk or draw away. His soul lunged for her. Caught her.

She screamed. And lunged back. Wrapping herself in him, beast and man.

He shouted her name, and she gyrated furiously. Reaching up, he caught her swaying breasts and rolled her nipples hard with his thumbs. A sound of infinite, elemental passion exploded from her. Fury and joy, need and offering, command and supplication. It was his mate, giving all of herself to him, demanding he give himself completely to her. It fused him irrevocably to her, and he was taken.

Wyc pulled her to his chest, banded his arms around her and clamped her roughly to him as his release ripped through him.

Bethany buried her face against his neck, bowed into him as her body tensed through another climax. Her cunt tightened and released its burning hold on his cock in time to the spasms rocking her in ecstasy, carrying him along the far edge of darkness and eternity.

When he felt powerless to give any more, she made a small, purring sound that ended on that incredible moan of hers, and her cunt pulled at him with one long, hot tug. He jerked in response to her body's final embrace and an unexpected spearing surge of pleasure tore through him. Another stream of cum shot from his cock and planted itself within his mate. She gasped, pushing herself up to look down at him. And smiled.

She brushed her fingertips over his Guardian tattoo. "It's changed colors," she whispered.

"The Guardian itself is no longer there. It's no longer needed. You're fully mine, as I am yours." He picked up her hand to kiss her fingertips. "If you were to check yours, you'd see the same thing."

He pulled her back down to his chest. She nuzzled against him, an occasional tremor still shivering through her.

Wyc stroked her back and soothed her through the final aftershocks of their lovemaking. While she drifted into sleep, he focused his senses fully on her. She was sated and deeply content. Exhausted but still vibrating with the fading echoes of emotion.

Never in his life had he unloaded twice from the same orgasm. There were elements to the Matching Ritual and Mating Rite that had been thought lost over the centuries. But he was finding more and more truth embedded in the folklore that surrounded the official ceremonial requirements.

He hadn't shared much of that with Bethany yet. She had enough to worry about without extra speculation concerning the validity of myths that he had grown up with. Especially the myth regarding the outcome of the first full joining between a matched Mystic and royal heir. Maybe that would be the one that really did turn out to be false or exaggerated.

Then he heard it. A voice, waking new to the world. A perfect blend of Bethany and himself. Male. A son.

Instinctively, Wyc wrapped a ferocious, protective love around him. The lifeforce of his child pushed back. Strong and powerful for one barely alive. He was glad. If the prophets' words were to be believed, his son's destiny would not be an easy one. Yet one his entire world would depend on.

He drew tightly around his son again with a bone-deep longing to shield his child and hold him safe from any and all harm. The confinement was immediately rejected with an attitude that came across with suspicious stubbornness. If his son had had eyes, he was certain they'd be rolling in irritation.

Moments alive and already incredibly willful. Just like his mother.

Wyc laughed out loud, rousing Bethany from her slumber. Blinking, she lifted her head to look at him, confusion drawing her brows together over amazing green eyes that held his soul.

"What?" she asked. "Is the Matching Ritual finished? Because if it's not, I need to rest before we do anything else."

Wyc brushed a damp strand of hair from her eyes and tucked it behind her ear. He thought about their homeworld she had yet to see. The place of royalty she was destined to assume. Her sisters they had to find and the son she didn't know she carried. He thought of the life with him she had yet to live. His smile faded to solemnity.

"No, babydoll," he said, and placed a lingering kiss full of promise on her lips. "It's not finished. It's only just begun."

Epilogue

೫

Rordyc ran his hand through his hair in frustration and fatigue as he climbed the back steps of the renovated rambling farmhouse. He had just spent nearly three weeks running possible leads to ground on Eavyn's location with little to show for it. For the first time he could remember, he was tired to the center of his bones of being alone.

It was more than just wanting to find his mate so he could get on with his life. It was the desperation of knowing he *needed* his mate or he had no life. None he was interested in living, anyway.

He blamed Wyc. Since Bethany had been found, his cousin had been more than a little insane and a bigger pain in the ass than normal—but also completely... Rordyc wasn't sure what word he was looking for. Content maybe? But it was more. He didn't know what the hell it was, just that Wyc had it, and he didn't. Even the hours spent on his favorite bike with the beautiful country surrounding him and the wind screaming in his ears hadn't distracted the restlessness that had begun to claw at his soul.

He opened the door to the kitchen and came to a surprised stop. "I didn't think you'd give up the cabin so soon," Rordyc drawled as his cousin looked up and met his gaze. He went to the refrigerator and pulled out a beer before joining Wyc at the table.

Wyc glanced around as he pushed the stack of papers he had been shuffling through back into a folder. In a voice pitched so that only Rordyc could hear should there be any others close by, he said, "We had a visit from a Predator up at the cabin."

The news sent a flare of shock through Rordyc. That Wyc was being careful with that information registered just as suddenly. "Anyone else know that's why you're back?"

"Amdyn. And, I assume, whoever sent the Predator up there in the first place."

"Any idea on how you were located?"

Menace flashed hot and promising in Wyc's blue eyes. "I'm working on it."

There was obviously more to the story, but right now, when their privacy couldn't be ensured, wasn't the time to get into it. Rordyc sipped his beer and sprawled more comfortably in the old, oak chair.

"Is Bethany here?"

Wyc pushed back from the table and ran a hand over his eyes. "She's upstairs. Sleeping."

Rordyc glanced at the clock on the microwave. "It's not even seven-thirty yet."

"She's needed more sleep the last couple of weeks."

With a frown, Rordyc asked, "Does she feel okay?" He hoped she wasn't having any unexpected side effects from the *Yes Master* antidote. It hadn't been used all that often.

Wyc's wolfish grin gave him his answer almost immediately. "My mate feels damn good as a matter of fact." He rubbed his palms over his thighs as if he couldn't wait to get back to proving to himself just how good she really did feel. He shrugged, the smug satisfaction dropping from his expression. "Myrra's assured me she's fine. A lot of women need extra rest during their first trimester."

"Congratulations." Rordyc was truly happy for his cousin. He focused on that and ignored the sharp jab of envy that speared through him.

"Thanks."

Pride filled the word, but there was some other emotion coloring the word. Rordyc watched his best friend carefully for a moment before realizing what it was. A knowing grin spread across his face. "You're scared shitless."

Wyc leveled a dark scowl at him and shoved out of his chair. "I'm going to laugh my ass off when your mate finally gets a hold of you and twists you all to hell and back."

Rordyc laughed. "Don't hold your breath on that one."

Wyc threw him a speaking look. An understanding that flowed between them that went far beyond what would ever be said. "Hopefully, I won't have to hold it for long."

Picking up the folder, Wyc left him alone in the kitchen. Rordyc pulled his wallet out of his back pocket and removed the clipping he had stolen from the library's research room close to two months ago. Following a different lead altogether, he had come across a picture of a woman standing with a group of people attending a charity affair.

There had been something—in her face, about her eyes—that had stopped him cold. Opened up a hole inside his chest and rammed through with the force of a freight train. Even now, after having studied the picture too many times to count, it had the same devastating effect on his senses.

At the time, he had tried to dismiss it and continue with his original search, though he couldn't keep himself from tearing out the page and stuffing it in his pocket. When he saw Bethany for the first time and recognized in her facial features nearly a mirror image of those to his mystery woman, his instinctive reaction made more sense. Hope that had been edging toward extinction fired to life again.

He was close to finding his mate. He could feel it.

His gaze scanned down the photo in appreciation of the curve-hugging gown she wore. Tasteful, sexy and designed to emphasize his favorite feminine attribute—breasts. And from what he could tell, hers were perfect. Not large compared to your average stripper or beer commercial babe, but the ideal size to rest soft and heavy in a man's hand. In his hand.

A dark, dangerous emotion slithered through him as it always did whenever his eyes moved off her to scan the rest of the picture. According to the caption, Janice Wyer had been instrumental in raising the foundation's needed funds.

He grimaced. The caption had been a misprint. Janice Wyer was an eighty-six-year-old philanthropist who donated regularly to nearly every charity in the state of Iowa. When he was able to eventually track the picture to the photographer, all the man could remember was that the woman in the picture was from out of town. California, he had thought. Or maybe Arizona.

Other than the fact that the charity function had served cheap champagne, there was one item the photographer was dead certain about. The man standing next to not-Janice-Wyer in the photo, the man with his arm around her waist—was her husband.

Why an electronic book?

We live in the Information Age—an exciting time in the history of human civilization, in which technology rules supreme and continues to progress in leaps and bounds every minute of every day. For a multitude of reasons, more and more avid literary fans are opting to purchase e-books instead of paper books. The question from those not yet initiated into the world of electronic reading is simply: *Why?*

1. *Price.* An electronic title at Ellora's Cave Publishing and Cerridwen Press runs anywhere from 40% to 75% less than the cover price of the exact same title in paperback format. Why? Basic mathematics and cost. It is less expensive to publish an e-book (no paper and printing, no warehousing and shipping) than it is to publish a paperback, so the savings are passed along to the consumer.

2. *Space.* Running out of room in your house for your books? That is one worry you will never have with electronic books. For a low one-time cost, you can purchase a handheld device specifically designed for e-reading. Many e-readers have large, convenient screens for viewing. Better yet, hundreds of titles can be stored within your new library—on a single microchip. There are a variety of e-readers from different manufacturers. You can also read e-books on your PC or laptop computer. (Please note that Ellora's

Cave does not endorse any specific brands. You can check our websites at www.ellorascave.com or www.cerridwenpress.com for information we make available to new consumers.)

3. *Mobility.* Because your new e-library consists of only a microchip within a small, easily transportable e-reader, your entire cache of books can be taken with you wherever you go.

4. ***Personal Viewing Preferences.*** Are the words you are currently reading too small? Too large? Too... ANNOYING? Paperback books cannot be modified according to personal preferences, but e-books can.

5. ***Instant Gratification.*** Is it the middle of the night and all the bookstores near you are closed? Are you tired of waiting days, sometimes weeks, for bookstores to ship the novels you bought? Ellora's Cave Publishing sells instantaneous downloads twenty-four hours a day, seven days a week, every day of the year. Our webstore is never closed. Our e-book delivery system is 100% automated, meaning your order is filled as soon as you pay for it.

Those are a few of the top reasons why electronic books are replacing paperbacks for many avid readers.

As always, Ellora's Cave and Cerridwen Press welcome your questions and comments. We invite you to email us at Comments@ellorascave.com or write to us directly at Ellora's Cave Publishing Inc., 1056 Home Avenue, Akron, OH 44310-3502.

THE
☥ ELLORA'S CAVE ☥
LIBRARY

Stay up to date with Ellora's Cave Titles in
Print with our Quarterly Catalog.

To recieve a catalog,
send an email with your name
and mailing address to:

CATALOG@ELLORASCAVE.COM

or send a letter or postcard
with your mailing address to:

CATALOG REQUEST
c/o Ellora's Cave Publishing, Inc.
1056 Home Avenue
Akron, Ohio 44310-3502

Make each day more *EXCITING* With our

Ellora's Cavemen

Calendar

www.EllorasCave.com

COMING TO A BOOKSTORE NEAR YOU!

ELLORA'S CAVE

Bestselling Authors Tour

erridwen, the Celtic Goddess of wisdom, was the muse who brought inspiration to story-tellers and those in the creative arts. Cerridwen Press encompasses the best and most innovative stories in all genres of today's fiction. Visit our site and discover the newest titles by talented authors who still get inspired - much like the ancient storytellers did, once upon a time.

Cerridwen Press

www.cerridwenpress.com

Discover for yourself why readers can't get enough of the multiple award-winning publisher

Ellora's Cave.

Whether you prefer e-books or paperbacks,

be sure to visit EC on the web at
www.ellorascave.com

for an erotic reading experience that will leave you breathless.